A F
To the

A novel based o
Television's saga
in the crucial middle years of W

A Family at War series

A Family at War
A Family at War: To the Turn of the Tide
A Family at War: Towards Victory

JONATHAN POWELL

A Family at War: To the Turn of the Tide

from the Granada Television series
created by John Finch

GRAFTON BOOKS
A Division of the Collins Publishing Group

LONDON GLASGOW
TORONTO SYDNEY AUCKLAND

Grafton Books
A Division of the Collins Publishing Group
8 Grafton Street, London W1X 3LA

Published by Grafton Books 1989

First published in Great Britain by
Mayflower Books 1971

ISBN 0-586-20921-2

Printed and bound in Great Britain by
Collins, Glasgow

Set in Times

A Family at War:
To the Turn of the Tide

'Go, go, go, said the bird: human kind
Cannot bear very much reality.'

Burnt Norton. ELIOT

PART ONE

'HOPE AGAINST HOPE'

CHAPTER ONE

May 1941

David's aircraft crept stealthily through the sky. The night had already wrapped it round and hidden it from the ground. He was being carried, gently, on velvet curtains through the sky, and his plane was heavy and loaded, ready and waiting, persistently seeking out its destination.

Sheila, Freda and Doris lay, half asleep and yet always with one eye open to the sky, under the Morrison shelter in Sheila's kitchen. Jean, Michael, Margaret and John George were in the Ashtons' shelter at the bottom of the garden. Once upon a time, Margaret had told her son that there were fairies there.

In the distance the steady crump of the bombs and the low moan of the air-raid siren were a recurrent memory and the all-clear a recurrent relief. They peopled their dreams, and were a constant reminder. For some there was the knowledge that their lives went on, for others there was the pain of lost friends, lost relatives and lost husbands, wives, sons and daughters. Children eaten up by the sea, consumed by the fire and destroyed by the night. And for some there was no more pain, no more fear, no more relief and no more memories.

The war brought everyone a kind of pain, of death, of loss or just the persistent toothache that never went away. The knowledge that there was more to come.

John George stirred in the corner of the Anderson shelter. Margaret looked across at him and saw her husband lying dead in a field somewhere in Belgium. She looked across at Michael and heard her son whimper. In a field, somewhere in Belgium she saw her husband lift his head.

There was no certainty any more. There never could be, and that was perhaps the most terrible thing.

She looked at Michael again. He was so tangible, so real, and she wondered how anyone could blame her, for he was a certainty. She felt his baby inside her. That was real too. His flesh, her blood, for better or for worse.

It was impossible to sleep.

Jean sat up. The silence disturbed her. She felt alone in the night and hidden away from everything. All around her she felt the unspoken messages that passed between Michael and Margaret. They cut across the thick silence like a knife. Her daughter and her lover. The word was distasteful to Jean and she felt it intruding into the fabric of what was left of their family life. She felt betrayed.

'I'll go and make some tea,' she said, and then added with a hint of bitterness in her voice, 'it's useless trying to sleep in here tonight.'

'Let Michael make it,' said Margaret.

'No, it's all right. You'll be wanting to get back to your little girl, won't you, Mr Armstrong.' Jean still called Michael by his surname as if intimating that she wanted to be as little involved with him as possible, to keep their relations strictly formal.

Her mother's intransigence annoyed Margaret.

'I sent her to my sister's a week ago,' said Michael, and then added by way of justification, 'to keep her away from the bombing.'

Jean glanced at him and left the shelter.

Margaret had not failed to catch the meaning behind her mother's words.

'You know what that means to her, don't you,' she said, 'you and me, an empty house.'

They looked at each other in the half light and knew what it meant to them both.

John George moved faintly.

Neither Freda, Sheila nor Doris could sleep. Occasional flashes lit the room and the breeze stirred the curtains.

'We've had five raids in a row now,' said Freda, 'makes you wonder why there's anything left.'

She didn't see the look that passed on Sheila's face. Any raid always reminded her of David. He was up there too, she thought. The war had taken him away from her, and she wondered to herself whether there was anything left.

'David hates coming back here, you know,' she said to Freda, 'he always did, but since his promotion he's been worse. I'm dreading him getting a commission.'

It had always been one of Sheila's worst fears that David

should get his commission. She knew that as long as he went on getting promotion, the further away from her he would grow. She hated even thinking about it, for she knew that as long as the war went on it was inevitable.

There was only one thing that would stop it, and that was unthinkable.

Suddenly she had an idea. It was one of those small ideas that spring from the depths of the mind like light relief, and which for a moment give some hope.

'I'm going to get us a new bed,' she said to Freda as if it was an idea from heaven, 'that old rattletrap upstairs is way past its time. God knows how many people have died on it. You practically touch the floor when there's two of you in it.'

She laughed at the thought and Freda giggled in sympathy, but the moment passed. Sheila thought of the last time that she had been in it with David. It was so long ago that the memory had faded. She tried to recapture it, but it eluded her like a fly on the window. Her mind passed on for she knew that there was no point in living in the past, and yet she often feared that the past was all she had.

'When's Margaret's baby due?' she asked.

'You know about it then?' replied Freda.

'She was round here the other day and it all came out. It's a pity she can't marry the chap. He sounds all right to me.'

Freda heard a note of bitterness in her voice as if the thought of another's happiness was too much for her to bear.

'He's nice enough, although I don't like him as much as John and I don't think Margaret does either,' said Freda. She floundered in trying to explain the situation, but it was too complex for her to put into words, 'we don't talk about it much at home, because of Mum.'

Freda paused for a moment and then decided that it wasn't worth the effort to go on explaining.

'We just sit there and try to pretend it never happened,' she said.

'Margaret of all people,' mused Sheila, 'I thought it was only me, or people like me who were supposed to do that sort of thing.'

For a moment Freda caught her eye. In the distance they heard a bomb explode. The almost gentle crump led them both back into their own private thoughts and, in the night, Sheila saw a picture of her and David, comfortable in their new bed.

That night, Edwin had been on duty at the warden's post. He'd been busy and had just returned from a nearby street, or what was left of it.

A mother dead with the door lintel over her chest and in her arms, a baby. Beside her another child, still breathing.

Nothing unusual. And yet, he thought, how odd to have to think that something like that was nothing unusual.

The chief warden looked up at him as he came into the room.

'Heard from your Robert yet?'

'Not since we had that telegram thing at the beginning of March,' replied Edwin, 'three standard phrases and his name from somewhere in the world he's not supposed to mention. It's not much for a worried mother, is it?'

Edwin thought of Jean and how she had never forgiven him for signing Robert's papers. He still couldn't see what else he could have done and anyway, he was the lad's father and felt the loss as much as she did. He just prayed and prayed that nothing would overtake their youngest son, for then he knew that Jean would never forgive him.

And so the night closed in on the Ashtons. Each one lay in their own private world of fears and recriminations, of worry and of blame. To each the war meant a different thing, and had made them face situations and problems that way back in 1938 none of them had ever dreamt they would be facing.

Nobody talked any more about the pretty fairies at the bottom of the garden.

Like all dreams, they had gone.

The next day, after the night was over and the dust had settled, a letter slipped through Sheila's door. She was in the living-room with Freda at the time, getting dressed, and Doris was upstairs.

'From David?' asked Freda.

'The gas,' Sheila replied.

She held the letter between her hands and twisted it round and round. It was as if the memory of David and the arrival of the letter formed something beyond their ordinary significance in her mind.

'I don't get letters from David any more,' she went on, 'I just get letters about him, but I don't even bother to look at them any more. They're anonymous ones. I just look at the envelope and then throw them in the fire.'

'Have you told him?' asked Freda.

Sheila thought what a simple logical question it was for Freda to ask, and what a complex irrational problem it would be for her to deal with. She closed her eyes and imagined tackling David about it. He had denied it once.

'I told him about the first one,' she said, 'they're about a girl and say that he got her pregnant. They say the same thing every time.'

'And you believe them?'

'When I told him about the first one he came out with some story about someone being jealous. I believed him then, in a way, becaue I wanted to,' Sheila paused and pushed back her hair from her face, 'after all, it's not something you want to believe, is it?'

At the same moment Doris came into the room. She was her usual self and Sheila thought how Doris seldom seemed to change. Doing up her dress, combing her hair and trying to put on her stockings at the same time.

Sheila turned to her and a feeling of fondness came over her for this chaotic disorganised and totally likeable girl.

'I was talking to Freda last night, and she says you've been bombed out,' she said.

'That first bad raid. We were in the shelter or else we'd have had it,' said Doris. 'I'm an unwelcome lodger at my sister's,' she added.

Suddenly Sheila felt lonely. She looked at the photo of David smiling innocently from the sideboard. It reminded her, not of him, but of the mornings spent waking without him and of the lonely breakfasts. It reminded her of the few times she had laid two places for the first meal of the day just in order to give herself a moment's hope.

'You could stay here,' she said, 'in the kid's room. I'd be glad of the company and we could share the rations.'

Doris paused. Why not, she thought, and accepted Sheila's offer.

'That's it, then. It's settled,' Sheila thought for a moment, 'you might as well move in now.'

Jean was in the kitchen when Sefton came round to see her, making some bread. She always liked it when he poked his head round the door, and smiled his funny lopsided smile at her. She had become very fond of her brother recently. The constant strain of Margaret and the baby, and of having

Michael hanging round the house so much got her down, so it wasn't surprising that she talked to Sefton about these things. The rest of the family seemed so unreceptive to her points of view. And anyway, she thought as if to justify herself, he is my brother. Sefton, with his arched eyebrows and almost perpetual air of surprise, was a good listener, and he paid attention to her problems. Jean didn't feel as she did with Edwin, that he was trying to get at her or to justify his own position in any way. She kneaded the dough carefully, as if the soft pliable movement of her fingertips among the heavy texture of the flour sapped the tension of her body away.

'I'm glad you told me, Jean. I knew she was in trouble of course but I thought, "wait to be told, Sefton, wait to be told." I must say that I wouldn't have thought it of your Margaret, I really wouldn't,' he thought for a moment and then said, in a far away, almost wistful voice, 'the last person on earth.'

'Yes, well there it is.' Jean sighed heavily. She wouldn't have thought it of Margaret either. These things happened between people, and as Edwin was constantly reminding her, there was no point in indulging in recriminations. Yet, she could never get it straight in her mind. She blamed herself, she blamed Edwin, she blamed everyone. Somehow, she thought, it could have been avoided.

'He'll marry her, of course, this chap,' said Sefton.

'In seven years?' replied Jean.

The facts of the situation stared her in the face. She often dreamt about it. A picture of John in her mind.

He had seemed so right for Margaret. So soft and gentle and loving, that she had thought it was as near to a perfect marriage as it could be.

And then the telegram.

Jean saw it in her sleep. She saw John lying with his face down in the dirt and herself standing over him. She turned him over and saw, burned deeply into his tunic, the frayed black edges of the material throwing into a kind of nightmare relief, three words.

'Missing, believed killed.'

And the flesh burned too. She could smell it.

Suddenly he was back in Liverpool, playing tennis with Margaret. The sun shone and he wore a bright, white tennis shirt. She saw his back, and then he turned and into the supernatural cleanness of the shirt were the same words. 'Believed killed.'

The uncertainty, the lack of knowledge annoyed her. She felt powerless, and she knew that that was what she was.

Jean turned to Sefton and stifled the momentary impulse to lean on his shoulder. She changed the subject.

'You never said how Tony was?'

Sefton, she knew, had been to visit Tony some days before, and since his return he had not said a word about what had happened. Jean thought it was about some business, but neither he nor Edwin, who had also gone, would tell her what had happened. It seemed like a conspiracy of silence.

'He's got himself a girlfriend,' said Sefton, 'but I'm not too sure what the situation is between them. I think he's rather keen on her as a matter of fact.'

Sefton poked his finger into the dough and it gave to his touch, leaving a small imprint behind. He was thinking of Jenny, Tony's girlfriend. They had sat opposite each other in the corner of a pub and talked while Tony had gone off to pack the suitcases that he and Jenny would take on the weekend they had planned together.

The weekend that Sefton knew, the moment he arrived there, that he had disturbed.

Jenny had leaned across the table towards him.

'You must be lonely in that big house of yours, Mr Briggs,' she had said, 'you should get yourself a woman. You're an attractive man, you know.'

A gentle smile played across her lips and Sefton remembered it. A soft sensual smile that meant a lot of different things. He treasured that moment for it wasn't often that other people took the trouble to really try to talk to him. To understand him.

'People along the road are talking, of course,' said Jean, interrupting his thoughts, 'you understand it's not for myself that I mind, it's for her.'

Sefton looked at her and wondered.

'When she goes out in the morning you can almost see her bracing herself for it.'

The look in Jean's eye told Sefton that she was finding it difficult to cope with what was happening. He wondered just exactly what went on in this family that made them all unable to come out with what they truly thought. There was the sound from the hall of the front door opening.

'That's probably Edwin,' said Jean, 'don't tell him I told you about it.'

Before Sefton had a chance to reply, the kitchen door opened.

It was Robert.

That afternoon, the sun shone for what seemed the first time for ages. The rain had disappeared and the dust still hung in the air. It was almost beautiful the way the beams of light shone through the piles of rubble, but then it was difficult to believe that out of that destruction could come any sort of beauty.

Sheila walked to work in the NAAFI and thought about her two children. She pictured them in her mind, away in Wales being looked after by another woman. Playing happily in the fields.

Peter kicking a football. Janet picking flowers.

She tried to smile inwardly and to be glad that they were away from it all. And yet she couldn't help thinking that, in being away from it all, the constant noise, the constant ear-splitting, wailing warnings of destruction, they were also away from her. One half of her, the half that took her through the day said that it was best. The other half, the half that tossed and turned in the night hoped that when she turned the next corner it would reveal them, laughing and happy, running up to her and shouting. A dream, that's all it was, a dream, and in a terrible moment she thought she might never see them again.

In the mud a small boy played with the stones and rubble. A young lad of about seven. As she passed he looked up at her and in his face there was a wisdom far beyond his years.

It was best that they should be away, she thought.

Earlier that day the delivery men had brought the bed round for her and had taken away the old one with its rusty sagging springs and its rotten mattress. She'd left Doris alone in the house to stand guard over her new acquisition. She was glad that Doris was there, after all, if she couldn't have the children then she might as well have some company, and she knew it couldn't be David. He was far away, drinking and smoking, talking to people. He didn't know the terrible loneliness she felt. The silent nights, the darkness and the faces of the children constantly recurring in her mind. He was all right. He had people to talk to.

David arrived in Liverpool on the afternoon train. He had a forty-eight and hadn't told Sheila that he was coming. He hoped that she would be pleased to see him. He knew that the most dangerous moment was the first one when he walked through the door. He looked out for the expression on her face. Surprise, happiness, laughter. One day, and he feared it, there would be the worst thing of all, no expression. Whatever he did, wherever he was, he lived in dread of that day, for he'd seen what it did to other men. His friends and acquaintances had come back from leave having found their wives with another man and having experienced the look of boredom, irritation or indifference that had greeted their arrival. They were the men he hoped he'd never have to fly with. From that moment the liveliest and happiest had become something else. They had become lost.

There were other reasons that David had come home as well, or rather one main reason and that was that he owed a friend five pounds. The friend, Teddy Main, was crying out to have it back. David had found himself in rather a difficult spot, but had managed to keep the wolf from the door until he returned from leave. He was sure someone would be able to lend it to him.

David regretted borrowing the money as soon as he realised that he was going to find it difficult to pay back, but what he was beginning to regret more was lying in order to get it.

That day, David had stood outside a door and heard Teddy Main talking to Frankie, David's best friend. A few words and phrases had seeped through the wood.

'He's all right,' Frankie had said, standing up for him, 'he'll pay it back to you in time, Teddy.'

'What I don't see, Frankie old chap,' replied Teddy, 'is why he's having any difficulty at all. After all, he's got an old man who owns a factory or whatever it is up North, so he shouldn't have any trouble.'

David hated himself for those lies and yet he felt himself being sucked into a vortex of social pretence. The higher up the social ladder he went, the more he felt he had to keep up with the people he associated with. It was a cruel vicious circle that he could see no way out of and which he knew he had to play.

When he got back to Liverpool, he went first to his parents' home. David usually did this, out of habit as much as anything else. He remembered the days when it had been his instinctive reaction, and when, after a row with Sheila he would leave the house they lived in and which he hated so much and go back to his parents' home.

He thought how young he had been then. A lot had happened since those days.

Things were different now, he thought. He knew they were, but wondered whether it was for the better.

When he got back, they were all sitting round the table. Robert was there talking ten to the dozen about his first trip, about the places he'd been and about the things he'd seen. David envied him his youthfulness and his enthusiasm, but yet he couldn't help still feeling like an uncle towards his youngest brother. It struck him as odd to see the young kid he remembered growing up so fast.

He looked at Robert's clean face that still didn't need shaving, and David realised something. Robert wasn't growing up fast.

He was being forced to grow up fast.

'We went to this place called Takoradi and then to Lagos,' said Robert, gesticulating with his hands, 'there was a swimming pool there, a big sheet of canvas in a hole in the ground.' He paused for effect, 'Every time someone jumped in, the lizards jumped out.'

'Uggh,' said Freda, pulling a face.

Jean was sitting in the corner, running her hands gently over the smooth polished surface of a small mahogany wood table that Robert had brought back as a present. She ran her nail in the crack between the ivory inlay and the wood.

'It must have cost a fortune,' she said.

'It cost me a pair of socks,' said Robert, smiling. 'As a matter of fact they were the ones that Freda knitted for me.'

He looked at his sister with a mock-apologetic expression on his face. The family laughed at Freda's indignation.

They were playing a game and they knew it. It was a game in which everything is said, in which anything is said as long as it is inconsequential and as long as it doesn't touch on a nerve that might hurt.

Sefton had been looking into his tea cup, ignoring the conversation, playing in his mind with his own thoughts.

'See any submarines, lad,' he asked.

Robert saw the wary look that his father threw his way. He

saw Jean look down and press her hands against the top of the table. He saw a nervous jump pass across Freda's eyes.

The question was too near reality, too near what might happen one day, and they all knew it.

'Not a sausage, Uncle,' he said quickly, 'in fact most of the lads at sea haven't seen one since it started.'

He was lying and he knew it.

David stood up.

'Time I was off,' he said, 'Sheila doesn't even know I'm coming.'

'Come on, lad,' said Sefton, who was just beginning to enjoy himself, 'have another drink.'

They were drinking the whisky that David had brought back from the camp, and providentially Sefton had passed David a note to go towards its cost.

'All right, I'll stay,' he said, 'just until Maggie gets back. It'd be nice to see her.'

There was a silence.

'I'll pour, shall I?' said Edwin quickly. He picked up the bottle and began to fill the glasses.

'Well?' David turned to the rest of the family, 'how is Maggie then?'

Another silence. David sensed that something was wrong with them all, but he couldn't fathom out what it was.

Everyone was aware that neither he nor Robert knew about Margaret, and they were all imagining what would happen when she walked in the room.

'We'd all be a bit better off if we could sleep at night,' said Edwin quickly, nervously, 'and you haven't asked about Sheila yet. She seems well as a matter of fact and I've got her a Morrison shelter. It looks a bit like a rabbit hutch, sat there in the middle of the kitchen.'

He looked round, wondering whether the moment had passed or whether he should go on talking, to avoid any more questions about Margaret.

Just at that moment, in Sheila's house, Doris was climbing into the shelter. Sheila was still at work and Doris was going to bed early, hoping for a good night's sleep.

'I suppose I'd better get over there,' said David to his father, 'Sheila'll be expecting me.'

'There's something I'd like to say before you go, lad.'

Edwin got up and turned to the assembled company. His

heavy reliable frame filled the room and he waited for a silence to fall.

'I'd like David and Robert to hear what Sefton's done for us,' he said, 'your uncle's given us the house. I know I've said it before, but I'd like to say it again.'

Edwin paused as if waiting to get his second wind.

'I've never been at the end of a more generous gesture,' he said finally.

There was a long pause. Sefton looked a little sheepish and embarrassed by Edwin's speech. Nobody noticed the sideways glance he took at Jean's face.

She was remembering the conversation she'd had with Sefton when all this had come up, and she smiled gently to herself. Her brother was a clever man, a very clever man, and he was cleverer than her husband. They all knew it. There was something else that Jean knew as well. She knew that Sefton, to put it in his own words, never did anything when there would not be a little dividend at the end. He could wait for the dividend, no matter how long, but in the end it would come.

That was the way he lived and the way he looked at life. It was his own style and with the man you had to take it or leave it. There was no separating the two.

Nobody knew quite what to say, so the silence sat as if in admiration of Sefton's generosity. There was a voice in the corridor and both David and Robert got to their feet, recognising it as Margaret's.

'No, of course you must stop,' they all heard her say. She went into the kitchen and opened the hatch.

'Robert, David,' she said, genuinely surprised, 'how lovely.'

They both saw the initial smile of greeting fade fast from her face as she closed the hatch again.

'Robert's been to West Africa buying tables and swimming with lizards.' Freda's voice, high pitched and broken by the tension, echoed across the room and bounced back into the silence from the closed hatch. Jean looked into her lap and gently set the table aside. Edwin put his hand to his hair as if to straighten it, but in reality it was a gesture of despair.

It was the moment they had all been dreading.

'Come on round, Mags, let's have a look at you,' said David.

The irony of his words was lost on Jean. She was thinking what a pity it was that this should be such a terrible moment for them all. Why, she wondered, couldn't they all be truthful and honest with each other.

Edwin leaned across the table to David, 'David,' he said in a whisper, 'we should have warned you. It's too late now, but . . . well just be careful what you say that's all.'

David looked puzzled. Edwin had assumed that from the atmosphere and from the glimpse that he'd had of his sister, he must know what was wrong.

David looked at his father, wondering what on earth he was talking about. Edwin was about to explain further when Michael came in the room.

'She's just popped upstairs,' he said, 'she thought she heard John George sneeze.'

David and Robert just stared at Michael, not knowing who he was or where he fitted into the picture. In the split second that he stood there and before Edwin intruduced him, an inkling of what might have happened flashed across David's mind.

After that, the tension broke and as always in a situation that they don't understand and can't manage, the people involved made their excuses. Sefton left. Freda went upstairs and Jean, saying she had a headache, went to bed. Margaret and Michael, the centre of the storm were almost forgotten and stood in the corner of the living-room watching the circus go on around them. They were the pivot and yet everyone tried to pretend they were not there. Edwin excused himself and went to do the washing up, not because he wanted to do it, or because it really needed to be done, but because it was a simple automatic task that would occupy his mind and take care of his fidgeting hands.

Edwin stood over the sink, his back bent and his eyes fixed on the dirty water and the plates. Carefully and slowly he washed the plates making a meditative circling movement with his hands. He tried to scrub them clean, cleaner than they could ever really be. The hypnotic repetitive task emptied his mind.

'David,' he said as his son came into the kitchen, 'you're just passing through. We're the ones who have to cope. Better to leave it as it is.'

'I want to know what's been going on, Dad. She's my sister after all.'

Edwin looked up. He felt tired and washed out, but not clean like the plates.

'She's pregnant,' he said flatly.

'Good grief,' David exploded, throwing his hands into the air, 'I can see that. Is it him, the chap she's with?'

Edwin nodded assent, and finishing the plates he began to wash up the knives and forks.

'He wants his neck wringing.'

'David, I don't want any trouble. I've enough with your mother as it is. That's definite.'

Edwin's temper began to run away with him and the strain of the past weeks told in the tone of his voice. Usually so calm a man, Edwin felt the rage within him boil and come to bursting point, but with a final effort he controlled it. After a moment he spoke calmly, slowly and with infinite care like a drunken man who knows his state and tries to separate each word.

'If I can bring myself to try and understand, I shouldn't have thought it was beyond you to try and do the same.'

David thought the hint was directed at him personally and he took it as such. He remembeed that his own marriage had started the same way one careless impassioned night in the park. There hadn't been the steady hail of bombs then, perhaps that was the difference.

'All right,' he said, 'I'll say it then. Fellers like me know about fellers like me. What I've done with my life is my business and it doesn't mean to say I like it that way. But it's different for our Mags, it's just different.'

'I know, son,' said Edwin, 'I know.'

He put out his hand and touched his son's shoulder. Both men knew that there was little point in carrying on the conversation. In the first flush of anger and indignation things get said that are later regretted and neither of them wanted to say things that they might later regret.

David sighed. He too felt suddenly weary. Tired and sick his head dropped from its usual upright proud position. For a moment he wished he were a child again. He wished that he didn't have the cares and responsibilities that came with adult life and for a second he felt sorry for Michael, sorry as a man who understands another because they have suffered the same situation. He knew he would never like Michael, and yet he knew that there would always be a bond.

He felt sorry as he felt sorry when he was over Germany. It was a sorrow that had to be shut off because it had no place in the present scheme of things. So many people caught up in the same device, in the same order of things, and never the twain shall meet.

Edwin sensed the thoughts that were going through his son's mind, and in a moment of closeness that was so rare he understood completely.

'It's not so good at the receiving end these days, especially these last few nights,' he said.

'It's not much fun at the other end either, Dad,' replied David.

He smiled at his father.

These moments were so rare, and yet they passed fleetingly, passed into the distance and were extinguished. Both men were so tired that neither tried to prolong it.

The raid started just as David left the house, but he decided to continue on home. After all, it was his only night with Sheila and he wanted to see her badly. He knew why he wanted to see her. It had been a long time. The feeling hurried him along through the darkness and the strange sounds.

Michael and Margaret were the only ones in the Anderson shelter at the bottom of the garden.

'You'll be all right,' she said as he got up and prepared to go.

'Don't worry. I'll dive for the nearest shelter if I hear anything coming.'

Margaret apologised nervously for the embarrassment that the previous few hours must have caused him. He seemed to take it well, she thought, pehaps too well, but she wasn't satisfied. There were so many questions she wanted to ask him, so many things that were important to her and yet they were all so difficult to ask.

'But we can't go on like this for ever, can we?' she said tentatively.

'Better to let things take their course,' he replied evasively.

She wanted to ask him what course he meant, and what things he was referring to. She felt like a ship adrift. Somewhere along the line she had latched on to him as an anchor and, although she couldn't express it, she felt that the anchor was drifting through the mud, uncertain where to put its hooks, where to grab on.

Michael looked up, wanting to be off.

'They're still buzzing about up there,' he said lightly.

As he left the shelter he pulled his scarf up around his face as if to hide it from the world. He leaned down and kissed Margaret on the cheek. She put her hand on the back of his neck as if to hold him just that bit longer. He felt the nerves tingle up and down his spine and for a moment he enjoyed the sensation, but then he quickly disengaged himself from her, fearing, in a way, what that touch meant.

It meant a certainty and Michael felt that, in a time of uncertainty when not even right and wrong were certain any more, when values had been turned upside down, that he was not entitled to hold on to anything.

David got home and let himself in with his own key. It was late and he wondered whether Sheila would be asleep by now or not. He looked round in the murky light and saw a funny black rectangular shape in the middle of the room. He remembered what his father had told him and realised that it was the Morrison shelter. He stood still for a moment and heard the sound of breathing. It came from the shelter. He thought Sheila must be in there instead of upstairs. He smiled to himself. A bed's a bed, he thought.

Quickly and expertly he took off his clothes, down to his underpants.

His whole body tickled with anticipation and excitement. Even the tips of his fingers felt as if they had little bits of nerve end sticking out of them.

Like a mole he burrowed into the shelter. It was like going underground. The shelter was warm and comfortable and there was a wonderful welcoming smell coming from the body that already lay there. He felt the cares dropping from his back and his mind lost its tenseness, his nerves relaxed. Everything went blank as he stretched his arm across the bed and whispered,

'Sheila? ... Sheila?'

For a moment there was no response, and David gently caressed the waiting shoulder, touching the places that he knew to the very last centimetre. He was going to make the best of this, he thought. He leaned over and kissed the back of the neck, just above the spine, his body pressed itself close, hard against the back of the other.

The body turned over sleepily and David made ready to kiss her mouth.

'Christ! !' said Doris.

'Sheila! !' said David.

They were both out of the bed in a flash. Moments, uncomprehending moments flashed past, and a million thoughts passed through David's mind.

A torch beam cut across the dark as David scrambled for his trousers and Doris pulled the bedclothes round her. It caught him full as he almost tripped in his haste.

'David?' said Sheila, half smiling, for she realised at once what had happened, or at least she hoped she did, 'what are you doing?'

'I'm trying to put my trousers on,' he said.

'And how did you come to get them off in the first place,' his wife asked him. She was already beginning to enjoy his embarrassment.

David opened his mouth to answer and then decided better of it. Hastily he picked up his trousers and the rest of his clothes and fled upstairs to dress again.

Sheila crossed over to the stove and put on a kettle for a cup of tea. She turned and looked at Doris who was still standing with the blanket wrapped around her.

'Tea'll be ready in a minute. I'll put a load of sugar in it. Sweeten him up a bit,' she smiled to herself and Doris smiled back. Underneath they both wanted to laugh out loud but David's presence upstairs stopped them.

'Was it awful for you?' asked Sheila.

'Worse for him I should think.'

'Don't let him catch us smiling when he comes in. He's embarrassed and it serves him right for not telling me he was coming.'

Sheila paused a moment and then added thoughtfully,

'He'll come back one day and find I've moved.'

'He's strong on you though, isn't he?' said Doris.

At the moment that she had awoken, Doris had been dreaming and David's arrival had coincided exactly with her dream, but it wasn't the dream that told her that David was strong on his wife.

'What makes you say that?' said Sheila, knowing exactly what Doris meant, but liking the reassurance.

They looked at each other and Doris knew she didn't have to answer.

While Sheila made the tea, Doris got dressed hurriedly and as they drank it together they laughed about the incident. By the time David had summoned the courage to face them again,

Doris had gone, saying that she would be back later.

'Is she going to be here every time I come home,' asked David.

'It's company for me that's all,' said Sheila. She felt herself on the point of saying that he didn't often come home and explaining about how she felt alone in the house without him, but the look on his face stopped her. To be truthful, it turned her knees to jelly.

'I've been dying for my own bed,' he said.

Sheila saw her chance and made the most of the moment.

'You're going to be disappointed I'm afraid, Davey,' she said affectionately.

His face dropped and she saw the old familiar prelude to a row pass over it.

'I've chucked it out and bought another,' she said.

David breathed a sigh of relief and took her by the waist. As he nuzzled her and kissed her neck she explained how she'd bought a new bed.

'I'll go and test the springs then,' said David, 'we can't sleep down here. Not tonight.'

'Oh, Davey, we can't,' she said, 'not till the all-clear goes. I'm terrified if I'm upstairs when there's an action.'

David tried to reassure her that the present raid was not a serious one. He used his superior knowledge to impress on her that it was only a diversionary raid and not one she should worry about. However much he pleaded she still wouldn't believe him and in the end he had to agree to come downstairs if anything started.

'You are an old devil, aren't you?' she said and smiled at him fondly, thinking how this was what it had been like between them before the bombing and the raids got in the way.

'Me? I'm just a fella on a forty-eight hour pass. Remember what you used to say? Like a second honeymoon.'

'Know all the right things to say, don't you, David.'

A few minutes later they were in bed together and for the second time in the last few hours David felt himself relaxing again. The fight, he thought, was almost won. He asked her how she had afforded the bed and she told him that she had saved up for it. She still had a few quid left in the post office. He remembered his debt, but let the thought pass out of his mind along with all other thoughts. He was involved, totally involved in the moment.

Just as he leaned over and kissed her, the sound of the bombs started again. She jumped up and rolled out of the bed as if she'd been stung by a wasp. He tried to grab her, but she escaped. He shouted after her but she was out of hearing in a flash, down the stairs and into the shelter.

The room was empty and David lay on his back, looking at the empty space beside him and then he looked up at the ceiling. Beyond it was the sky.

He smashed his fist into the firm new bed, and gritted his teeth. Then in a high pitched, uncontrolled howl he yelled at the invisible enemy.

'You rotten lousy bastards!' he screamed. 'You rotten lousy bastards!'

Later that night the all clear sounded and Sheila opened an eye. She peeped to one side and saw Doris, to the other side lay David, snoring gently. They were all three in the Morrison shelter downstairs. A little thrill passed through her body as she remembered the events of earlier and she leaned over and shook David gently by the shoulder.

'David, David,' she whispered gently.

But he was fast asleep and didn't stir. Sheila smiled to herself and went back to sleep.

There's always the morning, she thought and dreamed of clean sheets and new springs.

Early the next morning, Jean took Margaret a cup of tea. The all-clear had gone at about four, and Margaret had dropped off to sleep on the sofa in the living-room.

Jean stood over her eldest daughter and wondered at the peaceful smile that played over her face. She wished she knew what it was that, in sleep, could bring such a look to her face when her mind was so troubled.

Margaret woke and Jean gave her the tea. They talked inconsequentially as Margaret pulled on her dress that was lying on the floor. She patted her hair into place, and then paused, looking at her mother.

'I won't be back until after tea tonight, Mum,' she said, 'I'm going to see Michael.'

She looked at her mother and it was almost as if Jean knew what she was about to say. Jean's face flinched like a dog about to take a blow from its master. There was no point in beating about the bush, thought Margaret.

'You see, Michael has asked me to live with him and I'm going to tell him tonight that I will. It seems the only practical thing to do.'

It would be her anchor. Something she could catch on to and that would hold her still against the unbearable tide that was so strong and was sweeping her into places she did not know. She was afraid.

In half formed words and thoughts she tried to apologise to her mother for the pain she was causing her, but Jean's face had a rock-like expression, as if she had finally put up the barricades of reason to protect herself.

'I won't be able to be completely happy about it, I think,' said Jean, 'I'm made the way I am and we all seem to have some things that make us more unhappy than others. When I was younger I seemed to be able to talk more intelligently about these things than I seem to be able to behave when they happen.'

She looked at Margaret and realised that what she thought didn't in the end, matter at all. She took Margaret's hand and squeezed it as if gaining strength from the touch.

'You be happy, love,' she said, 'be happy.'

Jean left Margaret in the living-room getting herself ready to face the day, and went to the kitchen. Edwin was sitting at the table reading the newspaper. His breakfast things lay in disarray about him. Jean began to tidy them up and as she did so she told him what Margaret had said.

'Perhaps it's the best thing,' he said, hardly even bothering to look up from his paper.

Edwin went on with the paper. He was reading about Hess's landing in Scotland. The Germans seemed to be trying to establish that he was suffering from hallucinations and Britain that he was in good health.

Edwin looked at Jean washing up.

There are two sides to any story, he thought, it just depends what side you're on.

The door closed and Margaret went out.

It was about midday when Sheila came round to the Ashtons. She had left David asleep and it rather amused her to think what his reaction would be when he woke up and found her gone. There was still time though, she thought.

She went into the kitchen and found Jean ironing Robert's

dirty clothes. She asked Jean about Robert and was told about the adventures.

'You're looking better today,' said Sheila, 'I suppose it's having Robert home that does it?'

'Does it show?' replied Jean.

As Sheila was about to reply she saw her mother-in-law turn away and put her handkerchief to her eyes.

'You're crying because you're happy aren't you?' she said, and then added fondly, 'it's only natural ... it's not stupid.'

But Jean wasn't crying because she was happy. She was crying because she should be happy. It should be good, she thought, to have Robert home, and yet there was always a shadow cast over everything. There seemed to be some sort of divine balance operating in their lives. As soon as she was given one thing to be happy about, another thing cropped up to make her sad.

Sheila spent the next two hours pottering about helping Jean, talking to Robert and having a bath. When she felt ready and clean, she went home to David. He was there, waiting for her, but they both knew that this was no time for talking.

The new bed was beautiful and had a wonderful christening.

Afterwards they both lay back and lived for a moment or two in their own private thoughts. Gently she asked him when he had to get back. They had about two hours left.

Sheila tried to think of something to say, but words didn't come easily to her. She felt in her heart that it might be better if David went immediately. Somehow, they had reached the high point of his leave. The last few hours since he came home had been spent going up, they had been finding each other again after a long absence. Reaching higher and higher, they had just passed the peak, and as she tried to think of something to say, she realised that the longer he stayed the nearer they would get to rowing.

She fell back on old ground, and they talked about the children. It was a subject they had in common and which it was natural to talk about, just as two strangers might talk about the weather, or the raids on Liverpool. For the two strangers it would be safe ground, and for David and Sheila, anything that touched on their marriage was by no means safe. They touched on subjects gently, pressing the weak spots and then darting off again like fish sniffing round a bait.

There was a long silence and David rolled over on to his side,

'Sheila, love,' he said, 'can you lend me five quid?'

'You in debt, or something,' she asked.

It was a touchy place for him and he was quickly on the defensive.

'Just tell me whether you have or haven't, Sheila,' he said quickly, 'or otherwise, forget it.'

'We've got to think about the future,' she said, after telling him that she did have the money, and needling him by suggesting that it was the money he came for and not her, 'we've got to have something to give us a start after it's all over.'

He sat up, and put his head in his hands. A feeling of blank empty terror passed across his mind as it always did at the mention of a future.

'Future, what future?' he said, 'You know where my future is? You know where it stops? When I climb in that bloody plane, that's where it stops.'

He looked at her lying there.

'You know nothing, Sheila, you know nothing.'

'You can have the five pounds,' she said.

Tension dropped off him again and he regretted his words. He took her in his arms, and comforted her and himself.

'Don't leave me, Davey,' she whispered, 'please don't leave me.'

He savoured the moment of tenderness and stored it away in his mind for future comfort. This was what he would remember, he thought, when the future stopped one fine day.

One fine day, dropping out of the sky like an arrow. All about him, the space of the sky, and the split second knowledge that the future, that hope had just deserted him. Like old friends, like lovers, they would walk away laughing.

And then?

'And then?' said Margaret.

Michael was telling her that he had had a conversation with Edwin the previous night.

'I told him that I didn't know how much longer I could stay a conscientious objector, that's all,' he said.

'And then, you'll join up,' she said.

'I just wonder whether I have any option, that's all,' he said, 'when it's all over and assuming we win, I just wonder whether it won't be like that last lot. Just an accident of history. The great cause just a sham. The powers of darkness no darker than the powers of light.'

He was almost talking to himself, for Margaret's mind was on other things. Here she was, having come into her harbour and having got there, finding that the water was running out, about to leave her high and dry.

'I may as well go home then,' she said.

'Don't be silly,' he replied, 'not in this.'

The evening had passed and they were sitting in Michael's living-room drinking tea. It was late, about ten o'clock and the sirens had gone some time ago. Margaret felt surrounded by darkness, lost as if she was walking through a maze out of which she didn't know the way, and had no chance of finding it.

'Can't you see, Michael, that I have to go. You'd only be asking me to go through the whole thing again, everything I went through with John again,' her voice began to falter and the words became lost in the tears, 'I couldn't face it, Michael, I couldn't . . . I just couldn't.'

She sat still for a moment and he came over to comfort her. He put his arms round her as he had done many times before, but the certainty had gone from his touch and had gone from the feel of her body.

He thought of his child inside her.

She thought of his child inside her.

She thought of John George too, and of John, and she wondered whether he was dead, and if so, how it had come to him. She imagined a big explosion, and wondered if he had trodden on a mine, or been shot, or whether a bomb had hit him.

And she was there too, with him in the moment of his death.

A crash.

And the ceiling falling down.

And the maze that she was walking through opened up into a long deep dark well and she was falling down it, spinning, round and round.

And the silence.

Michael crawled out from under the rubble, and looked round, but he could see no sign of Margaret.

Everything was still and his voice echoed across the silence like the pathetic mew of a cat down a back alley as it comes to the end of its last fight.

'Margaret, Margaret.'

So this is how the world ends, he thought.

The uncertainty had lashed back and hit him in the groin, and he knew that he was lost.

Nothing, nothing was for sure any more.

And the future?

Michael collapsed among the rubble, and his hand stretched out of its own accord as if grasping for something that was out of reach, but not far away.

A spider crawled on to his little finger, knowing that it was safe.

CHAPTER TWO

May 1941

The all-clear sounded later that night.

The Ashtons walked up through the garden to the house like a band of refugees, coats and blankets over their arms, flasks hanging from their arms, and a look of downcast submission on their faces.

Jean was first into the kitchen.

'I'm going straight up to bed,' she said and did not move.

Robert followed. He put his dirty coat on the kitchen table and, leaning with one arm on the table he pushed his lank hair back on to the top of his head,

'I'll be glad to get back to sea if this carries on,' he said. He looked at his mother and saw the momentary shadow pass over her face. It's got to be said, he thought to himself.

Freda was at the sink, rinsing out the flask. She stood up straight for a moment and ran some cold water into the flask. Carefully she held it upside down and let the clear water drip out slowly as if she was measuring time by it.

'Margaret got a key?' she said.

Jean darted a glance at her, wondering if she had said it on purpose. She replied calmly,

'No, she hasn't, but I don't think we need wait up for her.'

'She's gone to Michael's, hasn't she?'

Freda's persistence was almost evil as if she was intent on twisting the knife where it had already punctured the skin. Jean was too tired to react, although she still felt the barb tearing at her flesh.

'Yes,' she said wearily, 'your father should be back soon. Tell him I'll see to the alarm, will you?'

Slowly Jean walked out of the kitchen. There was a stoop in her walk and a dragging to her feet that came from more than just tiredness. She paused at the doorway as if to say something more, but then she turned and went into the hall as if there was nothing more to be said.

Freda and Robert exchanged glances, but neither of them said a word.

There seemed little point in speech.

Behind him, the fading glow of fire.

Michael's house lay in ruins, the roof caved in and the windows blown out. Others in the street had suffered the same fate, and a pall of suffering hung in the air along with the smoke. It sat heavily on the shoulders of the stooped figures who wandered the broken landscape.

Some people scuttled about with a certain purpose to their movement. Michael felt no such purpose.

He leaned against a wall and was sick.

His last conscious memory was of shouting for Margaret and from there on he could remember nothing. Somehow he must have escaped, and somehow he was leaning against the wall of his house being sick. Quite why, he didn't know.

'You all right, son?' a voice said from behind him.

Michael turned and his eyes slowly registered the warden. He was writing things down and Michael heard himself answering questions. He wondered why. Slowly it dawned on him that it was light.

Early morning, thought Michael.

It struck him that a whole night had passed by, a whole six or seven hours lifted bodily from his memory and from his life and of which he had no recollection.

'Is it your wife we're looking for,' said the warden.

'No, no . . . just a friend,' said Michael.

He supposed he had told the warden Margaret's name earlier on and that they had been looking for her. Laconically, as if nothing mattered any more he wondered if she was dead. He remembered that there was something he ought to say. He searched his mind, right back into its inner recesses.

'She's pregnant,' he said.

Later on he found himself sitting in a hospital corridor. His arm was bandaged and there was a plaster on his face. By this time he had sorted things out in his mind. He knew where he was and what had happened. The corridor was busy with nurses and doctors, wheeling trolleys back and forth. It was like a shunting yard. There was a tap on his shoulder and the nurse smiled her warm practised smile.

'You can go in and see her now,' she said.

Michael got up, instinctively putting his good arm over the bandaged one. A man was wheeled by in a chair and Michael felt guilty at suffering such a small pain with so many others around who had suffered so much more.

Margaret was in the bed nearest the door. She opened her eyes and saw him standing over her. She blinked and the mists began to disappear.

'You've hurt your hand,' she said.

'It's nothing,' he replied, 'just a bruise.'

'I forgot to tell the nurse about the baby, it's important, they'll want to know.'

'I've told them already,' he said.

Margaret was in no condition to talk and Michael just sat beside the bed for a moment. A silence fell between them, and they both drifted off into their own private thoughts. After a moment, Margaret opened her eyes again.

'Is the house all gone?' she asked.

'Yes, all gone.'

'Nowhere to live together.'

She was beginning to fall asleep and the drugs they had given her were taking their effect again. As she struggled to speak, Michael leaned nearer her. Her words became blurred. The thoughts behind them were slipping away.

'You don't want to though, do you? You want to go away and fight.' She paused as if gaining strength. 'Poor Michael, you're all at sixes and sevens aren't you?'

It was as if she had achieved a final moment of clarity and the effort finally tired her. She drifted away into sleep, muttering as she went, speaking her dreams out loud,

'Nowhere to live together ... Uncle Sefton promised us a flat ... for John to come back to.'

He caught the name of her husband and turned away from her. He wondered how often she thought of John and whether it was when they were in bed together. For a bit he sat and looked at her as she slept, but then, finding it too painful he took his hand from her arm and went away.

He'd remembered that he had something to do. As yet her parents didn't know what had happened.

Edwin handed the telephone over to Freda and went into the kitchen where Jean was doing the last of Robert's clothes. She looked up at him as she smoothed the iron along a shirt collar. They both looked tired.

'I don't know,' he said, 'when Owen rang up before Christmas and I invited him to stay, Freda nearly bit my head off.'

Jean didn't seem to be listening to what Edwin was saying.

'Who?'

'Owen, the Australianised Welshman,' he said, trying to make light of the tension between them. Methodically, painstakingly she folded the shirt, and laid it on the sideboard. Then, with one hand still resting on the material she turned to her husband.

'She didn't come back last night then?'

The apparent casualness of her voice belied the tension that was beneath it.

'Margaret?' replied Edwin innocently. He could see now the kind of mood that Jean was in and was determined to do his best to avoid a confrontation. 'Well, it's just as well she didn't isn't it? Once the raid had started it was the most sensible thing to do.'

'You don't have to pretend with me,' she said, 'we mentioned it last night and now it's happened. She's gone to live with him.'

She paused and added as if it was an afterthought, 'I suppose she'll be coming back for her things today.'

As Edwin looked at Jean, he suddenly felt a rush of sympathy towards her. He put out his arm and touched her shoulder, but she flinched and drew away as if there was something indecent in his touch.

'Do you mind very much?' he said. He knew that it was a useless question, for it was obvious how much she minded. He supposed any mother would have felt the same.

'Yes, of course I mind,' she said, 'but I suppose it's the best thing for her and the baby.'

Jean hesitated before she mentioned the undeniable fact of the child. Somehow it offended her, but it was there and she had to admit it. Both of them were trying to keep as calm as possible. They talked about when she would give up her teaching job. The atmosphere became more and more charged. The words they uttered seemed strangely mechanical for such a subject.

'I suppose she'll hand in her notice when everything's settled between them,' said Edwin.

Jean looked up at him. His words struck a chord in her.

'Settled?' she asked, 'but I thought they were settled.'

Edwin paused for a moment, realising that he had not told her about the conversation he had had with Michael.

'There's a chance he might go into one of the services,' he said.

Jean was shocked. The fact that they were going to live together was bad enough, but to do that and then leave her for the services seemed heartless and cruel. Unthinkable.

'Don't you think he owes her a little certainty,' she said sharply.

'Yes, I do,' he replied. He saw the flame in Jean's face, and it ignited the anger that was smouldering in his own heart, 'what you've at last just admitted as the only way for them would have been settled long ago if you'd faced up to it.'

His frustrations at last found vent. He'd sat on the fence for months, trying not to express how he really felt for fear of upsetting Jean. Now his temper flared.

'Why else do you think they've held back?' he asked and then in the same breath he answered his own question, 'it's because they've been waiting for you, waiting for you to get used to the idea.'

The doorbell rang, interrupting their anger with its insolent tinkle. Edwin went to answer thinking that it would be Owen. A moment later he reappeared. His large frame filled the door, hiding the person behind him.

'Who is it?' asked Jean, not looking up.

Edwin stepped aside and Jean saw Michael standing there. His arm was still bandaged and the plaster was still on his face. This was the moment he had been dreading. It was the moment for which he felt most guilty. All the 'ifs' in the world were playing hide and seek in his mind, and in spite of his total ability to justify himself and to blame what had happened on circumstance he still couldn't help but feel that somehow it was his fault.

Worst of all he knew that they would blame him.

Jean looked at him. She saw the downcast look in his eye and with a mother's instinct she knew what had happened. It was her final justification for opposing them. To her there was something in Michael's face and in his way of walking that meant only one thing. Bad luck.

Jean walked through the door between the two men.

No one spoke.

Their two faces merged into one and out again. They floated indistinguishably in front of her.

She was crying.

Later that morning, Jean and Edwin sat in the corridor outside the ward where Margaret was lying. They were sitting in the same position that Michael had taken earlier. The only difference was that the corridors were quieter. Quieter almost than they had a right to be. Huddled together on the end of the empty bench they looked as if they were cowering together seeking warmth in each other's body. They spoke in whispers. And yet two people so close together could hardly have been farther apart. Their conversation was spasmodic, desultory, like a drip of water on a tin roof. The words they spoke had no meaning, unless their meaning was that they had no meaning.

'Sefton hasn't been round lately,' said Jean.

'He's too concerned with that pig of his,' said Edwin.

The mention of Sefton's pig made Jean want to laugh a long high-pitched hysterical laugh. It was so irrelevant, so ludicrous. A picture of Sefton's pig, sniffing and snorting in someone's back garden crossed her mind gratuitously. She imagined it, fat and ugly, smelling already of the bacon he would turn it into.

Then she thought of Margaret.

'John's been on my mind a lot lately,' she said.

'Yes, in mine too,' echoed Edwin.

'It's been such a time.'

'The years seem longer these days. Grey. All the same.' Edwin shrugged unable to properly collect his thoughts, 'October's a funny month,' he said.

'October?' asked Jean, wondering if he had forgotten that it was May.

Edwin wanted to tell Jean about the paper he had seen blowing along the street that day. Pieces running along in the wake of a car, falling over themselves like leaves. And how the water had seemed grey and colourless, without reflection. No clouds, no blue sky shimmering on the ripples. The year was at a point when it should be growing, be happy and fruitful. And yet there was no warmth. No warmth in his heart and in the heart of the small group of people who were his family.

They were like strangers in a foreign land.

The year felt as if it was dying a slow death in the moment when it should be sprouting life. With it, it was taking lives, his friends and acquaintances, and their sons too.

He wondered what winter would be like.

'Did Michael mention the baby,' asked Jean.

'No, I don't think so.'

'You realise she could lose it?'

Jean made the statement like a cooking recipe, or an instruction to a stranger as to how to get to the pier head. So calm so casual as if life had become that unimportant that it could be dismissed in the flick of a finger.

Which it can, thought Edwin, but it should not be in our minds to add to the destruction.

She went on in the same tone of voice.

'He's only marrying her because of the baby. A release. It would be a release.'

Edwin was shocked. She was talking as if the baby was a sock, to be discarded if there was a hole, or abandoned when it smelt.

'For you or for her,' he asked.

'I'm just trying to be logical, Edwin,' she said, 'I know she doesn't care for him and that he doesn't really care for her.'

'How can you say that? You don't know how they feel, how other people feel. No one can presume to know that.'

He thought of his own marriage and knew that he was right.

'You'd see if John came back.'

This was the last straw, and Edwin chose the most brutal words he could find. There was an almost childish delight for him in what he was about to say for he knew that she had gone far beyond the bounds of propriety, beyond all reason, and he felt the right to do the same.

'John isn't coming back. He's dead. Rotting somewhere in Belgium with two tags round his neck, and I'm not imagining it, Jean. You can't turn away from facts by thinking your way round them. Those tags will turn up one day, you know.'

He wanted to go on and talk of John's death in foul vile terms. He wanted to defile the memory of his son-in-law in his wife's mind, and to forcefully burn it out and throw it away in ashes. In filthy wet stinking ashes. It was like the devil inside him stinging him with its forked tail and taking him to the edge of an abyss. He wanted to say words that would sear themselves on Jean's mind and that were so hot and so fierce she would never forget them. He wanted to paint a picture of death and decay vile as a massacre and foul as a pile of stinking corpses.

He said only one sentence. In that sentence there was all the truth in the world, all the human truth. The core of what he was thinking.

'You wouldn't wish it on him would you? To come back to all this.'

There were no more words for what he wanted to say. They did not exist.

The language had failed him.

They sat in silence, and his sentence came back to him, flapping round his mind like an old rooster. He had made a human statement, and one that encompassed vast areas of silence.

After they went in, Jean was first to the bed. She leant over her daughter quickly and kissed her cheek.

'Hello love,' she said.

As she returned the kiss, Margaret looked over her mother's shoulder and saw Edwin standing there. She noticed a small tear in the front of his coat and the hat between his hands that got more and more crumpled as the years went by. She remembered it as a nice clean firm hat, but then she realised that the years had worn it as they had worn all of them. There was care written over her father's face, long painful lines of worry across his skin and in the sag of his belly and shoulders.

Margaret felt sad. She regretted the trouble she was causing them. Her heart and affection went out to the crumpled figure of her father as he stood there waiting for Jean to give him a chance to speak to her.

She wondered why the patterns of life were so hard on them all. Why, again and again, the prospects for them all were embroidered with so many stitches, so many pangs of suffering, and why the picture seemed to be always a sad one. Faded and frayed at the edges. No longer bright and beautiful with hope.

She remembered her teaching days. They were gone now and she wondered whether the happiness and satisfaction would ever come back to her or whether she would spend the rest of her life teaching from an empty soul, giving no love and humanity.

And getting none in return.

That afternoon, Edwin went back to work as usual. He crossed the ferry and noticed as he leant over the side of the boat, the dull lifeless light that the sky was casting on the water. In a way, it crystallised for him what he had been trying to say to Jean in the hospital. He knew his brain moved cumbersomely and it got slower and slower as time went on. It was no longer the agile creature that it had been as a young man. He had been trying to say something about time and inevitability. Not that he believed that man had no hold over his fate, but his life had run along lines which made him think more and more that the only thing to do was to run along with the tide.

One day it would turn, but he had given up fighting against it.

In times like the ones they were living in, there were so many imponderables that it seemed to him a question of adjusting to them and to accepting them. Not fighting against them and rejecting them.

He sat at his desk, vaguely fiddling with the cup of tea that was in front of him. There were a million things he could do. Like sorting out the filing or checking on some orders that he knew were getting behind hand, but he couldn't seem to put his mind to anything in particular. Anyway, he was expecting Michael in a few moments. He heard the sound of his steps coming down the rickety flight of stairs that led to the office. They stopped outside the door and in the frosted glass Edwin saw Michael's oddly distorted figure. It was like looking at someone in a badly shattered and bent mirror.

Which perhaps, he thought, was how he had been seeing Michael. Through the bent distortions of his preconceptions. There were so many things that got in the way of his understanding of Michael. He was Margaret's father. He had the pressures of the family to bend his view of the man.

'I should make more effort,' thought Edwin.

Michael pushed the door open hesitantly.

'You found us,' said Edwin, feeling as nervous as Michael obviously was.

'Yes, it was quite a nice trip across the river actually.'

Michael walked into the office carefully as if scared to offend even the old brown furniture.

Edwin invited him to sit down. As he did so, Edwin stood up. He walked across to the filing cabinet at the other side of the room and leant against it. Seeing no point in beating about the bush, Edwin broached the subject straight.

Michael understood what he was getting at immediately.

'You want to know if I'm going into the army or stick it out as a pacifist,' he said.

'Stick it out?' asked Edwin, slightly surprised at Michael's choice of words.

'Have you ever been a pacifist, Mr Ashton?'

'No, but I've had leanings,' said Edwin truthfully.

Michael gave a little knowing smile at Edwin's reply. It was something that he had heard so many times from people before, and he hated it for its sloppiness and lack of conviction. And yet, coming from this large man who sat in front of him it was almost an appeal for sympathy.

'It's not the same though, is it?' said Michael, 'of course, it's supposed to be quite a respectable position these days. There's not the same disapproval as there was from people in the last war, and not so many of us in jail either.'

He paused for a moment, thinking.

'I don't mind the odd anonymous letter, but what I do mind is losing my friends. The way they seem inevitably to drift away as if there was nothing else to be done.'

Edwin felt that the more he talked to Michael, the more he liked and sympathised with him. There was a conviction underneath what he said that Edwin admired, and there was also a pain at the circumstances to which his beliefs had taken him that showed the courage he had in him to be there.

Not the courage of a soldier in action, but a different kind of courage, a different kind of fight. And, Edwin thought, if you must evaluate it, a better fight.

'I hate fascism, you know,' said Michael after Edwin had mentioned the word, 'I hate it because of the bomb that nearly finished off Margaret and I. I hate it because of the torn flesh and blood that I see every day in the hospital. Sometimes it makes me want to get up and fight, and to do more than just shake my fist; but then what are you doing?' He paused as if expecting Edwin to answer, 'in the end it means that I'm doing just what I hate, doing the same things to human flesh and blood, to children like my Barbara . . .' Michael's voice trailed off. He didn't know how to finish the sentence. It was a sentence to which, perhaps, there was no end.

'It's madness, isn't it?' said Edwin.

'Yes, and it's a difficult madness to try and sort out. My beliefs aren't what they once were, I don't have a great unshakeable conviction. It's just very difficult.'

'She's going to be all right, you know,' said Edwin, trying to bring up the subject of Margaret tactfully. He picked up his tea and took a sip, but realised that it had gone cold. He put it down gently.

'It just needs time and patience,' he said.

'Yes, I suppose that's what it's going to take if I'm going to marry her.'

'If she was free now, would you?' asked Edwin.

'If she was going to give the same answer, then yes, I would.'

'Don't you think she would?'

Michael looked up and stared Edwin straight in the eye. He brushed his hand across his forehead as if brushing away a thought.

'I'm not sure,' he said. There was an unmistakeable note of frankness in his voice, 'it's just that I sometimes think it's only the baby, you know?'

Edwin knew what he meant and was about to answer when a tall figure in uniform came through the door. Tony looked clean and handsome and Michael looked up at him and contrasted his clothes, shabby and worn with the freshness of Tony's navy blue.

It was more than just a difference in clothing, it was a total outlook on life and it bit into Michael's conscience, shaking his resolution that little bit more.

'They sent me over to see father,' said Tony. 'His piggy's pregnant,' he added flippantly. He had sensed the atmosphere between the two men and his eyes darted from one to the other trying to sense exactly what it was that he had interrupted.

The conversation between Michael and Edwin was obviously over now that it had been interrupted, but for the sake of good manners, Tony took Michael on a guided tour of the works. Just before they both went, Tony popped his head round the door and said goodbye to Edwin. Michael did so too.

Edwin spent what was the remainder of the afternoon going through his outstanding work, and he was just about to leave early in order to get to see Margaret when there was another knock at the door. This time it was a nervous, hesitant knock. A woman's knock. Edwin thought briefly how funny it was that in all his years he had become very adept at trying to assess someone's character by the way they knocked at his door.

'Mr Ashton?'

Edwin at once recognised the neurotic strained tones of the voice. He knew it well.

It was Mrs Porter.

Pictures flashed through his mind in the second it took him to turn around. Pictures of Michael and Margaret and of his daughter lying, injured and pregant in the hospital.

'Come in, Mrs Porter,' he said.

Edwin thought quickly, wondering why she had come. He wondered if she had found out about Margaret, or at least heard something. She still knew people in the area and some-one could have passed the news on. Edwin was scared and his knees almost trembled with fear. This wizened, sticky woman had the knack of making him afraid.

'The truth is, Mr Ashton, it's been out of sight, out of mind since we left Liverpool, hasn't it?' she said, sitting down, 'the letter I had from Mrs Ashton was the first since Christmas and Margaret hasn't written since then either.'

Edwin explained tentatively that Margaret hadn't been too well. He daren't lie because he didn't know how much this woman knew, and anyway he was afraid she might sense that he was speaking in half-truths.

'He is our grandson, you know,' said Mrs Porter of John George, pursuing the subject like a hound on the trail of a disappearing rabbit. Suddenly her voice faltered and she reached for the edge of the table as if to steady herself. Edwin noticed a bead of sweat on her forehead and realised that she was near to fainting. He waited a moment for her to recover and then decided that he might as well tell her about Margaret.

'Mrs Porter,' he said, 'Margaret was injured in the raid last night and she's in hospital.'

'Is the baby all right,' she said immediately.

Edwin stopped. He looked at her for a moment thinking that it was the moment he had feared and that she knew about Michael. Then he realised that it was John George to whom she was referring.

'The baby, yes he's all right. Margaret was out you see, visiting a friend.'

Mrs Porter's mind slipped from subject to subject as if it could not stand to stay still for a moment. Edwin listened to her usual diatribe against Harry and took no notice. He sat there and let her talk for a few minutes. He looked at his watch surreptitiously. It was almost time for him to be getting back. They would be waiting to go to the hospital.

'Was there anything you wanted me to do for you,' he asked, assuming that she wouldn't have come all the way from Chorley for just a chat about Margaret. This woman didn't do things like that.

'Yes,' she fiddled with the clasp of her bag and produced a letter. It was crumpled as if it had been read over and over again. She held it in her palm, turning it round and round her fingers like a string of worry-beads.

'You see,' she said, 'I got this letter about John.'

John.

Edwin froze.

The mention of the name took the ground from under his feet, and for a moment he half expected the slight figure of his son-in-law to walk through the door.

All his assumptions fell about his ears.

He looked at Mrs Porter but there was no expression on her face to allow him to know what she was thinking.

'John?' he asked.

'From a man in the army. In Liverpool. He was out in France and he found it.'

She spoke so calmly that Edwin was amazed.

'I suppose you'd better read it, Mr Ashton. There's another letter inside it telling his father about my birthday. He always used to remind Harry about my birthday. He never used to let him forget about my birthday.'

She was repeating the phrase as if it was important to her, as if it gave her some much needed contact with John. The strain of telling him about the letter was beginning to show on her face, and that little twitch she so often had came back to the side of her mouth. The corner of her lips jumped as if divorced from the rest of her body.

Edwin read the letter. It read that the man who had found it had picked it up in a field.

Just that.

No mention of a body or anything that might give a clue.

She told Edwin that she had arranged to meet the man who sent the letter in a pub where he worked.

'I was going to offer to go instead of you if you wished,' offered Edwin, trying to gauge her mood, 'don't you think it might be distressing for you?'

'After what I've been through?' she gave a little choked and hysterical laugh, 'after the telegram and then the one that never came.'

'The one that never came?'

'We didn't have one to say that he's been definitely killed, did we? And if he had been killed then we'd have had one to say so, wouldn't we, Mr Ashton?'

She paused, 'And anyway, I know he's alive. I just know it.'

She said it with such certainty that Edwin knew there was no point in arguing with her. He didn't want to go through again what he'd been through with Jean. He looked at the hope burning in her eyes and felt sad for her. It was a hope that would last for ever, probably way past the time when there was even the remotest possibility that John would return. Probably way past the end of the war. He imagined her dead and felt that that hope would still be written on her face. He wanted to comfort her. To ease her pain.

'I'll come with you, Mrs Porter,' he said.

Edwin got up from his desk and put his coat on. They left the office and started the slow journey across the river. All the way across, Edwin wondered what he would say when they got home. He thanked his lucky stars that Michael was at work that evening.

Jean and Freda knew that she was in Liverpool as a telegram had arrived from Harry that afternoon. Cryptically it had said, 'Celia arriving. Look after her.'

'It doesn't necessarily mean she'll be in Liverpool today,' said Freda trying to look on the good side, 'it could be any time.'

Jean thought of Michael and Margaret and was thankful that Margaret's injury had necessitated a cage over her middle.

'We'll have to take her, you know,' Freda went on, 'she's bound to insist that she comes to the hospital.'

Jean put the finishing touches to the pie she was making for their supper and asked Freda to put it in the oven for her. She stood up, putting her hands to the small of her back as if to help her upright. She felt weary and remembered the satisfaction she used to get out of doing simple things for the family. Now, she felt that everything was a chore. They had become the moments she marked her life by and not the substance of it.

Empty movements, empty things surrounded her. The flesh and blood had gone out of the family.

'Supposing Michael's there,' asked Freda.

'He can't come tonight, he's on duty.'

'That puts off the evil day then.'

Jean moved over to the sink to rinse her hands. She paused with her hand on the tap.

'Which is just as well, because it might never come,' she said.

'How do you mean?' asked Freda.

She looked at her mother and noticed that the lines about her eyes were more pronounced these days and her actions slower. Freda saw the way the skin was pulling back from her eyes, straining at the cheek bones, and accentuating the round almost blank eyes. Jean was staring at Freda but not seeing her. She seemed to be looking straight past her into space. For a moment Freda thought she knew what her mother meant, but she put it out of her mind. People didn't think like that.

As they talked, Jean washed up and Freda sat on the sideboard. They were both talking, knowing that they were trying to avoid the implications of Jean's remark. It was one of those things that should never have been said and they both knew it.

Like people everywhere, they were faced with something and were doing their best to pretend it never happened.

Freda mentioned that she had taught Owen how to put on nappies during the afternoon. She had spent several hours with him, alone, and she was no nearer to being sure of her feelings towards him.

Inside her, she remembered the moment during the afternoon when he had put a hand on her knee, inside her she felt something stirring, but she wasn't quite sure what it was. It might have been an awareness of him and his physical presence, and obviously part of it was due to that, but there was something else too. She couldn't put her finger on it. It wasn't another man. But it was something that was around all the time, that was in the air. There was something inside her that was preparing her, but she didn't know what for.

Edwin opened the front door carefully, and hung his hat and coat in the usual places. He heard Jean and Freda in the kitchen, but the door was closed.

'Would you mind not saying anything about the letter,' he

said to Mrs Porter in a low conspiratorial whisper, 'we don't want to raise anyone's hopes, do we?'

'Hopes?' said Mrs Porter, not quite understanding.

'Just say you've come on business, to do with your old house.'

Jean and Freda came out of the kitchen and welcomed their visitor with as much enthusiasm as they could muster in the circumstances. Freda took her upstairs to wash and Jean and Edwin went to wait in the living-room. As they entered, Jean closed the door and stood with her back to it, her hands on the handle, barring the way to anybody else. Edwin sensed the blame on his wife's face. It was in the way she stood, and it told him that, in her own way, she held him responsible, not only for everything that had happened but also for the fact that Mrs Porter had arrived.

'Try and keep her happy,' he said, 'if for nothing else than for the sake of Margaret. If she's kept happy then perhaps she won't upset everyone so much. Besides she's an unhappy woman.'

'Has she said why she's come?'

Edwin lied and told her that it was on some sort of business she wanted help with. He was so vague as to the reason that he could see his wife didn't believe him, but they were too weary to pursue the subject. For the sake of a moment's peace, they let it lie fallow, until, thought Edwin, some future time when it would all be brought up again like unpleasant undigested food. He could foresee a conversation when Jean, and it could be years from now, would quite unexpectedly talk about this moment. She would repeat every word he said, down to its minutest inflection. She would know whether he was sitting or standing and she would know the title of the book he had in his hand. Her ability to remember everything and to recall every detail was something that amazed him. It terrified him too.

'Anyway,' he said, 'Michael won't be there. That's one blessing.'

'And one of us had better stay with Margaret all the time to see that she doesn't get too upset,' said Jean.

After they had gone out, leaving Owen with the baby he heard the sound of crying upstairs, and had to go and quieten it. His attempt for the first time in his life to change a baby's nappy was not a particularly great success and he was pleased to hear the doorbell go. He ran downstairs hoping perhaps that it was Freda, or if not, then some other member of the family. He needed reinforcements badly.

He opened the door to Michael, who introduced himself, being as surprised to find a strange Australian in the house as Owen was to find Michael at the door.

'Do you know anything about babies,' asked Owen apologetically.

Michael smiled and remembered that he did. He had tended his own child, Barbara, after his wife had died, and he expected that, fairly soon he would be getting back into practice. He looked at his watch.

'I don't want to miss visiting hours at the hospital,' he said, 'I managed to get a few moments off to go and see Margaret.'

He didn't pursue the subject as it was obvious that Owen didn't know what his connection with the family was. He felt it better not to go into detail, indeed, not to go into it at all.

'I suppose I'll get there before they leave,' he said, 'but I was rather hoping to find them still here.'

They both went up the stairs to do what obviously had to be done by the sound of the continuing crying. It took Michael only a few minutes to see to the child and Owen was left, lost in admiration and praise when he left for the hospital. He couldn't thank him enough.

No sooner had Owen settled down in the living-room to listen to the radio, than Robert returned.

'Chap called Michael was here,' said Owen, 'you must have passed him on the road.'

'No,' replied Robert, 'I didn't see him. Maybe he went the other way.'

'Shouldn't think so. He was on the way to the hospital. That's where you've been isn't it?'

Robert toyed with the idea of running out to see if he could catch Michael, but decided against it. He didn't want to involve himself too much. Leave it to them, he thought, and anyway he knew he always made a mess of things if he started interfering.

'Manage his nappy all right?' he asked Owen casually, falling back on the easiest conversation he could make.

'Yeh, but frankly if I hadn't felt so down for the chap I'd have left him, I think.'

'Down?' asked Robert, not quite understanding the phrase.

'Well, you know, him not having a father and that. It's pretty rotten.'

'Yes,' said Robert, 'it's pretty rotten.'

He thought of the conversation he had had with Margaret earlier in the evening. She had asked him if it embarrassed him, her having a baby and no husband. He had replied that it didn't make any difference to him. A gentle loving look had come into her eye and he wondered how someone with so many troubles, so much to bear could still have so much love left in her face and give it out so fully.

Once he had had a picture of his sister as a bit hard and as a schoolmistress not only in her occupation, but also in her heart. He knew now that that picture had faded and that another one had taken its place. A picture of someone who, for the rest of his life, he knew he would do anything for because he knew that she would do anything for him.

'Well,' he said to Owen, 'I met a smashing Judy at the hospital.'

He smiled at Owen and Owen smiled back, but their smiles were curious. They were not ones of humour, but of sadness for there had been a future in what Robert had said. Not an overt future, but an implied one. One of hope.

'Reckon she'll miss me when I'm gone,' he added wistfully.

The idea of people going away brought them both together. They had seen far too many people go, far too many people miss others who had gone and one day, they knew, it could be their turn. A kind of love broke out between them for a moment and Robert almost wanted to hug the strange man who sat in front of him.

He didn't, of course, but they had both found a moment of comfort in each other.

Comfort was something that Margaret had not felt at the sight of Mrs Porter coming into the ward. Fear, unease, foreboding had all sprung through her body, but not comfort.

'We should have been closer to each other you and I,' said Mrs Porter as she leaned over to straighten Margaret's pillow, 'we should have been closer.'

Had she lived a hundred years, Margaret could never be close to this woman. She was too selfish, cruel to those she pretended to love. The only love that Mrs Porter knew was the love of others for herself, and that she ignored. She seemed incapable of giving.

'How's Harry,' Margaret asked.

A look of hurt passed over the older woman's face as if Margaret had touched an old wound and exposed it to the sun.

'You always got on with Harry, didn't you? As a matter of fact he's not very well. You see he's always complaining about some pain or other. Just headaches, he says, but he should know some of the headaches I get and then he'd know what it's like. These days he just comes home and sits by the fire. Never says a word to me any more. Not a word. Just stares. He always was a starer was Harry. I expect he's staring at my things now, what with me being away I expect he's taken the chance to look through everything I've got.'

She paused for a moment and looked at Margaret.

'Yes, you always did get on with Harry, didn't you?'

Margaret was tired and she knew better than to believe what Mrs Porter had said. She thought of Harry sitting there in front of the fire staring into it and doing his best to shut out the sound of his wife's rasping grating voice. Margaret was no longer listening to the stream of self pity that was pouring into her ear.

'I thought when we'd left Liverpool that I'd leave it all behind me. The memory of those terrible days after we got the telegram, and even, as you know, as I do, that all we have to do is hang on and wait, and wait and wait ... and wait for someone, you know who I mean, to return.'

This last sentence brought tears to her eyes and she lay her head across Margaret's lap and shed them into the blanket. Margaret lay her hand across the back of her neck and gently tapped the shaking shoulders.

'Don't cry, please don't cry,' she said.

It wasn't out of sorrow for the woman that she said this. Margaret knew that if she went on crying like this that she too would do the same.

Her will would break, and then, control all gone she would break into a long scream and probably go completely, totally mad.

At that moment, she envied madness.

She wanted to be living in a world that was all her own and in which there was no responsibility. Whatever the terror of madness she felt that it must be preferable to the weight of sanity.

And the weight of this woman's head, the mother of her husband, lying on the place where another man's child was, at this second, growing.

Michael arrived to find Freda, Jean and Edwin waiting outside the ward, but he wasn't given the chance to get any further as Freda bustled him quickly out of the hospital muttering that she would tell him what had happened later.

They sat in a little yellow stained cafe. Rings on the tables where dirty cups had been. Freda had arranged to meet Owen there.

They had walked in silence through the almost totally blacked out city. The buildings rising either side of them like ghosts in the sky. The streets down which they walked were empty and Michael had felt like a truant out of school.

He wanted to stop still and listen for the silence and to be back again in his youth. It was a quiet night such as they had not had for some time, and the silence was to be valued, to be cherished and the stillness was not something that happened often these days.

He wanted to be out of time and alone, still in a place where things never moved and where the buildings, so solid and reliable were the only things in the landscape.

He wanted his own private landscape to be made of such things that had not the power to grow, to live, to move and to require nourishment.

He looked at a house and it didn't move. It didn't answer to his gaze. It didn't avert its eyes. It stood. Quite still. Quite oblivious.

He thought of the baby growing in Margaret's womb.

He looked at Freda. She was pretty. She raised her cup to her lips and looked across the rim at him. She had told him about Mrs Porter and now the conversation was scratching around the edge of something much larger, much deeper.

It was as if they were both walking round the rim of one of the coffee cups. Both afraid to fall in, but both knowing that, having started from the opposite sides of a circle, they would inevitably clash. The rim was narrow and then they would both fall in.

'You don't like me very much, do you?' he said.

'I never said that.'

'No, and because I've said it, you're embarrassed, and you're embarrassed because you don't like me very much, isn't that it?'

Freda averted her eyes. She wondered if it was true that she didn't like him and hoped that it was. She knew she felt something for him and if it wasn't dislike, hatred even, she was afraid of the alternatives.

'If you must know, Michael, it's that I don't think you're right for Margaret.'

'In the same way as you know you're right for Owen?' he asked.

'That's my business,' she said sharply, a nerve having been touched, 'will you stay with her if she loses the baby?'

'I think that's a heartless and unfeeling question, especially at this point in time and in the way you say it. As a matter of fact, I've been asked it once before today and the answer then was, and still is, yes.'

He paused and then added,

'Look, I don't want to fall out with Margaret's sister, so won't you give me the benefit of the doubt?'

'You don't know anything about Owen,' she said sharply and in self defence. She spoke as if she was trying to convince herself about it and trying to hide from something else that she didn't want to face. Michael wondered what it was she was hiding from and suddenly he saw an unconscious look pass over her eyes. She was like a scared, cornered cat and he'd seen the look before. It was one he didn't like.

Owen arrived a minute later and his jolly bumptious greeting saved them from further conversation. Michael looked into the remains of his coffee and felt that he had been saved from falling into something that was so dark and murky that he couldn't quite fathom it. He put it out of his mind.

Somehow, he knew that it would return. He didn't know when or where or even how, but he knew that it would.

Freda knew it too.

The pub was dark and brown, and the paint peeled from the walls in large slices. It had a musty, Victorian atmosphere as if the heaviness of the walls was hiding something.

It was just like a million other pubs.

Edwin and Mrs Porter sat in the corner at a brown wood table. They had caught sight of the man they wanted to see behind the bar, and when Edwin had bought the drinks, the man, whose name was Cowking, had said that he would be over in a minute.

Edwin looked at Celia. She still had the letter in her hand and the sweat from her palm was soiling it. The ink was beginning to run and the words become indecipherable.

'Mrs Porter,' said Edwin, 'will you promise me something. Promise me that you won't expect anything too much from this?'

'It makes no difference to me, one way or the other,' she said, 'I've come. I mean I'm not expecting miracles, believe me.'

Edwin wondered at her sudden change of tone.

'It's what happens in here that counts, Mr Ashton,' she said, touching her heart.

He could see that she was referring to the fact that she thought she knew that John was still alive.

Cowking, they didn't know his first name and somehow it seemed irrelevant, came over to their table.

He was an older man, about fifty and his hair was receding slowly from his forehead. It was grey, a silvery knowledgeable kind of grey and his arm was in a sling. He walked with a limp too. He looked as if the times, and the war had touched him physically. Not in the mind like it had touched Edwin and Jean, but in the body.

'The letter was from my son, Mr Cowking,' said Mrs Porter, hardly giving him time to introduce himself.

She went on to ask direct questions of him, and Edwin could see that for some reason the man was hedging round her questions. Cowking kept glancing at Edwin as if for help. By carefully timed looks, Edwin at last established some sort of communication with the man, and was able to convey that Mrs Porter was not the most stable of women.

'Where did you find it?' she asked finally.

'Mrs Porter, it's not going to be any help to you . . . it's like I said in the letter you see . . . I just found it,' his hand went to his injured arm instinctively, and he looked at Edwin who could see there was more to it than he was saying, 'like you might find anything on the ground.'

'Was there anybody there?' asked Mrs Porter.

'Nobody, nobody at all. I was lost and trying to find the way to my unit, or anybody else's for that matter and there was only bits and pieces around where chaps had been. Not far from Tournai it was.'

'Nobody?'

'No, I'm sorry ... I should have made it more plain in the letter ... there was nobody at all.'

Mrs Porter was silent for a moment and her face took on a glazed look, her hands, which had for ever been turning the letter round and round, lay still in her lap.

Suddenly she stood up with her hand to her mouth, and her eyes looked feverishly about the room.

'It's over there,' said Cowking, 'second door on the left.'

'She's on the edge, isn't she?' asked Cowking after she had gone out of the room.

'Yes,' said Edwin, 'it's a pity we couldn't have talked before you saw her; you see her son, John, married my eldest daughter.'

Cowking paused for a moment.

'My wife had a missing telegram about me you know, she lost two stone and God knows how many years of her life so you see I think I know how you feel, Mr Ashton.'

They both looked at each other wondering if there was any more to be said. Cowking was tense and he played nervously with the sling as if it was rubbing round the back of his shoulder.

'It's a right bloody mess isn't it?'

Edwin nodded and said yes with his eyes.

There was a pause, and then Cowking spoke suddenly, his words breaking out like a spring that has broken.

'I found it on him,' he said.

'On John?' replied Edwin trying to remain calm.

'Yes, if I tell you, Mr Ashton then it'll be up to you whether you pass it on or not.'

'Of course.'

Cowking looked round the room to see if anyone was listening. He took a deep breath and then the flood started.

'He was lying at the side of the road. No holes in him and no blood that I could see. Badly bruised though. I felt for his ticker as best I could. His pay book wasn't on him and I was just about to take off his tags when the jerry planes started coming at the road, and I copped this.'

He tapped his arm again, and Edwin noticed for the first time that the hand was missing.

'I staggered around a bit and then a couple of officers picked me up. I tried to tell them about your chap, but I was half fainting and the words didn't come easy. The letter was still in my hand but they must have taken it off me and put it with my things.'

He paused again to get his breath.

'That's it really,' he said, 'but there's just one other thing. Just before the planes came over and it's up to you what you make of it. It's that I had the feeling he wasn't dead, that's all and I can't make it any better than that ... it's just a feeling I had.'

He stopped speaking and looked down at the surface of the table, making little circles in some liquid that was spilt there.

'You can't tell a woman a story like that, can you?' he said.

'No, no you can't.'

'So now you know and now I know.'

'Yes,' said Edwin.

Cowking sat in silence as did Edwin. His finger moved round and round on the top of the table making patterns in the liquid. Lines that crossed over each other, and parallel strokes that merged into each other. A form emerged and as Edwin looked at it, he thought that it ought to make some sense, to mean something. He tried to find faces, things, concrete pictures in the lines that Cowking was drawing. But there was nothing there, no sense to it all somehow. Edwin felt that if he sat here long enough and watched that finger moving for long enough, he would find the secret to what it was describing.

But it would take a long time.

'It's a right bloody mess, isn't it,' said Cowking at last and Edwin saw that there were tears in his eyes.

Yes, he thought to himself, it is a right bloody mess and he wanted to cry, to be in harmony with the man but the tears wouldn't come for there was far too much else on his mind.

He hadn't the time to cry.

The next day, Michael managed to get to see Margaret. She was looking much better and at last he felt they could talk. He'd made sure to come at a time when her family wouldn't be there.

'No raids last night?' said Margaret.

'No, no raids.'

'Perhaps they think we've had enough?'

'Yes, perhaps they do.'

Michael spoke slowly for he was searching in his mind to get the right words for what he had to say.

'I want to tell you something,' he said.

Margaret looked at him wondering what it was. She was prepared for him to say that he was going to join up, after all, now, with things as they were it seemed to her to be a turning point. If he wanted to go, to go away from her, it was the hardest time for him to do it, and the hardest time for her to bear it. There were so many things now, so many responsibilities pulling them together.

The hardest time was always the right time, she thought.

'All that business about . . . well, about feeling I had to join up,' he said, Margaret braced herself for the worst.

'I won't be.'

She wanted to cry with joy, to hug him and to press herself against him. To show him how much it meant to her that he had said what he had. She controlled herself.

'Because of me?'

'Partly. Quite a lot as a matter of fact, and because of the baby, of course,' he spoke calmly, 'I shall have to just go on objecting, only a little less conscientiously. It just makes it that much harder. Why should I have ever thought it would be easy?'

'You're a funny man,' she said.

There was some news she had for him too and she decided that now was the right time to tell him.

'The baby's all right. I'm not going to lose it.'

She looked straight at him wondering what his reaction was.

It was a time, at last for honesty.

'It would have been a way out for you, wouldn't it?' she said, at last echoing what had been on everybody's mind, and which all the time she had seen in the faces around her and yet had known that no one had the courage to say it to her face.

'Why should you think I want a way out?' he said, 'I don't want a way out. Do you?'

The moment of honesty had passed like a meteor touching them only briefly. It had gone, but it had left its mark. It was a step, something achieved between them, and now they had to build on it. But for the moment they were back, treading old ground carefully, just like any two human beings about to start a journey together. They were back feeling their way into each other, wondering about what lay inside each other and fearing every next step for what it might bring. Excitement, love, anything, even rejection.

'There isn't a way out now, is there?' she said, 'not for either of us.'

And the way he turned his eyes and the way she felt her heart quiver told her that it wouldn't be easy. Nothing between them would ever be easy, nothing would be simple. Ever.

She knew that there was a future there, between them, and yet like all futures it would bring what it would bring. There would be only one time when they would know what that was, what that had been.

Margaret wondered for an instant about the moment of her death, and what, lying there no longer alive, just what it was she would look back on.

She placed her hand on her stomach and felt the baby there.

She hoped that what they had, what they had been through and what they felt for each other would at least leave something behind, playing in the sun.

Outside, through the window of the ward, she saw the sun shining and the lattices of the window casting a mottled shadow on the floor.

Somewhere, far, far away a dog barked, the strains of music played and a child cried.

She was in the park playing with her husband, John and their child John George.

Michael looked at Margaret and for a moment she was his wife, lying there, dying, fading away.

She was in the park playing with her husband, Michael and their child.

He looked at her and she was his wife, Margaret, recovering, growing strong.

And they both went through time, back and forward again. Wondering.

He put his hand on hers and she squeezed it hard, so hard to make sure it was still there, still real.

And they were in the present.

And then?

CHAPTER THREE

October 1941

October set in. That funny mixture, half summer and half winter the leaves dying from the trees and as they fall to the ground, the residue of the summer sun shining through their thinness.

Towards the end of June, Margaret had moved out of the hospital and was now living at her home. The injuries had turned out to be a bit worse than they had expected and she was to be bedridden until after the arrival of her child. For the sake of ease, Edwin had turned the front room of the house into her bedroom. It saved a lot of trouble that way.

Edwin closed the door quietly. It was early evening and Margaret was having a rest while she waited for Michael to come round. Faithfully, the father of her child still came almost every evening and looked over her. He sat beside her and watched the moving of her face, he touched her hand and talked to her.

They were all waiting, and a stillness had settled over the house. Expectancy wrote itself into everything they did as if the birth of Margaret's child was going to change their world.

In a way it was, but what way that was going to be, none of them could tell.

Edwin looked out of the window in the living-room. From a tree at the bottom of the garden, a leaf dropped. It swung, from side to side to side almost pausing in the air as if it was frightened to touch the ground. It seemed scared to rest and preferred to be caught on the currents of air that directed its passage. At last it touched the ground and lay there.

The grass imprisoned it. Quite still.

A dead leaf, rotting, worming its way into the ground.

The hatch opened.

'Michael's come. He's with Margaret,' said Jean.

Edwin realised that he hadn't noticed the noise of the front door opening. He looked at his watch. Half an hour had passed since he left Margaret's room.

It happened often these days. Edwin just found himself

looking out of the window, or at a book, but not really looking, not thinking, just staring into space.

Jean came through into the living-room with a cup of tea. She set it on the table that Robert had brought back from Africa. For a moment, she paused, looking at the table and she touched it gently with her hand. Her fingers ran over the smooth wood and she thought of her youngest son. The table had come to mean a lot to her, and the longer that Robert stayed away, the more she treasured it as a reminder of the fact that he had been away and had come back.

'You realise that he's on nights!' said Edwin, 'he won't have slept.'

Jean looked at him, wondering what he was thinking of.

'We could put him up here,' Edwin continued, 'until she's had the baby.'

He paused for a moment and saw that what he was saying was having no effect on Jean.

'I went round to his place the other day and it turned my stomach, Jean. It's awful for the lad. Awful.'

'It's just not practical, Edwin,' said Jean, 'and I've too much on my hands as it is.'

Jean's attitude to Michael hadn't changed a bit. She was still cool and distant to him whenever he was in the house. To Edwin it seemed as if she was trying to forget that he existed, to freeze him out of her mind. She hardly seemed to speak to him and Edwin noticed her doing small, stupid things like pretending to forget to make him a cup of tea when they were all together in the living-room.

A moment later, Michael came into the room and with hardly a word, Jean went back to the kitchen.

Edwin reached down and picked up his slippers. Slowly he took his shoes off and put the slippers on.

'I used to get this job done for me,' he said, 'Freda did it. The first night she stopped, I knew she'd grown up.'

He looked up at Michael. He was standing in front of Edwin with a troubled look on his brow.

'Have you heard from your little girl lately?' asked Edwin, trying to get on to a more personal level with him.

'She seems to be settling in a bit better now.'

Edwin thought back to before the war, to a time when evacuation and the separation it brought with it weren't there. It had been a time when families could live happily together, and when children weren't just a parcel, wrapped up with a card round their necks, in the care of people they had never seen before.

'We had an old couple next door before the war broke out. She died a couple of days before it started. Practically the last thing she said to Wilf was, "I hope you all come through it all right." We have, haven't we?'

Michael ignored the invitation to talk about his personal feelings that was implied by Edwin's story.

'Margaret hasn't seemed so well today,' he said, 'but the doctor's coming tomorrow.'

Freda came in, her arms laden with nappies and towels. She stopped short when she saw Michael. Her eyes met his and then flicked away quickly.

'Mum said there was a letter from Philip,' she said to Edwin.

'Yes, he met Jack Barraclough. The boy who used to live down the parade.'

Freda hesitated a moment, as if she was calculating her next move.

'That'll be a thrill for him,' she said, 'wasn't he the one who was always shouting about not joining up?'

'He was a nice lad, Freda,' said Edwin quickly.

He often wondered about Freda's hostility to Michael. In a way she seemed to have the same attitude as Jean, and yet it was different. Jean was passive, she tried to ignore the fact that Michael was there, while Freda seemed actively to try to say things that she knew would upset him.

'Anyway,' said Freda, picking up the things from the clothes horse, 'I'm going to get this little lot finished. When I want to be ruled by a baby, I'll have one myself, but not until I'm good and ready.'

She swept out of the room and Edwin looked to Michael.

'I'm sure she didn't mean to be personal.'

'I think she did, you know. She's a perfect right to her opinion of me, which is obviously very low.'

Edwin wondered at Michael's ability to accept these slights. He thought how terrible it must be for him to have to stand there and not be able to retaliate.

It was later that evening when Sheila came round. She had received a letter from David that day saying that he might ring her if he had time. She'd been glad to get the letter even though she hardly expected him to actually get as far as making the phone call. Something always seemed to get in the way of his plans, and when he did ring her it was usually from a pub. She could tell from the tone of his voice that he'd had too much to drink.

'I want to ask him what chance he has of Christmas leave 'cos I thought we might get the kids back for a few days.'

She hesitated. Edwin was sitting in his chair across the room from her. He looked so comfortable. So settled and yet she knew he had troubles of his own and wondered whether it was fair of her to burden him with hers.

'Unless,' she went on, feeling the uncertainties inside her growing stronger, 'unless it's too late.'

'Too late for what, love?'

'Too late for me and David. I thought if he saw the kids he might remember that he has a family. His letters get farther apart all the time, and it's only when his conscience troubles him that he does send me one. These days even his conscience doesn't seem to trouble him that much.'

Edwin saw the tears coming to her eyes, but there were no words inside him to comfort her. It seemed all of a sudden that he was tired and that the emotions and sadness left him powerless and impotent.

'It's not just the war though is it?' she said, 'our marriage was a mess before it started. I should never have married him. Mum didn't want him to marry me and she was right.'

Edwin wondered whether things would have been different, if David and Sheila had never married or would it have just been the same only with different people.

And then there was Margaret.

At one time in his life he had been head of a family and had done his best to steer the courses of that group of people along the way he thought was best. Best for him and best for them, but now it seemed that something else had taken over, something out of his grasp and way beyond his control.

Sheila had stopped talking and they were looking at each other in silence. Edwin fingered the newspaper that lay beside him nervously. Sheila had quietened down and the emotions had dropped from her face. She seemed calm and no longer frantic.

Their minds were following their own separate paths and yet they were both thinking of the same thing.

'You mustn't let Margaret marry that chap. Not if it's just

for the baby.'

'Margaret decides for herself, Sheila,' Edwin replied.

'I don't think she cares about him, not enough, not as she should.'

Edwin wondered.

He would have given anything to know how much Margaret cared for Michael. Her whole situation was so confusing that she could be doing what she was for a million different reasons.

You can only trust, he thought, trust that what people do will be for the best and will turn out in a way that will make them happy.

He knew that it was impossible to know what another person was thinking and he hesitated to judge anyone.

Michael sat by Margaret's bed. She was asleep and he held her hand. His thumb felt its way on to the slow pulse, and he started to count the small beats. They were normal, healthy beats and he counted for several minutes.

He was counting the blood running through her veins.

He was timing her life as it made its way slowly forward.

For every pulse, there was a moment of time and in every moment of time his life and hers became more inextricably intertwined.

A slow web was forming that would drag them together and bind them in its cocoon.

It was forming inside her belly, growing larger, making a cord that he knew could never be cut.

Her face was still, as if the life inside it had halted for a brief respite, had stopped and was waiting for an eyelid to flicker, for a word to be spoken, for a life to come out of her.

It was a still moment and suddenly he felt a small shiver run up his spine.

He felt afraid.

The moment was too still, and the air was too calm.

It was as if they were the last two people left on the earth.

Too still.

Too calm.

'Are they still going to send her to this place in Shropshire about her back when she's had the baby?' asked Sheila of Jean. Jean was making some sandwiches which they were going to have instead of supper.

'It's all arranged,' she said.

'You'll miss her.'

Jean paused and cut the pile of sandwiches slowly with the knife.

'Does she seem quiet to you?' she asked.

'A bit.'

'She said something this morning ... I don't want to say anything to the others. She said she hadn't felt the baby move. For days.'

Sheila looked down. She knew what this could mean.

'She said she felt heavy. Very heavy,' said Jean.

Tony was on leave that day and decided to go and see his uncle in the evening. He had a curious fascination with the Ashton family, and would have given a lot to know how they worked and what they thought. There seemed to be no honesty among them, and as people they seemed to be unable to talk to each other without hiding behind lies or excuses.

Tony thought of himself and his father. His father was an honest man, but in his own way. Tony thought back over the years of his childhood and remembered the tortuous arguments and disagreements that he had had with Sefton. It had taken him years to master the technique of sitting back and watching his father's machinations.

He laughed at them now.

'Aunt Jean still hostile, is she?' he asked Edwin.

'She tries for Margaret's sake, but it keeps creeping through. Freda can hardly stand to be in the same room with him and Sheila thinks it's all a terrible mistake. I daresay it seemed like that at the beginning, but it happened and there's nothing we can do about it. Why can't they learn to make the best of it?'

The way that Edwin said the last sentence, accentuating it, sounded to Tony like a plea. It was as if he was crying out against the insanity around him.

Edwin went on, 'I've been trying to persuade Jean to let him stay the night, but of course she won't. Pretends she's too busy.'

The hatch opened and Freda popped her head through.

'Anyone not want saccharine in their cocoa?' she asked.

'Sugar ration not stretching?' said Tony.

'It did till we got a permanent visitor in the house. I don't know why Mum didn't ask him for his ration book.'

'Michael offered it to her and she turned it down,' said Edwin sharply.

She withdrew her head quickly and closed the hatch door with a bang. Edwin and Tony looked at each other, and in spite of everything, they smiled.

Tony understood what his uncle meant by saying that the women of the household seemed to be ganging up together.

A moment after, Freda came in with the cocoa and Edwin took one to Michael in the front room.

Tony had always felt close to Freda and sometimes wondered how he would have felt to her if she had not been his cousin. She was an attractive young girl and he liked her vivaciousness. They had gone out together quite often when they were younger. Played tennis together, gone to dances and visited the seaside. They were times he remembered with a good deal of affection, but things had changed now. They had both grown up a lot and then, he thought, there was Jenny now.

Jenny with the long blond hair with whom he went away for different kinds of weekends.

Jenny, the girl he had asked to marry him.

And who had turned him down.

'Whatever happened to that sweet little girl who used to have a crush on me?' he asked Freda.

'What girl?' she said.

'You.'

'Me? Certainly not.'

'I hope you realise that you've just shattered one of my most pleasant illusions.'

Tony paused. The conversation had started off as a light-hearted banter, but a note of seriousness had crept in. Without being asked, the laughter had gone out of their faces and they were looking at each other warily, straight in the eyes, afraid to tread on ground that might prove difficult.

He tried to joke his way out of it.

'What's his name then? You've got all the symptoms of the big romance, Freda.'

She looked at him and a cruel sneer passed across her mouth. She ran her finger round the edge of her cup and a strand of hair fell across her face. She didn't bother to push it back.

'You think it's very funny don't you?' she said, 'Little Freda having a crush ... Little Freda going out to dances ... little Freda dating an Australian airman ... well, I'm not little Freda any longer. You don't know anything about me, any of you.'

She stopped for a moment. The words had come out of her mouth as if by themselves. They seemed to have drained her.

Suddenly she got up. Tony, realising she was upset went over to her and stood behind her, gently putting his hands on her shoulders.

'Leave me alone,' she said, 'oh, leave me alone.'

And she rushed from the room, slamming the door after her. As she opened the door, Michael was standing there about to come in. She stopped in front of him and looked at him for a moment. Flashes of hatred came from her eyes as if she was trying to burn him up. She looked trapped, caged in, twisting and turning like a fish in a man's hand, trying to escape from something that was holding her in, from something that was gradually strangling her.

Jean heard her raise her voice from the kitchen where she was talking to Sheila. They both heard the living-room door bang and the fast hurried steps going up the stairs.

They paused in their conversation, but did not comment.

'I'll have to get the bus whether he rings or not,' said Sheila.

'Nonsense, you can stay the night,' Jean replied, 'then if David rings you'll still be here.'

'If you're sure ... I mean if it's not putting you to too much bother.'

'Of course,' said Jean, 'it'll be nice to have you.'

Jean felt no sense of shame at having invited Sheila to stay when she had already refused Michael. She liked Sheila and felt sorry for her. It was her duty to look after her, she thought.

There were no obligations like that to Michael.

Edwin came in with the cocoa he had taken to Michael.

'Anybody want this?' he said.

Michael popped his head round the door.

'I'll have to be off in a minute,' he said.

Edwin plucked up his courage.

'Jean ... can't we ask Michael to stay the night. He must be worn out.'

Edwin was sure that Jean wouldn't refuse the request, especially with Michael in the room.

She looked round coolly and eyed her husband and Michael standing there. They looked like a pair of stuffed dummies to her and she felt no sympathy for either of them.

'I'm afraid we can't dear,' she said, 'we haven't a bed and anyway, Sheila's staying. Didn't I tell you?'

Edwin was amazed with the innocence with which she said it. He wondered how someone could be so straightforwardly mean and cruel.

It seemed to him that there was nothing left between them. No decency, no humanity, nothing that he believed in and that he had tried to live by.

It seemed to be a long string of lies, a perpetual line of pretences and petty feuds.

An empty shell.

His family like lost people wandering around in the desert, miles away from each other, with the sun beating down slowly killing them, drying them out until they were shrivelled up into tiny balls of skin and bone.

And all of them having lost the will to live.

'He's ashamed of me, Dad,' said Sheila as she stood by the kitchen door with the hot water bottle under her arm, 'I should be proud of him, what with him expecting a commission, a husband with a future, but I'm not. I'm just scared of him growing away from me.'

'You're just disappointed he hasn't rung,' said Edwin trying to smooth things over.

She turned to go out of the door and paused.

'You know whose side I'm on,' said Edwin.

'Yes, yes, it helps, Dad, it helps.'

She smiled weakly and slowly went through the door, closing it after her quietly.

It seemed to Edwin as if she was summoning up the courage to face the darkness and spend the night alone.

Which was how she felt.

Edwin stood still for a moment, but he was disturbed by Jean who came into the kitchen after she had heard Sheila go upstairs. He thought for a second and then asked the question that was expected of him.

'Why did you ask Sheila to stay the night after you'd refused Michael?'

'She's family,' said Jean simply.

'Family,' echoed Edwin.

He wondered how much that word meant and how valuable it really was.

It was outdated, it had lost its value and it meant nothing any more. It was the residue of sentiments that they no longer felt, or if they did feel them, then Edwin thought it was no longer any more than a pretence.

'I'm beginning to think she's a victim of this family, and it looks as if Michael might be well on the way to becoming one too.'

'If there's a victim, then it's Margaret surely,' replied Jean.

'Jean, they're going to have to spend their lives together. Why not accept it?'

'If I was as sure of that as you seem to be then maybe I would. I promised Margaret I would and I don't break promises easily, Edwin.'

She was thinking that Margaret had told her earlier in the day that she felt heavy, that she hadn't felt the baby move.

'It's a promise that you're going to have to keep in the end,' said Edwin.

It was a quiet night. There were no raids, no interruptions, no alarms to the peace which should have been sleep for all of the family.

Their sleep was only fitful and came to each of them in small bursts. The house was a house full of people, all sheltered under the same roof and gathered together weaving their lives in and out of each other.

Margaret lay with the heaviness of her child inside her, bearing down out of her about to be born into a world that hardly seemed fit to accept an offering of yet another life.

Her child seemed to be waiting for the gift of its life with an unearthly calm as if it was pulling back, afraid to announce its own existence.

And Michael. After he had walked home from the Ashton's, he sat in his chair, unable to go to bed for he knew that sleep would pass him by that night and yet also unable to read a book or the newspaper. He felt caught in a vacuum where action was impossible.

They were waiting. All of them. Waiting.

It was about seven o'clock in the morning when Margaret felt the sweat break out over her brow, and something inside her push down.

She called for her mother, and, hazy as her brain was, she often thought of this moment afterwards.

At that moment she had wanted to tell them all that she was afraid.

To scream out and say that she was fearful of what the future would bring.

'It's stopped now,' she said to her mother later on, 'I thought I felt it move again last night after you'd all gone to bed.'

Jean patted her hand.

'Don't worry, the ambulance'll be here soon,' she said.

'Michael was awfully tired last night. Don't you think that someone could have asked him to stay?'

Jean explained that Sheila was staying and that there would have been no room. Margaret couldn't help but notice the way her mother avoided her eyes as she said it.

'Mum, that time last May when we thought I might lose the baby . . . I'd have still wanted to stay with Michael, you know,' Margaret hesitated and took her hand away from under her mother's, 'so you will keep on trying to understand, won't you?'

Jean was silent. Inside her, there were too many answers to her daughter's question and she couldn't find the right one.

Michael came round after the ambulance had taken Margaret away to the hospital. The family were waiting at home and had arranged for one of the nurses to ring from the hospital when anything happened.

'Freda,' said Michael finding himself alone in the kitchen with her, 'you don't like me very much do you?'

'I don't know you very well, do I?' she said.

'Can't we be friends? For Margaret's sake? I do care for her you know and I'm not going to let her down.'

Freda looked up at the face in front of her. It was a strange face with heavy dark features and she recognised in it a genuine desire to make amends and to understand.

'I'm sorry,' she said, 'I've been rude and thoughtless. I think we can be friends.'

'Shake hands on it?' said Michael, smiling.

Freda stretched out her hand in answer to his question. Her fingers touched his gently and she felt a shock. For a moment she was numbed and then the panic overtook her. She withdrew her hand and muttered confusedly, asking him to make some coffee or tea. She put her hands to her head and rushed from the kitchen.

In the hall, she stopped. Her fists were clenched and she felt herself biting them.

Their conversation in the cafe came back to her and suddenly everything seemed to make sense.

'I'm having an affair with a married man,' she said to Sheila.

It was late in the afternoon and still there was no news from the hospital. Freda was passing away the time by doing the ironing.

At first, Sheila was incredulous, and for a few moments she thought that Freda was really serious.

'Does his wife know?' asked Sheila.

'He doesn't know either,' Freda replied.

'He doesn't know? But you said you were . . .'

'I just wanted to see what you'd say, that's all. I wish the ground would open up and swallow me.'

Sheila suddenly realised what it was that Freda was saying.

'You mean you've got a crush on a married chap. Well, thank goodness for that,' she paused, wondering how serious it was and how she could go on without hurting Freda's feelings, 'Are you going to do anything about it?'

'I didn't even like him at first and I still don't sometimes. I suppose it's because I can't have him, so that's that, I don't really mean to talk about it. I don't even like to think about it.'

It was as if she could hear herself talking, as if she was outside herself saying things that had a life of their own. She controlled herself.

'Don't worry, I won't mention it again, not to anybody.'

They both heard the phone ring in the hall and a moment after Jean came into the kitchen.

'Freda would you wake Michael. He's asleep in the front room.'

Freda went to do what her mother asked, and on the way she realised that she would have to master her feelings for as long as Margaret and Michael were together, she would always be reminded of what had happened the moment he had touched her hand.

It took Edwin some time to get to the hospital from his

office and when he walked in he saw Jean sitting alone on a bench in the corridor. She looked small and hunched up, her coat wrapped round her as if she was sheltering from the wind. He approached her slowly and sat beside her.

'Can we see her?' he said.

'Michael's with her.'

'Is she all right?'

'Yes she's all right.'

Their conversation was staccato and bare like the walls of the hospital. There were pauses in between what they said to each other, and Jean had hardly turned to look at Edwin.

'The baby was still-born,' she said.

The words sounded so hard to Edwin, so cold that it was almost a sin to have to speak them.

So many hopes disappeared with them.

'You knew, didn't you?' he asked Jean, 'Sheila told me that you'd said Margaret hadn't felt the baby move.'

'That could've meant anything,' she turned to him, and pulled her coat tighter round her, 'you're thinking of what I said when we were sitting here once before aren't you?'

'A release, you said it would be a release.'

'It was a terrible thing to say.'

'We all say terrible things to each other sometimes.'

There was a moment between them, a moment of reconciliation and of honesty in which they admitted the lies and deceptions that had passed over the last year. Edwin felt them all wash away and something of a cleanness came over him. He was glad and he wondered whether it would be possible to forget and in a way to begin again.

'I don't think anything will part them now,' said Jean.

It seemed to Edwin that Jean had at last come to accept what was inevitable, what had been inevitable for some time.

It was just sad that it should take all this for her to come to think that.

Michael sat beside Margaret in silence. She was drowsy and still under sedation. Her lips moved.

'John George has a cough,' she muttered.

He held her hand for a moment and then laid it gently on the bedclothes.

He wondered what she was dreaming of, and whether pictures of her husband were in her mind.

A link between them had gone. The child would have been

tangible, and would have existed to show them and the world that they had a right to each other.

And now it had been taken away.

The hopes and everything that they had built their lives and expectations around had disappeared.

He wondered how they would fare without a future.

The world seemed to conspire against them, and as he thought this, a feeling lifted inside him.

He knew that he would fight, in his own way, to the very bitter end. He would not let her go.

Margaret slept.

She was empty. The growing inside her had stopped and there was a stillness in the air about her. She was floating above the world, her whole body was light as air and the currents took her away. There was nothing underneath her, nothing to hold her down.

She was empty.

Empty.

PART TWO

'GIVING AND TAKING'

CHAPTER FOUR

January 1942

'... The Soviet Union is determined on the utter defeat of Germany; so are we. The Soviet Union is determined to do all that is in its power to ensure that Germany cannot launch further wars upon the world; so are we. Out of the untold suffering of the present war, the Soviet Union wishes to gain a lasting peace for all its people; so do we. For these common objects we must work together to win the war and the peace. With the experience of Moscow talks fresh in my mind, I am convinced we can do both.'

Edwin turned off the radio and sat for a moment, thinking. For some odd reason, he thought of Napoleon, and then realised why. Eden had been talking about Russia, and the winter in Liverpool was cold.

He looked out of the window and saw that it was raining. The house was empty and the drops of rain echoed against the glass. It was almost hypnotic and one of the phrases from the radio kept running through his mind ... 'the untold suffering of the present war ...'

He repeated it over and over to himself until the rhythm of its words kept time with the rain.

His mind felt dull and battered. It wasn't the air raids or the constant news of the war that he read in the papers and heard on the radio that bombarded him. It wasn't even the news that some friend's child had died.

It was the look on the faces of his family, and the fact that Margaret was still in hospital, her back not yet healed.

It was the silence that sat where John Porter should have been.

It was the crying of John George.

Edwin sometimes wondered whether the baby didn't know more than any of them; and whether its cries weren't for food or for its mother at all.

He wondered if it was crying for all of them.

New York sat behind him as Robert walked along the deck of his ship. The evening was closing in and the lights of the tall buildings began to twinkle along the skyline.

'Sparky?' said Robert opening the door to the wireless room.

'Back already,' answered Maitland.

Maitland was a young lad, third radio officer and a friend of Robert's. He had fair hair and a chin that didn't need shaving. He was taller than Robert and he carried his height in an unwieldy manner as if he was ashamed of it. His voice was too high, not squeaky and unbroken, but tense and nervous. He was an intelligent lad, probably more so than Robert, but he seemed frightened of others and didn't have the confidence that made Robert popular.

Maitland envied Robert his ease of speaking and manner. He wasn't jealous and the envy never showed itself aggressively for he was glad to have Robert as his friend. He felt protected.

'You know that silk stuff that third got from Macey's?' he asked. 'I went round to take him something in his cabin a moment ago and he just sat there, tearing it up.'

'His judy'll give him his cards.'

'She has done. That's why. There was some mail waiting when he got back. She must have written to him. Thomas told me it was another bloke.'

'They were engaged,' said Robert.

They both observed a sympathetic silence for a moment. This sort of thing happened every day. It was just another incident, but the two young lads felt sad.

It was cruel.

Robert forced himself out of the melancholy.

'Take 'em or leave them, that's my motto,' he said. 'They're not all like that,' replied Maitland with all the wisdom in the world, standing up for the whole female half of the human race.

'Yours is all right, I can tell that from the photo,' said Robert.

'You can?'

'You can tell with some ... you can just tell,' replied

Robert.

It was a game they often played with each other. Robert knew it made Maitland feel good to be complimented on the crumpled photo he kept in his wallet. It was probably only an old photo of his sister, and the things he said about her only fantasies, but it didn't hurt to play along.

They both needed the security of each other's confidence and friendship.

For underneath everything they said was the knowledge that the next day they would be starting back across the Atlantic. It was cold out there and rough, and at first Maitland had been sick.

Underneath the waves and the grey, furious sea there were shapes floating stealthily, and sometimes a white vapour trail wrote itself along the surface.

Thinking of that, with the fear of it in the back of their minds all the time, both Robert and his young frightened friend knew they needed each other.

Anything to take their minds off it, anything to lean on.

Even if it was a crumpled photograph of your sister.

Later that evening, the doorbell rang in the Ashton's house. Freda answered it. She wondered who it could be at this time of night. Carefully, slowly she turned off the light and drew back the blackout curtain.

'It's me,' said Michael.

'Oh . . .' she replied, 'come on in.'

'I thought they might like to know how Margaret is.'

'They're in the back room. I'm making some cocoa if you'd like any.'

Quickly, Freda turned and went back into the kitchen. She still found it almost impossible to talk to Michael about even the most simple things.

'Hello Michael,' said Edwin, 'we wondered who the dickens it was.'

He led him into the living-room, and as they entered, Jean looked up.

'It's good of you to come,' she said.

'I'm sorry, I know it's late but I thought you might like to know how she was.'

Michael had seen Margaret earlier that day. The hospital was some way away from Liverpool, and was in fact quite near to David's base. As Michael arrived he had met David on his way out. Their conversation was perfunctory for they never had very much to say to each other but Michael gathered later from Margaret that David was soon to be up for his commission.

They had talked mainly about Margaret's brothers. She had just received a letter from Philip.

'I just wonder,' she had said, 'whether we'll ever be a family again. Philip says that sometimes, just now and then, he gets homesick. He closes his eyes, and tries to imagine that he's here.'

'I know I haven't met him, but from what you've said I should think Philip probably has more imagination than David or Robert.'

Michael could see that Margaret was wondering just what Philip would think if his wishes were granted and he could come home. It would certainly be different, and not nearly the same as he must imagine it.

'Robert's just a boy,' she said, 'I dreamed about him the other night. He was holding a little wooden train that he had bought for John George and he kept telling me he wanted me to be his next of kin. He was standing in the sea at Scarborough where we used to go on holiday. He had his trousers rolled up.'

She paused for a moment, and Michael remembered the odd scared look in her eyes as if there was something she wanted to grasp, to explain, but which was just out of reach.

'You don't have to go back tonight,' said Jean disturbing Michael's train of thought, 'you can stay here, in Margaret's room.'

Edwin looked over at his wife and caught the hint of a smile in her face. She knew she had just said something to make them all happy.

In the kitchen, Freda was standing listlessly watching the kettle boil. The steam rushed out of the spout and yet she hadn't the will to turn it off.

She was thinking of Michael.

Every time he came round, she found herself rushing away to her bedroom, or to the kitchen, or anywhere to be somewhere else but in the same room with him.

Her mind was confused, and the worst thing was that she had nobody to talk to about it. Her conversation with Sheila in the previous autumn had been the only time it had passed her lips. For the following months it had remained, boiling inside her.

She was gradually realising that she would have to go away.

That same evening, David was in the pub with his friend, Frankie. The bar was crowded and it was near to closing time. David was just back from seeing Margaret and he and Frankie sat in the corner of the room away from the crowd.

Frank looked at his friend. He knew him well enough by now to see that things weren't right with him. David was sitting with his head low and his hands cupped round his pint of beer.

'Where is she?' said David, 'you know, the little redhead in the siren suit?'

Frankie saw that David was trying to pull himself out of a mood. He made a witty answer and David smiled, then lapsed back into silence.

'It's all slack and ashes, Frankie,' he said.

'What is?'

'Me and Sheila.'

David thought back to Christmas.

He'd managed to get leave and spent some time at home with Sheila. His children had been there. Janet and Peter. It was ages since he'd last seen them and they'd grown up so much he hardly recognised them.

It was more like meeting someone else's children than seeing your own again. There had been a distance between them that he'd found it difficult to bridge. Somehow, the more he had tried to be friendly, the more he'd tried to go out to them, the more they had seemed to retreat from him.

He remembered the look in young Peter's eyes. His son had been waiting for him on the doorstep of his home and David knew the moment they met that Peter was expecting, not his father, but a hero. He'd asked him what it was like to fly and what it was like to kill people.

He'd tried to explain that it wasn't like it was shown in the films, that men weren't heroes, that they were only doing a dangerous and messy job and that they all hated it.

The tension had conveyed itself to Sheila until in the end David had been forced to go back early because he couldn't bear the rows and arguments any more.

He remembered the little, lost figure of his son standing

outside the door to the bedroom, overhearing every word that he and Sheila spoke to each other.

On the train, leaning out of the window, waving goodbye to his son, his daughter and his wife as they stood on the platform.

The train drawing slowly away from them and then, just as it turned the corner, he'd caught sight of something he would never forget.

He'd given Peter a model aeroplane for Christmas. Sheila and Janet waved and his son turned and threw the plane on to the track.

It was as if the image had been shattered for ever, and the link between him and his son broken.

'She doesn't even want me to get my commission, you know,' he said to Frankie, 'she doesn't want me to do anything with my life. All she wants is for me to stay the same as I was, the same as when I married her.'

Frankie looked at his friend. He could sympathise but there were other things in David he could see and they made him understand Sheila's attitude. He tried to put it gently.

'Maybe she doesn't want you to go the same way as Teddy Main.'

'You told me he bought it over Cologne,' said David.

'His mother came to the station after that. I talked to her,' Frank looked at David and a note of urgency crept into his voice, 'Teddy's old man died five years ago and his mother kept a little grocer's shop in the back streets of Birmingham. Remember how he kept telling us how stinking rich he was, laying the accent on and chucking his pay around? He'd been subbing off his poor old Mum for years, Dave.'

'He put on a damn good show then,' said David defensively.

'You don't really think that. You're your own worst enemy, David, and don't use that phoney accent on me either. Maybe that's what Sheila's afraid of.'

David knew there was a good deal of truth in what Frankie said. The smile slipped from his face. It was a spiral, an eddy that caught you. David knew he was in it. The more he wanted his commission, the more he wanted to get on, the more he felt he had to pretend.

He knew he could never go back to the docks and to the house he'd lived in before the war. It wasn't good enough and his life since then had taught him that there were other things, better things.

And if he had to play a game to get them, then he would play it, whatever the cost.

He knew there would be sacrifices to be made along the way.

'I had an odd sort of telephone call this morning,' said Edwin to Jean as they were going to bed.

'What about?' she asked.

'Some chap from London saying he wanted to come over and do a check on Harry Porter. I tried to ask him why, but he wouldn't say anything. Just a formality was all he'd tell me. Kept repeating it, just a formality.'

Jean took the kettle from the stove and filled the bottle. She screwed the top in.

It seemed an odd thing to her that someone should want to inquire about Harry, especially from them. There was so little they really knew about the Porters.

The mention of the name made her tense. It brought back John to her mind. She had spent so many months, so many years trying to forget him, that any mention of the name brought a strange kind of fear to her and she began to sweat.

It was as if he was watching them. Watching them and waiting.

She felt him very close.

'I'll put a bottle in your bed,' she said to Edwin, 'the nights are getting cold.'

'Yes,' he replied, 'it's pretty cold out there.'

An uneasy feeling came between them. Lately, things had been much better in the family. Edwin sensed that Jean had accepted Michael almost completely. She was no longer tense when he came into the room, and the days when she seemed bent on ignoring him were over.

Sometimes, Edwin would reach out and hold her hand. There would be an answering pressure from her fingers.

Yes, he thought, things were getting better between them all.

He looked at the window and outside he could hear the wind. It was a cruel sound as if a ghost was howling, trying to reach them all. The wind got at the cracks in the window and it rattled.

A moment of foresight, of premonition came over him. He shuddered for it was too terrible to think about.

Edwin turned and picked up the bottle. Clasping it to his

chest he concentrated on its warmth and went to bed.

He wanted to sleep and to forget.

Robert too would have liked some warmth to keep out the biting cold of the Atlantic. He was standing by the ship's rail talking to Maitland. They were both shivering with their arms wrapped round their bodies in the illusion that it might give them that extra bit of comfort.

It was more than just physical comfort they needed.

'The DEMS bloke told me that the stuff we loaded in the drums is aviation spirit,' said Maitland.

'I'd keep away from him if I were you,' replied Robert, 'he's a real moaning minnie.'

Maitland wasn't to be deflected from his train of thought by Robert's hesitant attempts at good humour.

'95 octane stuff, he said, that's pretty explosive isn't it?'

'Look,' said Robert, 'I've been at sea for more than a year now and I haven't seen a thing apart from the odd scare and the occasional depth charge.'

They both leaned over the rail in silence and watched the black of the sea rush past the side of the ship. Robert preferred not to think of what might be under the surface. He liked to forget about the things he'd seen in his year at sea and wished what he'd just said to Maitland was true.

'You cold,' he asked.

'A bit,' his friend replied, 'where'd you get that duffle coat?'

'Ten bob off a navy bloke that was skint in Freetown. It's all right isn't it?'

Maitland looked out into the dark. They were on the edge of the convoy and there was nothing beyond them except the sea, and perhaps somewhere, but a long way off, there was land.

'Feels a bit exposed on the edge, doesn't it?' he said.

'Nothing between us and Greenland.'

Maitland peered, putting his hand over the top of his eyes, searching for something. Something that would bring them a bit of comfort, something to tell him he was not alone.

'I can't see the escort that peeled off,' he said.

A moment later a pattern of depth charges, dropped just astern, told them what the escort was doing.

They froze for a moment hardly daring to breathe, and the noise of explosions reverberated dully through the ship.

Lurking out there, they now knew, was something that brought a sick feeling into their stomachs. Robert tensed his ears, listening, trying to catch a sound.

But there was nothing above the throbbing of the ship's engines, nothing above the whistling of the wind and the slapping of the sea. He could only hear the habitual sounds that he was so used to. He strained for other sounds, anything to take away the forbidding silence that he felt underneath him. All around him.

'Don't worry,' he said, 'they're only depth charges, it's just the navy smelling them out.'

They were both tense, waiting and frightened and they knew it. There was no point, though, in admitting it. It only made things worse.

The next evening, when Edwin came back from work, he found Sheila waiting for him. She was in the kitchen making some tea.

'Hello love, what are you doing here?' he asked.

'Getting your tea ready. It's orders. Mum's next door visiting the sick.'

It was some time since Edwin had last seen Sheila and he knew that she didn't come round these days unless it was for a reason.

'Expecting a call from David?' he asked.

'Sort of; the usual thing; he might and he might not.'

She was evasive and pretended to concentrate on peeling the potatoes.

'Things didn't go too well at Christmas, did they?' said Edwin.

Sheila looked up at him and Edwin saw the answer in her eyes. He wished there was something he could do for her.

'Has Mrs Porter been lately?' she asked, changing the subject.

'Just before Christmas.'

'Do you remember her coming last summer, after Margaret was injured?'

'Yes,' said Edwin wondering what Sheila was getting at.

'I was on a train that day and I met her on her way over. I'd gone down to see David only there was nowhere to stay so I had to come back the same day. She told me she'd had a letter about John, and that she was going to see the chap who'd written it.'

Sheila saw the worried expression on Edwin's face and

realised that he was wondering whether she'd told anybody.

'Don't worry,' she said, 'I haven't told anyone, because I thought if there was anything in it then someone would have said.'

'Nothing came of it,' he replied, 'in fact no one knows about it except me and Mrs Porter. I didn't say anything to Jean or to Margaret. You see, I didn't want to raise anyone's hopes or anything. It was just something someone had found.'

As Sheila put the peeled potatoes into the pan, the phone rang. She practically dropped them in her haste.

'That'll be David,' said Edwin, 'off you go. I'll see to the potatoes.'

Sheila picked up the phone expecting to hear her husband's voice at the other end. Instead it was a gruff official voice asking for Mr Ashton.

It was difficult for her to hide the disappointment when she called Edwin to the phone.

However badly she got on with David, and however much she feared what the future might bring, there was still the old same excitement when she thought of him and the same loneliness when she thought she might lose him.

It was always the same. He did things for her that she knew no other man could do.

It only took the two men fifteen minutes to get round to the Ashton's home. Their names were Brent and Dimmock. Both in uniform, they carried official looking cases and asked if they could talk to Edwin alone.

'They're just making conversation at the moment,' said Jean to Sheila, 'I'm sorry we've got to sit in here, but they said it was confidential.'

Jean was making some tea to take into Edwin and the two men.

'Why don't you go into the front room,' she said to Sheila and Freda who had just come in.

'It's like an icebox in there,' said Freda.

'Oh well, please yourselves.'

'You don't come round much these days,' said Freda to Sheila after Jean had carried the tray out.

'You could come round and see me,' replied Sheila, 'anyway, Doris says you've been a bit down in the dumps these days.'

'Does she?'

'I thought it was to do with that man you told me about in the summer. Remember? The married one.'

Freda didn't answer. There seemed no point in talking about it when it was impossible to explain fully just what she was feeling.

'It's over now, is it?' asked Sheila.

'Sometimes it is and sometimes it isn't. It's a bit like a cold. One day it's finished and then the next day it's back again in full force.'

Sheila jumped when the front doorbell rang.

'That'll be David,' she said.

'Silly, it's the door.'

Sheila watched Freda go to answer it and thought just how much it meant to her for David to ring. Probably it meant more than she would admit.

Freda answered the door to Michael. As he stood there in front of her she knew that the feeling would never go away. It would never be allowed to go away. She had caught a perpetual cold that, she felt, might be with her for the rest of her life.

Jean was pouring out the tea. She glanced at Edwin, and smiled. He smiled back and shrugged his shoulders. Neither of them could quite understand what it was the two men wanted.

One of them, Dimmock, was tall and thin. He sat in the armchair and smoked his pipe, sucking on it slowly and asking considered questions. The other, Brent, was small and hardly said a word. Edwin could feel him taking in the room and assessing the answers that he gave to their questions.

Brent was like a mole and Edwin felt him burrowing under the surface of their lives.

'You go to work by ferry then, Mr Ashton?' asked Dimmock.

'Yes.'

'A good start to the day.'

'It blows the cobwebs away.'

Out of the corner of his eye, Edwin caught a glimpse of Brent looking at the photos on the sideboard.

'Is this your daughter, Mr Ashton?' he asked.

'Yes, that's Margaret.'

'And this is Porter's son?'

'Yes. He was posted missing at Dunkirk. Believed killed.'

Jean looked up. She was sitting quietly in the corner drinking her tea and not missing a word of the conversation.

'Forgive me for asking,' she said, 'but how did you know that it was John.'

Dimmock seemed slightly taken aback, and glanced quickly at the other man. It seemed to Edwin that he was reproaching him for making a mistake. Brent looked away and put the photograph back on the sideboard.

'They showed us a picture,' said Dimmock.

'You've seen the Porter's then?' asked Edwin, surprised.

'Oh yes, we paid a fleeting visit. She's a bit disturbed, wouldn't you say? Difficult to talk to.'

'She lost her son, Mr Dimmock,' said Edwin, 'it does seem a bit unnecessary, all this. I mean Harry had a good record didn't he? In the last lot.'

'Yes, it seems a bit unnecessary to us too sometimes,' he paused imperceptibly, 'he was in the signal wasn't he?'

'Infantry, I thought,' said Edwin.

'I meant the son, Mr Ashton.'

'Yes, he was.'

'Made his own sets and things did he? A lot of the T.A. blokes did that sort of thing.'

'He made our youngest, Robert, a crystal set a long time ago.'

Brent was still standing behind Dimmock and Edwin noticed him trying to catch the other man's eye.

'You haven't forgotten that we're due at Formby in the morning, have you, Peter?' he said.

'So we are. 19TC,' he looked at Edwin, 'do you know it?'

'It was where John was before he went to France.'

'I daresay quite a few chaps passed through there on their way to the rude awakening,' replied Dimmock casually.

Edwin was a little confused by the conversation. It seemed to him that the two men were more interested in John than in Harry. There was something about the way they were talking, and the forced casualness with which they referred to John and steered the conversation round to the subject which made him suspicious. He couldn't work out what it was that they wanted, and a nagging doubt was forming at the back of his mind.

'It sounds as if they're going away,' said Freda to Michael. They were still in the kitchen, and Sheila had gone upstairs. Freda was trying desperately to make conversation to Michael.

She feared a silence falling between them.

'I just dropped in to say that I've found a flat for Margaret and I to live in,' said Michael, 'it's nothing to shout about. I hope she'll like it. It's on the ground floor and there's a bit of garden at the back.'

He paused trying to sense Freda's reaction, but she had turned away and was busily drying some plates.

'You won't mind, will you?' he said.

'It's nothing to do with me,' she replied.

'You're part of her family. She cares for you all. If we can't learn to be friends, then she'll be unhappy.'

'We've accepted it haven't we?' said Freda. The words sounded foreign to her, as if someone else was speaking them. They were the right words for the occasion, but she knew that they were only another lie. She could accept that Michael and Margaret would live together, but she would never be able to think about it without feeling sad. Her reasons for feeling like that would never be what others thought they were. They would never be the same reasons as her father's or her mother's or those of any other member of the family.

'Do you still find me such a terrible person?' he asked.

'No,' said Freda, 'you're not a terrible person at all.'

And she knew she meant it.

Later that evening, Michael went to catch his bus and Freda went to bed early saying she had a headache.

Edwin popped his head round the door and saw that Sheila was in the living-room, half asleep. She was still waiting up for a phone call from David.

Edwin hoped he would ring this time. It was things like this that made him feel distanced from his son. He wondered whether he would have hated David if it had been Sheila who was his daughter and David who had come from another family.

He went into the kitchen. Jean was making some cocoa for them all before they went off to bed.

The visit of the two men and its surrounding doubts had brought them together in a way that they had not felt for months.

'They said they would come again tomorrow didn't they?' she said.

'After they've been to Formby. God knows why. Two perfectly fit chaps like that with a good military training should be put fighting with our Philip instead of running about the country asking a lot of stupid questions. What do they know about Harry Porter now that they didn't know before they came.'

Edwin was scared to voice his real feelings about the visit. Instead he channelled his frustrations into a vein of anger.

Jean took the kettle from the stove, and paused for a moment. She spoke quietly.

'As a matter of fact I got the impression that they were more interested in John than in Harry.'

Edwin looked at her and for a moment they found a peace together. For once they had the same fears and doubts. Their lives seemed to be moving, binding into one, and they were building a little fortress to protect them both from what they saw against the horizon.

'It seemed like that to me too,' he said.

The image of his son-in-law lifted itself from his memory and appeared once again alive in front of him. His heart was joyful and glad, but that feeling was dowsed in the same moment.

It was something he couldn't hope for, and it was something he feared.

He tried to banish the thought to the back of his mind, but it wouldn't go.

The phone rang. It interrupted his thoughts, and he thanked it for doing just that.

There were some things that didn't bear thinking about.

Jean answered it.

'It's David,' she said, 'go and get Sheila will you?'

David had been in the Turk's Head with Frankie for some time that evening. He had just heard that he'd be getting his commission, and he was celebrating.

'Aren't you going to ring home?' asked Frank.

'I'm just working up to it,' David replied.

They were playing snooker ... Frankie was winning. He sensed that David's mind wasn't on the game.

David stood up and rested his cue on the edge of the table.

'What's your ambition then, Frankie?' he asked.

'Civvie Street,' he said, 'it can't come soon enough for me.'

'What'll you do when it does come?'

Frank lined up his cue and then firmly pushed his ball across the table. It broke up a group of reds and potted one neatly.

'Dunno,' he said, 'haven't thought about it really. After all, what's the point? We'll all be ready for old age pensions by the time this lot's over.'

He paused and looked at the table, wondering which way to shoot next. He was doing well, but hadn't left himself in a very good position.

'You know what I want, Dave? I want to go to bed when I feel like it, eat when I fancy, have someone bring me my slippers, and for people to knock on the door when they come to visit.'

'You want the earth, you do,' said David.

Frankie looked up at David and saw that he was slowly chalking his cue. He reckoned he was probably thinking of Sheila.

'You wouldn't mind staying on,' he said.

'No,' replied David, 'I wouldn't.'

'Squadron leader Ashton eh?'

'What's so funny about that?' said David sharply.

'Nothing. You've got it in you if that's what you want.'

Frank leaned back over the table using the cue round behind him. It was a difficult shot and he missed it.

'Damn,' he said.

David wasn't there. Frank looked across the bar and saw him about to dial a number. He noticed David hesitate with his hand over the phone and then pick it up sharply.

Frank was sorry for David, knowing as he did how things were between him and Sheila. He often wished that somehow David would make more effort to try to understand his wife. Frankie was unmarried and he missed having someone he knew he could rely on. It seemed a waste for people to carry on like David and Sheila. There was so much they could have, so much they could grasp to help each other, but David seemed intent on turning his back on that side of his marriage.

'Hiya,' said David when he heard his wife's voice at the other end of the phone. There was a pause. She sounded so faint, so far away, the distance between them was so tangible. They were miles away from each other. Even when they were together, there was still this kind of distance between them.

'I had a letter from Peter,' said Sheila, 'he wrote that he was thrilled to see you at Christmas.'

'You're making that up aren't you?' said David, 'I'm just

another fella to our Peter now.'

There was a silence at the other end of the line. Sheila had lied about the letter from Peter. It hadn't mentioned his father at all.

'I'm getting a commission, by the way,' he said.

'Congratulations.'

Sheila didn't sound enthusiastic. David explained that he would be getting three weeks off to buy his kit. He also said that it meant more money and that from now on he would be paying Sheila her allowance direct.

'I can manage,' she said, 'if you just pay the kids' money.'

He sensed a resentment in her voice as if she was trying to prove she wanted to be independent from him. She seemed to be trying to say that she could do without him.

'You don't want me to get on, do you?' he said, 'you want me to stick in the same old rut and come back to the same old rut, don't you?'

Sheila was near tears. She had been looking forward to this phone call, but as usual it had turned into yet another row between them. There was a certain amount of truth in what David was saying. It wasn't that Sheila didn't want him to get on, it was just that she was scared of him leaving her behind.

She wanted to say all these things and to explain to him exactly how she felt, so that he might be able to understand, but whenever she did try to explain he always misunderstood her. A tear dribbled down her cheek. It was a tear of desperation, the feeling that however hard she tried, she would never get the chance to explain to him properly. If she couldn't explain, then things would go on drifting away from her. She didn't mean to provoke rows with David, they just happened against her will.

Almost in answer to her thoughts, the pips began to sound. She heard his voice over the fast noises that were threatening to cut them off.

'I've no more change,' he was saying, 'see you when I see you then.'

Hard as she tried she couldn't bring herself to answer him, to say anything at all.

'Sheila, Sheila,' he was raising his voice at the other end of the phone. Suddenly the line cut dead.

Slowly Sheila replaced the receiver. Gently it rested in its little cradle and she left her hand on it. To take her hand away from it was the final break of communication between them. She wanted a miracle, she wanted to hear his voice again.

Edwin heard the silence in the hallway, and when she didn't appear he went out to see if everything was all right.

He sat on the stairs beside her. She had her head in her hands. She spoke, her voice muffled by the tears and the hands which she kept over her face.

'I sometimes feel I've got nothing left, Dad,' she said, 'what with the kids being away and David being away too.'

'It won't last for ever,' he said. She put her head against Edwin's shoulder.

'He says he's got his commission. He won't come out when it's all over. It's the best thing that's happened to him . . . now he's only got to get rid of me and then he'll have everything he ever wanted.'

'You shouldn't worry, love. He'll be cock-a-hoop for a bit then he'll turn to you. When it's worn off, or something happens to upset him, he'll turn to you.'

'He won't, and I can't even blame it on the war. It was touch and go with David and me before the war even started.'

'The war split you up. It broke up the family too. You've just got to stick it out. That's what we've all got to do. Stick it out.'

There was a note in Edwin's voice that startled her. An urgent, feeling tone to the way he spoke his words as if he was saying something that was close to his heart.

'This war's done things to my marriage that I wouldn't have dreamt possible,' he went on, 'Jean has never really forgiven me for letting young Robert go. You wouldn't notice it, but it's in everything she does. You learn to live with it, and sometimes it goes away, but in the end it always comes back. She's never forgiven me.'

Edwin didn't mean to say this, but he couldn't help himself. He knew that these were the private thoughts he ought to keep to himself. They were the things that occupied him in his sleep, that made him toss and turn in the night, and which he thought about as he sat in the living-room, staring out into the darkness.

The two men came around early the next day. There was a different look on their faces this time. They walked straight into the house and sat down in the living-room.

'My wife's out at the shop I'm afraid,' said Edwin.

'What sort of chap was he, Mr Ashton?' asked Dimmock.

'Harry?'

'No, John.'

Edwin wondered for a moment.

'A quiet lad. Really a very ordinary chap. He joined the territorials for the summer camps. I think. Just a very ordinary chap. But then they all are aren't they?'

They were looking at him. Edwin felt that they were sizing him up. Scrutinizing him.

'We've decided to come clean,' they said, 'it's that we've been picking up this radio transmitter from Belgium and they've given the identification as John Porter.'

This time it was Brent speaking. He stood in front of Edwin with his hands behind his back.

'It doesn't mean a thing at this stage, Mr Ashton. In fact it's more likely that either the resistance or the jerries are using his name. Probably picked up his tags. Hoping to get something out of us you know.'

It was Dimmock speaking. Then Brent chipped in again.

'On the other hand, if he was alive they could be using his experience to build them a transmitter and his knowledge of languages.'

There was a pause.

'What we need is a list of personal details. Some things he'd know about and that the jerries wouldn't. Then we could be quite sure and with a bit of luck we could confirm or deny finally that he was either dead or alive.'

Edwin heard them as if in a dream. He had suspected that this was what they might be getting at. Now, finally it had been placed in front of him and it was time to face up to the fact that John could be alive.

In his bones he felt that it was true.

Somehow he knew that he had spent the last year or so rationalising his fears and his hopes.

It had been bad enough almost knowing that John was dead. It was worse, after all this time to almost know that he was alive.

Edwin remembered what he had said to Jean in the hospital corridor. He had asked her if she would wish it on John to return to things as they now were.

He wouldn't wish it on anybody.

Somewhere, far away in the middle of the Atlantic, with the cold seas swirling and heaving there was an explosion.

Robert was playing chess with Maitland at the time and, as usual his friend was winning.

The small chess men scattered over the cabin floor.

Robert and his friend were thrown to the ground.

And then the hurried, scurrying activity.

The lifebelts. The chaos. The night all around them and the drumming of feet, hurrying away from the streaming water.

Men holding their heads in their hands. Offering themselves up to the sea.

It was the moment when they came face to face with the reality which they feared and which they did not talk about. So many jokes, so many false reassurances, so many silences as they looked at the sea and wondered where their friends had gone.

Robert jumped.

And the sea held him, breathless, waiting.

Edwin looked at the two men. He found it impossible to speak. His mind was whirling around seeking some solution, looking for a way to react. He was searching for the words with which to speak.

He could not say anything.

How, he asked himself, do you speak when you don't know what it is that you are thinking of.

At the same moment in time, during the same hour, with the same night and the same wind, cold, and the rain beating down on the windows, the same rain; the waves rolling and beating, the night holding your eyes back so you couldn't see farther than your hand.

At that moment, Robert jumped. He landed among the other small red lights bobbing on the collars of their life-jackets.

His arms thrashed out. His legs moved.

He clambered through the sea, he fought through the darkness, he struggled towards a small raft, already overcrowded.

He forced himself to look through the darkness, trying wildly to find a point of hope, searching in the sea for something to help him.

He was alone although there were many others not less than a few yards from him.

There was no one to talk to. To lean on.

There were no crumpled photographs of your sister, or your girl, or your mother, or anybody to help you through the waves.

And there was the oil from the ship, clogging up your lungs.

The oil and the sea.

It was difficult to even breathe.

An explosion and the men had gone. Edwin looking through the glass of his windows seeking, hoping for a signal to tell him what to think.

Somewhere out there, he thought of John.

He wondered was he dead or alive?

In his heart he knew he was alive.

He knew he had to be for that was the way things were.

Edwin, searching for what to think, for what to do.

Edwin, the night around him and the rain beating on the window.

Robert, the night around him, and the sea searching for his mouth, sucking him in.

CHAPTER FIVE

January 1941

ROBERT

A raft bobbed on the sea not far away from him. He could just see the cluster of little red lights that milled about it. They would come into his vision and then disappear. At one moment they were within his world and then a small mountain would rise in front of him and exclude them.

His arms thrashed out. In spite of the cold, the shock and the numbing chaos of the last few minutes, or it could have been hours for he had lost track of time, Robert felt a need in him to get to that raft. He wasn't thinking about it. His brain was dead and an intuitive force took him on. It made his legs move and his arms go round. His fingers dug into the sea as if it were a rock he had to climb.

Somehow he felt his body moving on. He passed others who were doing the same.

He passed some who were simply lying still in the water.

He heard the voices getting closer. There was a scurrying activity going on all about the raft. Robert fought his way through the fighting men until he could hang on to the side. He stretched one hand out and grasped. His fingers closed round a piece of rope and he let his whole weight hang on that slender link.

For a moment he thought he was safe. He had something to hold on to.

Slowly his brain came back to life and he began to be able to distinguish some of the voices. Almost as if he was dreaming, he recognised the cockney lilt of Hopkins, and the scouser voices of Walker and Rawson.

There were other faces he couldn't recognise.

The cold was beginning to get at him and all over his body he felt a sticky clinging substance. It stuck to his face and his hair. It was in his mouth.

Oil, the oil from the ship was seeping into his clothes and his body. It was in his mouth too.

He heard someone cough raucously. The noise was hard and rasping.

It was himself. He could hear his own cough, trying to dislodge the heavy substance that was clogging up his lungs, that was making his breath hard to come by.

A head lolled against him, and the extra weight almost made him lose his frail handhold on the raft. He looked round and saw that it was Maitland. He was in a worse condition than Robert and barely had the strength left to hold on.

Robert heard the voices on the raft. He caught dislocated phrases that came out of the night and wandered round his brain. They weren't like ordinary speech. They didn't seem to relate, to tie up to each other.

'Christ it's cold.'

'The tanker's still burning.'

'Can you get Sparky on?'

'No room lad. Hang on though.'

'Bloody corvettes buggered off. She got the blokes off the other two rafts and then buggered off.'

'She'll be back. She'll get something on the radar and then she'll be back.'

'Young Sparky's first, mate; anyway it's no warmer up here, honest.'

Robert recognised Hopkins's voice. He was speaking in a whisper, but it carried above the other sounds.

'Rawson? It's Malloby, he's gone.'

Rawson got up and crawled carefully to the other side of the raft.

'You sure?' he said.

'He's gone.'

They put their hands either side of the dead body, and tried to lift it but it was difficult to move. There was a dull reluctance in its weight.

'Shove him off,' said Rawson.

Robert heard a dull splash as the body slid into the water.

Rawson looked over in his direction and Robert's heart leapt. He wondered if it was his turn to get on to the raft.

'All right, lad, let's see if we can get your mate up shall we?'

Robert did his best to see to help them lift Maitland up. It was difficult. There seemed little life left in the body of his young friend. He gave them no help.

After a bit, Maitland slid to relative safety and lay there like a stranded whale.

Every so often, Robert heard the splash of yet another body being dumped in the sea. He was desperate to get on to the raft. Slowly the numbers of the men around it dwindled. Some were thrown off and drifted away into the darkness until all that was left was the little bobbing up and down of the red light on their life-jackets and then that would disappear. Some just loosed their grip on the side and slid away, noiselessly, into the water.

After a time, with the raft still full, there were only about four or five of them gripping to the side.

Hopkins looked up. Not far away he saw a red glow. It was the oil that was floating on the water. It had caught fire and was drifting towards them.

Hopkins stared at it in disbelief. He focused his eyes and tried to control his brain into an orderly pattern of thought.

'The fire's drifting this way,' he said.

Rawson looked up too.

'It's us that's drifting into it,' he said.

A strange voice came from one of the other men on the raft.

'Where's that bloody corvette,' it said.

Rawson got up on to his knees and crept to the side of the raft.

'Everybody on to one side. We've got to start pushing. We've got to move this bloody thing or else.'

He nodded at the fire. In spite of the cold and their tiredness the men clinging to the side understood what he meant.

Rawson looked at Robert.

'Come on up, Ashton.'

'I'm all right,' replied Robert. He didn't know why he said that, it didn't even sound like his own voice.

'I said come on up. I've got big feet and with them behind us we should make seven knots.'

Robert clambered up on to the raft, helped by several pairs of hands. His breathing came with more difficulty all the time and the oil that was deep in him clogged up his lungs. Every time he took a breath it was like trying to suck the air in through treacle.

He lay on the wood of the raft, hardly able to move. Dimly

he heard the splashing as the others tried to kick the raft into movement. Slowly they began to move and as Robert glimpsed out of one eye, he saw the flames reflected in their faces, playing in their eyes.

On the one side was the fire and on the other was the water.

In the middle a raft, small against the ocean and on it several tired and weary, almost beaten men.

When dawn came, the sea was calm. Deathly still and the wind was gently making small ripples on top of the swell. The raft lifted and settled hypnotically.

Only eight men were on it now and among them were Robert and his friend, Maitland.

They had spent the night huddled against each other for warmth. There had been a few half hearted attempts at a song or two, and the occasional joke.

Now the efforts to keep themselves awake had faded and they all sat in silence, feeling and hearing only the steady lap of the sea at their raft. Always reminding them that it was there, waiting for them, ready to claim its next victim.

'All right lad?' asked Rawson.

'Yeah,' said Robert.

'How's your oppo?'

'He came round in the night, then he went off again.'

Robert felt the heavy weight of Maitland's face against his chest. He held him like a baby.

'Bloody corvette never came back,' said someone.

Rawson looked out across the sea and blinked. They were surrounded by bodies floating in the water, and bits of wood, cases, crates, logs, and odd bits and pieces, and bodies.

There, not that far off there was a boat. It was one of the lifeboats from the ship. It had a sail on it and was moving towards them.

'It's one of ours,' said Rawson.

'Be no bloody warmer there than we are,' said a despairing voice.

Rawson looked down at Robert. He saw the pain over the young lad's face and heard the breathing that was coming more and more faintly from his lungs. It was obvious that there wasn't much time left for him. Rawson smiled at Robert. compassionately.

'We could be a lot worse off,' he said, 'a lot worse off, eh lad?'

Robert tried to smile back, but he could hardly hear the words that were directed at him. They didn't seem to enter his brain. Everything was becoming hazy, foggy and indiscernible.

Robert tried to smile again. His face wouldn't move.

The boat drew up alongside the raft and the men scrambled into it. Some of the officers from the ship were already there. The first sparks had an emergency set and was tapping away incessantly.

They lay Robert and Maitland along the seats on either side of the bow.

Robert was coughing harshly and without a break. His whole body moved, shuddered with each retch. He was conscious of very little.

'Young Ashton sounds bad,' said Rawson to one of the officers, Russell.

'Oil. He was in the water for sometime wasn't he? It'll have got to his lungs.'

'Nothing we can do?'

'It's in his lungs. It's corrosive that stuff. Eat him away,' Russell paused. He felt bitter, not so much for himself, but for the sense of impotence, the fact that he could do nothing.

'What am I suppose to do?' he said sharply.

'Nothing we can do,' said Rawson, echoing the senior man's words.

'Hang on to this will you?' said Russell, giving the tiller to Rawson, 'I'll go and have a look at the lads.'

Carefully he manoeuvred the length of the boat, stepping over the legs of men who had hardly the strength to move. He sat down beside Robert.

Robert's eyes were closed when Russell got there, but he felt the weight of the man as he sat down beside him. Russell looked at Maitland, and pulled back the lids from his eyes. The pupils rolled up. He put his head to the lad's chest. There was nothing.

Maitland had gone some time ago.

Russell nodded to one of the men sitting near him and gestured that they should put the body over the side. He looked at Robert and saw that he had opened one eye.

Gently, Russell drew a blanket over Maitland's face. He

smiled at Robert trying to inject some hope into the young lad's face.

'Just to keep him warm eh?' he said.

Robert hardly gathered what was going on. The pain in his chest was becoming unbearable and the constant coughing and retching were wearing down his will. He tried for a while to keep up his spirits by thinking of his home, of his parents and his family.

But somehow the memories faded.

They eluded him and became unreachable. The people he knew and loved wandered across his mind. They wandered into his brain and then out the other side.

He tried to catch them and to tell them to stop still for a moment. He tried to hold on to them, to keep them in his grasp, but they just got farther and farther away.

He saw his mother's face smiling at him and waving.

He shook his head and felt his brain explode.

The next time that Russell came up the length of the boat, he saw that Robert had gone as well.

Someone was playing a mouth-organ, and a few voices sang rustily. The boat drifted across the calm sea. The strains of the music played out and were taken away by the wind.

The two bodies splashed into the sea, and were taken, drifting along with the music, away from the boat.

Soon they were out of sight.

With only the occasional note of the mouth-organ for their requiem, and two or three voices singing, out of tune.

Underneath the seat there was a small piece of crumpled paper. It was a photograph of a girl. The sloshing of the salt water made it soggy until you could no longer distinguish who it was in the photograph.

It could have been anybody.

It didn't matter who it was.

Mother, girlfriend, sister, they were no longer relevant.

The comfort they had given had ceased to be of use.

Some weeks later a telegram arrived at the Ashton's home. Edwin opened it and Freda read it over his shoulder.

Their faces fell and, as one, they both cried for their brother, their son.

They could only know what the few bare words meant to them.

Robert was dead.

They would never know what had happened, what lay behind the words on the official form.

Only one person knew what they really meant and he was gone.

CHAPTER SIX

March 1942

The two months after they heard of Robert's death passed slowly for Edwin. It passed slowly for the rest of the family too.

They hardly ever spoke of it. At first there had been the tears, but after a while they had dried up and been replaced by the silence.

It was quite simple really, for there was nothing to say. At one moment, Robert had been there, in all their minds and now he no longer existed.

The fact that he no longer existed was one that none of them could really believe. On the face of it there seemed to be so little that you could say, and yet underneath there was everything to say. All the emotions crying out to be given voice, all the pain asking to be told to the world.

Except that there were no words which measured up to what wanted to be given voice.

Thus, the silence.

The long drawn out pauses over tea when Edwin and Jean were alone together.

The glances across the table when the family were all together, full of recrimination and blame.

It was Jean who blamed Edwin for the death of their youngest son, for, if he had not sent him away to sea, if he had not signed the papers, then perhaps Robert would be here today, she thought.

All this happened between them and no one spoke a word.

The days and months after Robert's death passed very slowly for them all.

One day in March, Edwin received some more sad news. His father had died. Edwin had a more gentle reaction to this than to the death of Robert. He'd loved his father deeply and admired the stubbornness with which he stuck to his working-class principles. His miner's pride came out in everything he did, and Edwin often envied his father, wishing he had inherited that strength of mind.

The old man had been ill for some time and the news of his death came almost as a relief to Edwin. Not a relief in the way that he was glad to be rid of the constant worry of his father, but a relief for the man himself.

Edwin had often noticed of late the look of bewilderment in the man's eyes. As his father looked about him and read the news of the war, and as Edwin explained that Philip was abroad, fighting, and that Robert was dead, his father had seemed unable to understand what it was all for.

An honest reaction, thought Edwin.

And then he wondered at his calm acceptance of the old man's death. He questioned it and thought that, perhaps, he was becoming immune to the meaning of such things.

He felt as if he had become immune to pain.

Edwin sat in his brother-in-law's living-room, waiting for Sefton to get back. He held his hat between his knees and stood in the middle of the room. He still felt like an employee begging favours when he went to see Sefton. He would never be on an equal footing with the man, there was too much resentment between them and a backlog of slights which made it impossible for them to look each other straight in the eye. Edwin had been used by Sefton and he knew it.

'Sit down, Edwin,' said Sefton as he came into the room, 'I've been to Preston for the day.'

Sefton looked at Edwin and noticed the way he hunched his shoulders and still wore the shabby old mack that he had had for what must be more than fifteen years.

Sefton knew, always had known, that Edwin was one of life's under-managers. He would look after things and give orders, he would do what he was told and others would do what he told them, but he would never be the one from whom the orders came.

Sefton felt affectionately sorry for his brother-in-law. He knew him well and the man was no Churchill. Sefton admired Churchill more than any other man and secretly compared himself to the country's leader.

'How's Jean taking it?' he said.

'Not too well I think,' replied Edwin, 'she says very little about it as a matter of fact.'

'Does she think he might,' Sefton paused, knowing he was on tricky ground, 'come back?'

'No. She's never stopped hoping for John, but there's no point in hoping for Robert. We had a letter from someone who was on his ship. Said they were in a boat. We don't hope any more for him.'

Edwin looked at the photograph of Sefton's wife, long dead, which had pride of place on the mantelpiece. He wondered how Sefton got through the evenings with no one to talk to. He wondered if he ever thought back to the days when he had someone to lean on.

'I'm needing a couple of days off,' he said, changing the subject, 'just to clear up my father's affairs over in Yorkshire. Not much to do, but it takes time.'

'Of course, Edwin, of course,' he smiled condescendingly, 'Tony turned up yesterday with that girlfriend of his. They've come to stay since he's got a spot of leave. She's a nice lass, and she's got a lot more sense than he has if you ask me. I don't know, some of the young people today.'

'They're doing all right, Sefton. They're doing a dirty job that we let them in for, just like our fathers let us in for the last lot.'

He paused, thinking. He wondered why it had to be. He asked himself why Robert was no longer with them. There didn't seem to be an answer.

'The sins of the fathers,' he said, 'how many more generations.'

Edwin didn't quite know what it was that he meant, but he knew that there had to be some reason for it somewhere.

Margaret got back from the hospital that day. Her back was now fully healed, except for the odd twinge of pain. She had been out in the afternoon with Michael looking at the new flat he'd found for them both. They got back to the Ashton's house the same evening.

They took their coats and hats off and hung them in the hall.

'I wish Spring would hurry up,' said Michael, shivering.

'It's been Spring for ages,' replied Margaret, 'and by the way you didn't tell me where the coal was kept in the flat.'

'It's in a bunker round the back.'

Michael paused and held Margaret by the arm. He had something to say.

'Won't you come tonight?'

'Just give me a few more days,' she said, 'for Mum, because

of Robert.'

'All right.'

Michael wanted to get everything settled. He had spent too long with Margaret not knowing where he stood. He wanted to get her away from her family and to have her to himself.

'I can hardly believe you're back,' he said, 'it's been so long.'

'Me too. It's going to be like it should have been isn't it Michael?' She spoke pleadingly. Desperately, Margaret wanted to be reassured. She wanted him to tell her that everything was going to be just as it was meant to be.

He took her in his arms and kissed her. It was the best way he knew of giving her the reassurance she so much wanted.

Freda watched them from the kitchen door and her heart sank. She could never forget what it was she felt and seeing them kiss made it almost unbearable.

'John George woke up and then went back to sleep,' she said.

Michael went upstairs to look after Margaret's son. It was an excuse, for he felt the tension when Freda was talking to them.

'David rang up,' said Freda, 'he can't come until tomorrow.'

'Is he really going to stay here?'

'Well, he certainly isn't going home,' replied Freda.

The previous month, David had come back for a day of unexpected leave and found that Sheila had gone out with Doris and Freda for the evening. He had waited all night at his house for Sheila but she hadn't returned until the morning.

David had assumed the obvious thing. He asked her if she had been with a man and his wife hadn't denied it.

He had rung a few days before, and told them all that he wouldn't be staying with Sheila the next time he came home.

'Where's Mum?' asked Margaret.

'Upstairs, switching the rooms round to make a place for David.'

'She seems to be all right, doesn't she?' asked Margaret hesitantly.

'Yes, well, you wouldn't know would you? I mean you weren't here when it all happened were you?'

Margaret thought she heard a note of blame in Freda's voice as if she was blaming her for escaping her responsibility by not being there to help.

'Did we hear any more than just ... just the telegram? I didn't dare to ask.'

Freda dropped her eyes as if the memory were too painful.

'Dad had a letter from one of the officers in the boat. He said that Robert died in his sleep. He said that he was a brave boy ... he said he was very brave.'

Freda's face screwed up. Her eyes closed and she rested her face against Margaret. They put their arms round each other and clung there for comfort.

Freda was whispering, choking over the words.

'I've never felt like this before ... I know now how you must have felt about John.'

She moved away from her sister, and then looked her in the eye and spoke with great calm.

'How did you bear it Margaret?' she asked.

Margaret didn't know how to reply. Her feelings about the past years were so mixed. There had been Michael to think about.

'I don't know,' she said, 'I don't think I did bear it exactly. I just turned my back on it. As if ... as if there had never been anything between me and John.'

It was true. That was what she had tried to do. There had been no other way but to try to forget. Sometimes it came back to her in her sleep, or when she was walking down the street and she would see someone who looked like John.

To forget. To put it out of her mind.

Any other way was too painful.

Besides, you couldn't live in the past.

There was always a future. There had to be.

Upstairs, Jean was in Robert's old room.

She was sifting through the remnants of the past.

There was a cardboard box. In it were the droppings of a life. The schoolchild's rulers and notebooks. Some pencils.

Jean still thought of her youngest son as a child.

She opened the book and read the childish handwriting.

'ROBERT ASHTON. AIGBURTH. LIVERPOOL. LANCASHIRE. THE WORLD. THE UNIVERSE. THE WORLD.'

That was how it read.

She couldn't cry for her eyes were dry. The past. Robert, her youngest son who had been lost at sea and who would never come back.

There seemed so little point if this was all that was left of a life. If, after all the years and the effort and the love, all that was left was a book and in it was written a name. Just a piece of handwriting to remind her.

The remnants of her son.

There seemed so little point.

It was dark by the time Edwin got home that evening. He always felt depressed when he went to see Sefton because it reminded him of the thirty odd years of service to the man.

Recently though, he hated the prospect of coming home to the guilty atmosphere of his family.

He opened the door and the greyness lifted from his brow when he saw Margaret waiting for him. She hadn't changed and she was smiling.

He thought how nice it was to be smiled at for once and greeted with a hug.

'Hello love,' he said as they embraced, 'it's lovely to see you.'

'I'm sorry about Grandad,' said Margaret.

'It was to be expected,' he paused, 'I'd better go and see your mother.'

'She's upstairs,' Freda's voice came from the kitchen, 'and there's a message for you by the phone. It came this afternoon.'

Edwin picked up the scrap of paper and read Freda's almost indecipherable scribble.

The message was from Dimmock asking Edwin to ring.

He looked at Margaret as she went to the living-room to talk to Michael. He could just hear their low whispers. He hardly knew what to think. In a few days the truth would be known and whichever way it went, it would be sad. There seemed no alternative that could bring any joy to even one of them.

Jean was still in Robert's room when she heard the footsteps on the landing outside.

'Is that you Freda?' she said.

'It's me,' replied her husband.

He could hardly help but notice the way her face dropped as he entered the room.

He told her that he was catching the half past eight train the next morning, and she said that she would pack his case.

'Jean?'

He reached out for her arm, but she flinched.

'There was a message for me. It was from Dimmock. You remember Dimmock?'

'Yes.'

Edwin braced himself, deciding it was time he told Jean what he knew. The knowledge of the possibility of John's return lay heavily on his mind and he wanted so much to share it with someone.

'There was something I never told you. They didn't go into detail, but they'd heard something that made them think John might be alive.'

'Go on.'

Jean was standing quite still. Her eyes were closed. She looked as if she was waiting for someone to hit her. Afraid of the blow, but resigned to its force.

'They said that soon they'd be able to let us know definitely. One way or the other, whether John was dead or alive.'

'Why are you telling me this now?' asked Jean.

'Seeing Margaret. Whatever happens, she's going to need us both now.'

Suddenly Edwin felt weary and lonely. He needed someone to talk to.

'I wish you'd come with me tomorrow. It's a lonely task, closing the door on part of your life.'

Jean was hardly listening to his words.

'You know he'll try to get her to stay with him. If John comes back then he'll try to persuade her to stay with him.'

'But we don't know,' said Edwin. He found himself fighting against his real feelings, trying to convince himself.

'Dimmock told me that it was just as likely that the Germans had found his tags and were using them to make some game of their own seem genuine. But he said that we'll know soon.'

'We know now,' said Jean, 'I've always known, I'll pack your case and mine for tomorrow.'

She left the room and Edwin stood there alone.

In his heart of hearts he knew that she was right, but he wasn't yet ready to admit it to anyone but himself, and even that was difficult. Things as big as this didn't bear being faced until they were inescapable.

But Jean was right.

In her own way, Edwin thought that she was braver than he

was.

He would have liked to have her kind of courage, but he couldn't help thinking of the cost of that courage to other people.

Tony woke up the next morning with a hangover. He felt terrible. It wasn't only because of the hangover that he felt bad. It was because of the way that his father behaved when he brought a girlfriend home.

Tony arrived back from taking Jenny out the previous night to find Sefton was still waiting up for them both. They had made polite conversation and drunk some of his father's blackmarket Scotch. However hard he tried, Tony had been unable to make his father go upstairs and leave them alone together. Then to cap it all Sefton had put them both in rooms at opposite ends of the house and with his own bedroom in between.

He walked downstairs carefully. Every step made his head ache and his mouth tasted like an old boot. He was dying for a glass of water and a quiet breakfast.

To his chagrin, Sefton was already there, reading the paper.

'Good morning, father,' he said.

'Tony,' replied Sefton, hardly looking up, 'did you sleep well?'

'I was a bit sloshed as you well know.'

They sat in silence for a moment and his father's serenity annoyed Tony. He wanted to shock him into speech.

'Do you always sleep with your door open, Father?' he asked.

'And how do you know that?'

'I paid an early morning visit to the bathroom.'

Tony paused. He was feeling very antagonistic towards his father. He hated his patronising attitudes and his habit of still trying to treat him as a child.

'What's the idea?' he said.

Sefton sighed, and explained pedantically.

'Ever since we had the burglary I've slept with the door open. I've become a very light sleeper these days.'

They both knew why he had kept the door open, and they both knew he was lying. It was a game they played often.

'Good morning,' said Jenny sweetly.

Sefton looked up and smiled one of his sickly ingratiating

smiles. Tony winced.

Jenny was about twenty-eight years old, blonde and very beautiful. She was an expert at using her charms to play people along. It was easy for her to get anything she wanted out of people by just smiling, and Sefton was easy prey for her.

'There's a sight for sore eyes,' said Sefton, 'and a better thing for someone to wake up to than this man over here.'

'Isn't it time you were going, Father?' said his son.

'Yes, I suppose it is. Will I have the pleasure of seeing you this evening?'

He directed his question at Jenny, and she nodded quietly saying that they had nothing planned. As soon as Sefton left, Tony's frustrations burst out.

'Slimy old devil,' he said and imitated his father's way of speaking, 'I hope I shall have the pleasure of seeing you this evening.'

'Just good old fashioned manners,' Jenny replied, 'you seem to have a hangover this morning, Tony.'

'A hangover . . . yes, and a very ancient one.'

He looked at her and realised that she was not going to side with him against his father. His teeth grated with the thought of the way that they would be ever so nice to each other.

Jenny was a clever girl and already she had sensed the tensions between father and son. She was also beginning to see the similarities between Tony and his father. It interested her to see just how far their antagonism went, and what exactly it derived from.

'FEATHERSTONE' said the sign on the station platform. The train pulled to a halt and Edwin took their cases from the rack. His heart jumped when he saw the rows of cottages stretching into the distance. He looked up and overhead the machinery pulled its dirty little buckets up the slag heaps on thin wires.

This was the place he had lived in as a child. In one of the back to backs he had spent what were meant to be the happiest years of his life. Rows upon rows of identical brick built houses, stained with the black grime of coal dust. The faces too, of men also stained with grime from the pit, their backs bent from years of labour in confined spaces, walking with their hands in their pockets, the stoop of their shoulders telling a tale that it was only possible to understand if you had shared it with them.

Such a man had been his father. Proud of the fact and Edwin had shared this life for twenty years or so until he had left for Liverpool.

It was something that he understood and which was part of him.

They walked down the road from the station and past the oddly shaped miners' welfare building. The clock in its small obtruding entrance had stopped. They passed the small shop that Edwin's grandmother had kept and which in his youth had been a secret store of illicit sweets.

Small things came back to him. Things he had forgotten, but which now appeared, crisp and sharp in his memory, revitalised by what he was seeing.

The time he had fallen over and grazed his knee. The time that he had thrown a stone through a neighbour's window and then run for his life. He had never owned up and the moment plagued his conscience for months.

He had a key to the house and they went in.

He looked around the room and noticed that, even now, the dust was beginning to settle, was starting to make its own death mask on the inanimate objects about the rooms. The rocking chair that used to travel backwards and forwards incessantly had stopped. With no inhabitants, the room was lifeless. It was a memorial to a life that had just passed.

Jean looked round and thought of Robert.

'Your first look at where I came from,' said Edwin, 'the first time you've been here in our thirty odd years of marriage.'

'I'll make some tea, Edwin. You brought the milk didn't you?'

Edwin took a bottle of milk from his case and handed it to her. She went towards the kitchen, but paused before she opened the door.

'What time are you ringing them back?' she asked.

'About seven,' he said, 'there's a telephone along the road.'

When Jean came back with the tea, she handed him a cup. It had no handle and the saucer was dusty. Edwin held it fondly. He remembered it.

'Was it always like this?' she asked him.

Jean was looking round and she couldn't stop the disdain which she felt from showing on her face. To Edwin it was the same as it had always been. Small and a bit dark with windows that let in very little light. Cramped, but enough. He knew it too well to question it.

'It smells,' said Jean, 'it's awful.'

Edwin knew it smelt, but they were smells to which he had grown accustomed and to which a lot of other people had also grown accustomed. It was part of the life there. In the end you forgot about it.

'Of course it bloody well smells, the whole place smells. There are burning slag heaps on the back door step. I used to wake up in summer when there was a wind and I could taste the ashes in my mouth. You don't have to tell me that it smells!'

He was shouting at her. There were memories that he didn't want to be reminded of, parts of his life that had become blurred and were best left that way. Besides, remembering some of the squalor of the place brought the indignities of his parents life to mind. His conscience plagued him, saying that he had ignored them, not done enough to help them.

'I'm sorry,' he said, 'but you saying that makes me feel guilty, and then I take it out on you. I neglected them you see, and my conscience tastes like the ashes that blow in the window.'

He paused and looked at Jean. She was still standing and it was obviously an effort for her to sit down. She looked out of place there, uncomfortable and ill at ease. Nothing about her fitted the place, and there was no sympathy in her for it.

'They felt it,' he went on, 'that you never came here. They felt that you were spurning them.'

'I didn't understand them,' she said honestly, 'they weren't my people, you see.'

In this place, in the furnishings and the memories they held, and in the way that he and Jean reacted to it, Edwin suddenly saw the difference between him and his wife. He saw the way that their upbringings clashed and the way that the past histories of their lives before they met had so many different ingredients, it almost seemed unthinkable that they had spent so many years together.

'No,' he said, 'they weren't your people.'

They passed the afternoon and early evening looking through the house. Edwin found so many things to remind him of his past that it made him want to close his eyes. He found it painful after a while even to pick up the objects that were scattered about the room.

It was like a map to his roots. A whole world lay there in front of him and he could chart the geography of his life in that room. He talked to Jean about his father and tried to explain the pity that he felt and the admiration for his way of life. He tried to get over to his wife the guilt that sat on his heart when he thought of this place. A guilt that made him think he had deserted something to which he belonged.

'I'm boring you, aren't I?' he said.

'You can't expect me to be fired by your old battles, Edwin,' she replied.

'But they weren't my battles, that's the trouble. I was living in a middle class house in a middle class Liverpool suburb having my bread buttered on both sides,' he paused and looked at Jean, 'you really don't understand me, do you?' he said.

He was near to tears. Years had passed away since he had felt his guilt, his desertion so strongly and now he was faced with it again. He needed someone to share it with, but there was no one but his wife. She didn't understand, and she didn't even seem to want to.

It pained him that, after so long together, they should still find so much distance between them, so many spaces and vacant words, so little compassion.

'Isn't it time you went to phone?' she said.

Edwin put on his coat and walked down the street. Everything was the same and he was back where he felt he belonged.

But he knew that it was too late.

Besides, there were other problems facing them all and there was too little time to regret the past.

It was all about him, the past which was occupying his mind at that moment. It was in the slag heap which was still just discernible against the evening sky. They were monuments to his memories. Edwin felt that they had been put there to rub home to him the sum total of what his life now meant.

He had sold himself to the family into which he had married. He had given up his life for the thirty pieces of silver.

The silver that kept him in a nice house. The silver that came from his brother-in-law's pocket.

He felt the comfort that sucked him into its bosom, the

complacency that kept him there.

Inside him he knew that the sparks were dying. Years ago they had been very real sparks, very hot sparks.

There had been a time when he had cared for the injustice which kept his father bent and toiling in the mines for a pittance of a wage.

He had cared about the grime in the curtains of the house his parents lived in, the ash that blew in the window, and the tramping feet of men, bowed down by care, and subjugated by the position into which they had been born.

He had cared.

But the fires were going out and his soul, turning slowly and inevitably to ashes, was dying.

What he wanted was a reawakening, and that was something which would never come.

He paused and looked around. It reminded him of his other responsibilities.

Edwin picked up the phone.

'Did you get through?' asked Jean when he returned.

It was more than an hour later. Edwin had spent the time wandering around, desperately searching in the memories of his youth for some kind of strength.

'Yes,' he replied.

'Well?'

A long silence as Edwin fingered the old miner's lamp that had swung from his father's hand. He put it down and rocked the chair slowly.

But there was nothing to tell him what to think.

'He's alive, isn't he?' said Jean.

She knew. She always had known. For Jean the hope had always been there and she had never really let it slip from her mind.

'All this time . . . alive . . . all this time,' said Edwin.

Jean was so calm. Edwin put his head in his hands, incapable of speaking, of saying anything.

John. So long, so many months, so many days, so many hours, so many miles away.

Alive.

'All this time,' he repeated.

He thought he saw the ghost of a smile pass over Jean's lips.

'We'll have to tell her now,' she said.

Margaret was at the sink, washing up, when David got back, and she explained to him that their parents had gone over to Yorkshire to finalise grandfather's affairs. Michael was in the sitting-room, reading.

David took his sister aside. He closed the hatch that opened into the living-room so that they wouldn't be overheard.

'Is he staying here,' asked David.

'Michael?'

'Yes. I mean, where will I sleep?'

'You shouldn't be staying here,' said Margaret, 'but since you are you could do us all a favour.'

'What?' asked David.

'Go and see Sheila.'

David was determined not to be persuaded to go and see his wife. His last visit home had been disastrous and he had no desire to repeat it. He was sure she wouldn't want to see him either.

In the end, however, he promised to go and see her the next day, but that was more to keep Margaret quiet than anything else.

Sheila got back from the NAAFI later than usual, and as she walked down the narrow dark little alley to her house she saw that the light in the front room was still on. She paused a moment, annoyed with herself for being so forgetful. It must have been on all day. She put her key in the door and realised that it was unlocked. She opened it and then stopped and listened. She thought she heard a sound rather like the munching of a biscuit.

'What are you doing here?' she said in amazement.

It was Colin.

Colin Woodcock came from Manchester but worked twice a week in Liverpool as a draughtsman in a factory. Sheila had met him on her night out in Southport. That night, they had been two lonely people who had spent the evening together for comfort and friendship.

After they discovered that she had missed the last train home, he had suggested that they go to an hotel. Sheila was tempted and yet there was something in her that made her say no. As long as David was still in the back of her mind, however vaguely, she would always refuse offers like this.

At the same time there had been something in David's

attitude when she'd got home the next morning and found him waiting for her that made her let him go away thinking that she had spent the night with a man.

He'd jumped to the conclusion so quickly, so easily that she'd done nothing to disillusion him.

Afterwards she'd regretted it, but she would never forget the pleasure that ran through her veins when she realised he was jealous.

It meant that he still cared.

Colin was good looking in a gentle manner with brown straight hair that flopped over his forehead. He was everything that David wasn't. Quiet and shy, he was unassuming and didn't try to force himself on you. Sheila liked him for that and she also found him attractive. It was the gentleness in his hands that attracted her. She felt that with him, life would be peaceful and easy.

But there was still David and it was the memory of the fire she felt when he was near her that made her keep Colin at a distance.

'I missed the last train home,' said Colin, 'and I managed to get the key from the neighbours.'

'You missed it on purpose didn't you?' she replied. Half of her was angry because she knew that she couldn't throw him out at this time of night and half of her was pleased. He was so nice and it was good to have someone who cared near to you.

'I could kip on the floor?'

Sheila looked round wondering what was the best thing to do. Then she saw the Morrison shelter in the middle of the room. She lifted the side.

'In there,' she said pointing.

He started to take his trousers off and to fold them.

'And you can keep your trousers on, Colin.'

He looked and smiled at her, then, getting down on his hands and knees he crawled into the shelter. She shut the side, and smiled back. It was safe to do that now.

As she went out of the room, on her way to go upstairs, she turned and saw him wave at her. He looked like a caged animal. Sheila realised that she was already fond of him and a little arrow of fear went through her as she wondered whether it would grow to anything more.

We're all like that, she thought, we're all caged animals.

Momentarily she felt David grasping her heart. It contracted and gave a little jump. He had a grasp on her that she knew would never let go. She too was in a cage. A cage that had been built round her by her husband ever since they first met. Sheila wondered whether the time had come to break out of that cage or whether it would go on holding her for the rest of her life.

Tony sat with Jenny in the kitchen. It was getting late and they had just come home. Earlier that evening he had had a fearful row with Sefton about Jenny. Tony felt that his father had transgressed the bounds of propriety completely in the questions that he'd asked about their relationship.

Tony, too, was beginning to feel fenced in. The sharp eyes of his father constantly watching his every movement, constantly trying to gauge what he was thinking, and constantly wanting to know his every feeling. Tony felt like a business which his father was running, with its every fluctuation open to Sefton's scrutiny.

'You're a bit childish you know,' said Jenny.

'It's because he treats me like a child and therefore I sometimes find myself behaving like a child. Is that so unnatural?'

Tony was rummaging about the kitchen trying to find something to eat, but he was having little success.

He turned and looked at Jenny. She was so aware, so cool and composed so calm he felt that she too was watching him and weighing him up.

'You're not waiting for an old fashioned proposal are you? Me down on my knees?' he asked.

'No, I'm not old fashioned,' she replied, 'it's you who's the old fashioned one.'

'Because I want to marry you?'

'These things take time, you know, Tony.'

'But there isn't any time. I find time very precious these days.'

It was true for as far as he was concerned, time might run out at any moment. It was the moment that was for grasping. He felt the need to throw away the shackles of his life and to hold something firmly, to grasp on to it, to have something new.

He looked at Jenny. Her face was immovable and Tony felt no reaction coming from her.

'I think we'd better just pack it in, don't you?' he said.

'If that's what you want,' she replied, 'but just remember

that it was you who said that and not me.'

Tony wondered what it was that she wanted from him, and then he wondered what it was that he himself wanted.

He didn't know, but he was certain that he needed some sort of change. He needed to break away from his father and the age old influence that Sefton had over him.

Edwin lay awake, thinking, and Jean was beside him with her eyes open. They hadn't slept for a moment and they hadn't spoken a word either.

Outside the night held the small mining town in its grasp. The darkness sat on the slag heaps and Edwin felt the dust of years settling down over the town and over his body.

The moon shone dully through the window.

He could hear the tramp of heavy boots. It was a sound he knew well. Many times before he had lain awake and listened to the night shift coming home. He half expected the sound of his father opening the front door and creeping stealthily into the house.

'What are we going to do,' whispered Jean, 'about Margaret?'

'What else can we do but tell her. What she does then and who she decides to live with is up to her.'

'She's John's wife.'

'Yes,' Edwin sat up and drew his knees up to his chest, 'and you're mine. Look at us now. We can't sleep in the same bed without staying awake. We can't agree on anything. We count so little to each other after thirty years of marriage so why should her short term mean anything to Margaret?'

'You've tried too hard, Edwin, you've taken it all on yourself and you've shut me out. The way you've decided things without consulting me.'

Edwin knew she was thinking of Robert. He would never be forgiven.

'You make me sound a complete failure,' he said.

'You're a good man, it's just that I let you go on. I never helped you enough.'

'You mean you've let me blunder on.'

He paused a moment and thought of the dark outside. Suddenly he felt lost and near to weeping. Not knowing which way to turn, not knowing how to deal with the situation, not knowing what to do.

'I don't know where I am, Jean. I'm lost and I want to comfort you, and when I do that you seem just to turn your back on me. We should be mourning Robert together, we should be sharing the danger of John's return. I mourn Robert, I do . . . I want help . . . help me.'

He was crying now and his head was on her shoulder. Like a small child this large man, usually so strong, so firm was shaking like a leaf. His shoulders heaved and the tears flowed from his eyes. Jean held him in her arms and stroked his hair gently.

'We're all lost,' she said.

Jean looked over her husband's shoulder, and in the distance she saw a grey flat world that she could no longer understand. It stretched way away into the horizon, lifeless and blasted. On it there was nothing, no trees, no greenery, no life.

Just herself and miles away, small and lost was Edwin. Her husband.

Shadowy figures peopled this world that she couldn't understand.

She heard the voice of Robert, her youngest son, crying out to her.

She saw John appearing larger on the horizon.

Robert receding.

John appearing.

Giving and taking.

The sound of Edwin weeping.

The lustreless empty feel of his head on her shoulder.

And his body like a child.

'We're lost,' she muttered again, 'all of us.'

Everybody was lost and wandering, seeking out a future they didn't know and looking for a past that they could hold on to.

There was no force to keep them together, and so they drifted away into the night and the darkness, children crying to each other across the abyss, men shouting warnings, and no one hearing the words or the sounds of the other.

Lost.

Sheila was lost too the next morning when David came round and found Colin there having breakfast. There was nothing she could do this time to dispel the obvious conclusion that he jumped to. He walked into his house and saw this strange man there with his wife.

It seemed to him that there could be nothing further to be said, so he left immediately without saying hardly a word.

After he had gone, Colin turned to Sheila and said quite simply,

'I'm sorry.'

She didn't answer. Colin was not to blame and the fault was hers.

In a different way, she too was sorry.

It was a deeper sorrow, one that stemmed from the history of the past, from the circumstances of the present which seemed inevitably to have led to a conclusion.

She wondered was the conclusion as simple as it seemed. She wondered what would happen to them all.

Sorrow, flat bare sorrow, lying out in the rain stemmed from what had happened.

Who was to blame?

No one or everyone?

She wondered what would have made a difference to them all, what it was that could have led to a different ending.

'You look awfully unhappy, Dad,' said Margaret when they were alone together later that day, 'what is it?'

'We've got another bridge to cross, love.'

'Yes?'

'It seems there's no end to them nowadays,' he paused, 'you see when we were away, we had some news.'

They looked at each other and Margaret understood. The feeling had been with her for days, it had been in her dreams and in her thoughts. Whenever she looked at Michael she had seen John. When her baby cried it was like listening to a voice from the past, screaming out to her, getting nearer, approaching across the wastes of their lives.

She understood. The feeling rushed through her body, and she felt as if slowly she was being torn in two. Every nerve end stretching to its full finite limit until it was about to crack, to split open.

Her whole body screaming in pain, her mouth open wide, the noises reaching from her head, the screams opening up and out out out into the sky, filling the heavens with her unheard pleas for peace.

She was dying, falling down, things collapsing about her

ears. Carefully constructed defences knocked down with one blow.

She wanted peace and rest, and she knew it would never come.

There would never be an end to the suffering.

No end to the pain.

And no help from anyone but herself.

They were all lost, defenceless.

'It's John, isn't it?' she said quietly.

A moment's calm settled over them all.

PART THREE

'FROM THIS DAY FORWARD'

CHAPTER SEVEN

May 1942

At the small window marked inquiries, they told Edwin to go down the long passage that he could just see behind the half-open door.

The passage was a musty colour and the paint peeled from the walls. There were occasional benches along the side and on them sat the occasional soldier. They merged into the background. The noticeboards had meaningless, official pieces of paper pinned to them. They flapped slightly in the breeze as Edwin passed.

He had such a piece of paper in his hand and he showed it to the officer in the room to which he had been directed. There was a long trestle table in the middle and three men sat behind it. They had blank faces and the one in the middle just nodded when he saw what Edwin handed him.

About thirty men sat or stood around the room. They all looked tired and worn out, their heads sagged to their chests and there was a lifeless quality to their eyes.

It was a very silent room apart from the occasional cough or the odd shuffle of a foot.

Edwin looked round at the faces, but he couldn't find the one he was looking for. He turned to the officer and spoke to him quietly.

'Shouldn't he be here?'

The officer nodded in the direction of the wall behind Edwin. He turned. There was a knot of men standing in front of a bench. Edwin peered at them.

In the midst of the group, one of the men was sitting with his head between his knees. Edwin looked at him, recognising the lank straight hair.

'Hello John,' he said, going over and standing in front of his son-in-law.

They went in silence to the station. John spoke hardly a word. He looked a completely different man to Edwin. There were bags under his eyes, and whenever Edwin asked him a question, he didn't seem to have the strength to reply.

He was like a ghost, empty and reactionless. His hands trembled so much that it was impossible for him even to light his cigarette, and when Edwin did it for him, John just let the thing hang between his fingers.

Sitting on the train, John watched the smoke curl up from his cigarette. He saw the ash grow longer and longer until it dropped off and landed on his trousers. He felt a burning feeling at his fingertips and noticed that the stub was scorching his flesh.

Somewhere he heard a man at his side. A big man with a vaguely familiar face who had come and taken him away from some sort of institution where he had been for a length of time.

The man was speaking, telling him things that John recognised and yet which didn't seem to mean anything. Names and words passed across his mind and he tried to place them, but everything was too confused. Nothing fitted into place properly. It was all too much of a blur.

Too hazy.

All he knew was that he had spent an endless amount of time in places he didn't know and at the moment he felt that he was being taken back to where he belonged.

But he didn't know where that was or who the people were that lived there.

He didn't care.

'The baby's marvellous,' said the voice.

John looked up, startled. He recognised the man who had led him away and across the crowded station, who had sat him down in a train and with whom he was now travelling.

It was his father-in-law. John thought back. The word, baby, meant something, but he wasn't sure what it was.

'John,' said Edwin, 'of course I'm mad. You weren't with us then.'

John spoke. It was the first thing he had said since Edwin met him.

'Was it a boy?' he asked.

'Yes,' said Edwin.

John smiled and thought of Margaret. He remembered now where he was going and who was going to be there. His wife whom he hadn't seen since he was sent to France.

And his son. A boy.

John wondered what Margaret had called their son and hoped that it was something nice.

Outside the countryside rushed by and John tried to focus his eyes on things through the train window. However hard he tried all he could see was a constant blur. In the end he gave up. He gave up listening to the voice at his elbow and he gave up trying to concentrate his mind. He let the feelings flow over him, and he was like a pebble in the tide, he was being carried backwards and forwards. He didn't will it and yet he didn't fight against it. It just happened.

He was a leaf.

He was a pebble.

He was anything he wanted to be. It seemed so easy to abdicate responsibility. He felt nothing and let himself be carried on.

Sleeping, he dreamt of his wife. He dreamt of Margaret, and he saw his son. They were all walking together, hand in hand and happy as he had never been. The pain dropped from his eyes and he was in her arms again like a baby. Everything was peaceful and the rest sunk over him. It engulfed him until he no longer existed.

He leant forward and in his sleep he kissed Margaret and held his son. He thought he felt the life seeping back into his veins.

'Another kiss,' said Michael as Margaret swung off the bed and started to pull her slip over her head. He held her hand, not wanting her to go away. They had just made love.

'It's best in the afternoon,' said Margaret, 'you can hear all the busy world outside and you're out of it. Your mind stops working.'

'You can forget your problems,' said Michael. He understood what she was talking about, 'but when you get up, they're still there.'

He paused. However hard they tried to forget it, however hard they tried not to talk about it, it was always in their minds.

'You won't face it will you?' said Michael, 'they'll be back here tomorrow. Your father and John. I think it would have been better if you'd come to live here before. If you'd burnt all your bridges.'

It was the same argument they'd had thousands of times over the previous month and a half ever since Margaret got the news that John was alive. The same things being said over and over again. Michael wanting Margaret to move in with him and wanting the constant reassurance that it was him she loved, that she still wanted him. And Margaret, fearing the final decision although she knew it was what she wanted. She was sure it was, and yet inside her she couldn't do it until she had seen her husband in the flesh. Somehow it was too cruel for him to come back after all he must have been through and find that she had deserted him.

Margaret thought it would be better to tell him to his face, it would be more honest and truthful.

'You'll have to tell him at once,' said Michael.

'He's only on leave for four weeks or so and then he'll have to go back. It doesn't have to be now or never.'

Michael sat up. The fear of delay was in his eyes, the fact that he knew the longer they left it, the more difficult it was going to be.

Margaret paused by the door.

'Where're you going,' he asked.

'To the shops.'

This was the most difficult moment for him, for there was the constant thought in the back of his mind that, after she had left the room, she wouldn't come back.

'Margaret. I beg you; realise that you've got to hurt him. There's no sparing either of us. The longer you leave it, the harder it's going to be. In the end it could become impossible.'

They both knew that they were thinking the same thing. Ever since they first met, their relationship had been dogged by circumstance. Things had happened that had forced them apart, every plan they had made seemed to have ended in disaster. Events had conspired against them.

Now her husband had returned and Michael was determined not to let it all fall apart yet again.

Margaret didn't know her own mind. She wanted Michael and yet there was a seed in her brain that couldn't bring herself to face the final decision.

She preferred not to think about it.

Jean was at the sink. She had just finished tidying up the front room. Her mind was ill at ease and she wanted someone to talk to, but Margaret was out, Freda working, and Edwin had gone to London. She occupied her time by cleaning the whole house. She told herself she was doing it because John was coming back, but she knew that it was just to fill in the minutes. Although she knew she was alone, she wanted to avoid feeling it.

The doorbell rang and she jumped.

'Edwin said not to expect them back until tomorrow afternoon. You know what the trains are,' she said to Sheila as they walked back into the kitchen. The kettle was boiling and Jean made a cup of tea. She put one down in front of Sheila.

'I called twice at your place, and left messages for you to come round. I was worried when you didn't come,' she said.

'I'm not very good company these days,' Sheila replied.

Jean felt sorry. Sheila was like a daughter to her and always had been since she first got married to David. David hadn't told her what happened when he went to see Sheila the last time he was home, but Jean was pretty sure that things were bad between them.

'You see, Sheila,' she said, 'I had to see you because I'm beginning to feel that I don't know my children any more. David . . . we hardly see him and he's like a stranger when we do and then there's Margaret. I never know what she's thinking these days.'

Jean was thinking of her own marriage as well. Their trip back to Featherstone had been a sort of stopping point in their relationship. It had been an admittance of failure, and it was as if they had turned round to each other and said that after thirty years together there were still huge gaps of misunderstanding and vast areas of each other that they did not know.

'If you want me to go and grovel to him, I'm past that,' said Sheila, 'and what's more, he doesn't even seem to care any more for the children. He hasn't been to see them in a blue moon.'

Sheila finished drinking her tea and got up. She looked at Jean and wanted to be able to help her, wanted to be able to say nice things about David and to tell her that the marriage was a happy one. There was no point in lying, she thought, or even pretending in any way. They had to face up to the facts.

'Don't be surprised if I don't come again for a bit. I've got to sort things out,' she said.

'Just hang on, love,' answered Jean, 'he'll be back to you soon. You'll see.'

Sheila smiled. She wondered whether David would be back and whether, if he did come, she would still be there.

She thought of Colin, and then of David. They were two such opposite people. Sheila wondered which one she would have chosen if she had the chance to begin all over again. She knew it would still be David, but she regretted the mechanism inside her which made that the only inevitable choice.

David was on a train, travelling to a small town not far away from his base. He was going back to a part of his past about which he often thought, but which he hadn't had the chance or the inclination to visit for some years.

After the last time he saw Sheila he was convinced that their marriage no longer existed as such. There had come a point where it seemed that they had no more to say to each other, or where there was little worth in questioning what had happened.

It was two years now since David had seen Peggy, the girl who had borne him a child just after he had gone into the R.A.F. He had never seen the child either. He couldn't forget that it was a part of him, that child whom he had never seen and when his marriage and his two legitimate chidren seemed to be flowing out of his life he had suddenly got a strong desire to try to recapture a part of his past which had never come properly to fruition. There had been a promise there which he'd never fully experienced and it was that promise which drew him steadily nearer to the house where Peggy lived with her father and the child.

David remembered the soft submissive look in her eyes and the warm trusting feel of her hair. When he had first known her and before she had discovered that he was married and she was pregnant, Peggy would have done anything for David. It was that absolute trust and comparative peace that he wanted to discover again.

He knocked on the door of the little grey stone station master's house where she lived. A man opened it. He was in home guard uniform and was about fifty, thin and tall with a straight back and firm eyes.

'Come in,' said Mr Drake, 'come into the parlour.'

David introduced himself and for some reason he gave his

name as Porter. He knew that if he used his real name, Peggy's father would probably throw him straight out again.

'Is Peggy here?' he asked.

'No, she's down at the church hall making preparations for the bazaar, but she won't be long I don't expect.'

They made a fairly desultory conversation for a few minutes, talking about the war and the latest topics of news. David felt uneasy. Mr Drake was eyeing him and down as if he was comparing him with some picture he had in his mind. David felt he knew more than he was admitting.

The door opened and a small girl with long dark hair came in. She was about two years old and reminded David of Peggy. He saw something of his own face in her and found it difficult to restrain himself from hugging her. He was faced by his own daughter.

'I expect you want some water, Junie,' said Mr Drake, 'if you'll excuse me, Mr Porter.' He gathered the little girl up in his arms and left the room. David wandered round for a minute, looking at the snapshots that were displayed on the mantelpiece. There was one of Peggy and the little girl playing in a field. David picked it up and slipped it inside his pocket.

Peggy stood in the doorway, dumbfounded.

She had spent the intervening years doing her best to forget David and to piece together a new life. Now, here he was standing in front of her without warning.

'David,' she said.

Behind her in the doorway, David saw Mr Drake. His expression had changed and instead of the almost obsequious kindness which he had shown David at first, there was a look of indignation.

'I've been hoping to meet you one day, Mr Ashton. In fact I thought it might be you when you first came in,' he said.

Peggy asked her father to leave them alone, but he insisted on staying.

'You've caused a lot of misery in this house, Mr Ashton, what do you want with us now?'

David found it a bit difficult to speak. He hadn't really worked out what kind of reception he was going to get but it had been obvious it wouldn't be a good one. It was different to be confronted with it.

'I wanted to see Peg, and the kiddie. It is mine you know.'

Peggy's father was on the verge of losing his temper. He

found it unbelievable that someone could just walk in like this where he had been the cause of so much heartache.

'You think you can walk in here two years later and say you want to see your kid. She's nothing to do with you now, Mr Ashton, so I'll ask you to leave before you do any more damage. I won't have my daughter upset by you again.'

David turned to Peggy. She was standing near the fireplace, twisting her hair in her hands. It was a mannerism that David remembered, and was one he had been fond of. It accentuated her vulnerability.

'Peggy,' he said, 'it's your life, not your father's.'

She paused a moment before she spoke. David saw the tears that were creeping nearer the edge of her eyes.

'I'm getting married,' she said, 'in four weeks' time.'

Her father looked at David.

'Now will you go?' he said.

David looked round the room and caught Peggy's eye. She turned away from him. But in the moment that he had caught her eye, he'd seen a note of hope underneath the imploring look that told him she wanted him to go.

He would come back the next day.

'You can stay,' said Michael to Margaret as they lay lazily on the bed, 'he won't be back till tomorrow.'

'Not tonight, Michael,' she replied, 'not tonight of all nights.'

A hint of urgency crept into the way he spoke and the way he held her hair, bunched up in his hand. He pulled her back on to the bed and lay over her, looking straight into her eyes. She saw the insistence and the desperation.

'Yes, Margaret, tonight of all nights.'

'You won't believe I've burned my bridges, will you?'

He pleaded with her and when he kissed her she realised how much she didn't want to lose him. Her will weakened and she wanted to crawl inside him and to lay there, protected. She wanted to do anything that avoided having to face the future. She wanted to ignore the facts that in the end she would have to deal with.

Decisions seemed almost impossible and the easiest way was to acquiesce, to not take any decision at all.

'Well, I don't have to be back until tomorrow afternoon,' she said, 'I'll stay.'

He smiled at her. It was a little battle won, a small moment of triumph and it was the way he hoped things would continue to happen.

The train had taken a long time to get to Liverpool, being held up several times along the line. Edwin had expected to have to wait until the next day to be able to take John home, but he was glad that they'd let him out at once.

They'd hardly spoke at all on the journey, except in small bursts and John's questions had been mainly about the baby.

Most of the time they had both looked out of the window. For some of the time, Edwin had slept. Occasionally he'd looked up and seen that John's eyes were open. He was looking vacantly into space, his eyes flicking as the landscape passed. Edwin wondered what was going on in his mind. He wanted to know the experiences he'd been through and why it was that every so often his face would screw up in pain as if the thoughts that were passing through his mind were too painful to bear thinking about.

They got off the train. The platform was littered with men in uniform, standing still or bustling about with their packs. One or two of them were just motionless in the crowd, looking around the station. They seemed stuck to one spot, unable to believe their eyes.

John descended from the train slowly, carefully placing his feet one in front of the other as if he was unsure of the ground. Edwin helped him down.

'Welcome home to Liverpool, John,' he said, taking his pack from him.

Edwin wondered what kind of welcome it would be.

Freda was helping her mother prepare the house for the next day. Jean had got out the best china as Mr and Mrs Porter were expected to come over to welcome John home. The plates were laid out carefully in the kitchen and Jean was wiping them all down.

'You've volunteered to help scrub the hospital wards haven't you?' she asked Freda, 'the house will seem empty without you.'

Freda didn't reply. She was in two minds herself. She wanted so much to get away from the atmosphere of her home. The constant tension was getting her down and making her bad tempered. A few days before she had volunteered to become a nurse as she knew it would not only mean living away at the hospital, but also there was the possibility of getting away from Liverpool altogether.

On the other hand she felt guilty at doing this at a time when she knew that the family would need her most. John's return was going to be harrowing for them all. Even the thought of it set her nerves on edge and she felt she would go mad if she didn't know that she was soon going to be able to put it all behind her.

'Why don't you go up to bed,' she said to her mother, 'and I'll wait up for Margaret.'

A shadow passed over Jean's face as she thought of Margaret with Michael. She had hoped that the news of John's return would lead Margaret to break off her affair with Michael. It would have been so much simpler if she had. Jean couldn't understand how her daughter could carry on with another man and at the same time know that her husband was returning.

It seemed so callous.

'I hope she hasn't missed the bus,' said Jean, covering up her worst fears. In Margaret's state of mind, she wouldn't put it past her to spend this night away from home. Jean wondered whether she ever thought of the pain that she was causing to the rest of her family by her behaviour.

But then, she thought, no one in this family seems to think of the others much these days. They all seemed to have settled down into a selfish frame of mind in which they didn't help with the family life. They had all split away from each other until there seemed little to keep them together except for force of habit.

They heard the door open.

'That'll be her,' said Jean, relieved.

She walked into the hallway, and Freda followed her.

They stopped still. Freda looked over her mother's shoulder.

'Oh my God,' she said, and then put her hand over her mouth to stop herself from saying more.

Edwin was helping John to take off his coat. He hung the pack up on the stand by the door.

They were back and Margaret wasn't there to welcome them.

Jean walked up to John and kissed him on the cheek. Over his shoulder she could see the puzzled look on Edwin's face. Calmly she explained that Margaret had gone to see a friend and that she would probably be back later.

They led him into the living-room, and sat down. Jean was talking quickly, covering up the silences and desperately hoping he wouldn't ask any questions about Margaret. Jean found it hard to lie.

John sat there silently, hardly speaking a word. Indeed, it seemed to Jean that he wasn't even listening to what she was saying. He got up and wandered, in his vague sleep-walker's manner, over to the mantelpiece. He picked up a photograph of John George and stared at it.

'Would you like a sausage or something?' asked Jean.

'I'm all right,' he said slowly, 'sorry about Robert.'

Jean glanced at Edwin as she always did when the name of their youngest son was mentioned. It was an involuntary action which she could not help.

John looked up. It was as if something in his mind had suddenly focused, and become clear. There was, for the first time since he had entered the house a shine of life in his eyes.

'Where's the baby?' he asked.

'He's been asleep since six o'clock,' replied Jean.

John looked at them both, almost accusingly. He looked as if he thought that they were trying to keep the child from him.

'I want to see him now,' he said firmly.

Jean and Edwin glanced at each other and Edwin led John out of the room to take him upstairs.

Jean went back into the kitchen. Freda was preparing some food.

'Your father's taken him upstairs to see John George,' said Jean.

Freda took the lettuce from the sink and shook some of the water off. It spattered on to the floor.

'She's a bitch,' she said, 'I always stuck up for her before, but now he's come back I don't understand how she can go on. It's common decency not to. Staying in another man's bed tonight of all nights.'

'Don't talk like that.'

'You mean you don't want to face facts?'

'All right, maybe I don't want to face facts. Maybe I've faced enough facts . . . maybe I never want to face facts again.'

Freda was surprised by the anger in her mother's voice, the frustration in the way her lips pursed themselves and the tightness in the way she was clutching on to her dress as she spoke.

'I'm sorry, Mum,' she said.

Edwin left John in the room with his son and came downstairs quietly. He could hear Jean raise her voice from outside the kitchen, and his heart sank. He wondered what effect the coming tension of the next few months would have on them all.

'That's a sick boy we have there,' he said as he came into the kitchen.

They had all seen by now how ill John was, and they wondered whether Margaret would have the heart to leave him when he was in that state.

Upstairs John sat by the side of his son and watched the tiny face as it slept. His mind wandered over many things, but stopped on none of them. He found it difficult to collect his thoughts. They constantly wandered over the past years. It was so strange to be back in the place where he had spent so many happy evenings and nights.

Everything was strange. There was so much he didn't remember, like the colour of the wall-paper and the pattern on it. He felt the bed, and that was strange too.

He was sitting with the lights off. In the darkness he felt safe and secure. He didn't want to see the lights or hear the voices of the people around him. He only wanted the silence and the quiet. He wanted no sensations to pass in front of his eyes or molest his brain.

He wanted to sleep, to be unconscious and to wake up in a place where he understood what was happening, where he didn't have to take in any impressions or stimulus.

He wanted peace, sleep and quiet. To be where nothing mattered and he was left alone.

It was at about midday when Mrs Porter arrived at the Ashton's. She explained to Jean that Harry couldn't come as he was busy. There was something about the way her eyes skipped from object to object that told Jean that she was lying.

They went into the living-room.

'I'll call him,' said Jean, 'he's been sleeping late.'

'Who?'

'John. They arrived back last night.'

Mrs Porter's hand went to her head as if she were about to faint.

'And I wasn't notified?' she said incredulously.

Jean explained that it had been too late to do anything about it. By now, she had known this neurotic woman long enough to be prepared for her foibles, but she hardly wanted to have to cope with her on top of everything else that was happening.

'I can hear him moving about. He'll be down soon,' said Jean.

'I can't understand some people, they've got no consideration for others,' she looked at Jean, 'it's very kind of you I'm sure to even let me come at all. I'm only his mother aren't I?'

Jean hoped that Mrs Porter wasn't going to make matters worse than they already were. She knew that John was in no fit state to cope with his mother's overbearing affection. Jean wanted to do everything she could to protect him.

Mrs Porter was pacing the room like a caged animal. Every so often she would stop and look at Jean as if she was about to say something, but then she would think again and continue to walk about.

She came level with the mantelpiece and Jean saw her pick up a photograph of Margaret. Her heart sank.

'And where is Margaret by the way,' she said.

Jean hadn't time to make the various excuses she had planned in her mind. The door opened and John came in.

Mother and son looked at each other silently for a moment, and then she went over to him and touched his cheek with her hand. Her arm went round his shoulders an she nuzzled her face into his chest. She was like a lost animal seeking shelter, burrowing further and further into some small oasis of warmth. She muttered her son's name over and over again and she buried herself deeper in him. Her hands explored the face and skin of the son she had thought might be lost, whom it had been possible she would never see again.

Somehow Jean noticed that John was not answering back to his mother's embraces. He had put the baby down on the couch and was looking over her shoulder at it all the time. He was totally transfixed by the sight of his son.

Jean went over and picked up the baby. As she carried him out of the room, John pushed his mother away from him and stood in her way.

'Will he be warm enough?' he asked.

Jean looked into his eyes and wondered what was behind the blank vacant stare that showed through them. John repeated his question. He looked at the baby and as Jean went out of the room he followed her with his eyes. There seemed to be a magnetism that drew him to the child and which excluded everything else.

Mrs Porter led him to the couch and they both sat down. She continued to lean against his shoulder and to shower him with affection. She tried to draw him to her and to make him look her in the face. She asked him questions and told him that she would look after him, but however hard she tried, his eyes kept going to the door and he kept on talking about the child wondering whether it was warm enough, or whether there was anything he could do to make it more comfortable.

After a moment, he got up again and pushed his mother away.

'I must make sure it's all right,' he said, and walked out of the room.

Mrs Porter sat there with a shocked look on her face. She realised that she had made no impression on her son and that his mind was elsewhere.

She was hurt and she lowered her head into her hands. Strange whimpering sounds came from her mouth, animal noises like a cub calling for its mother.

She was crying for the past when she had been able to lavish the pent up affections of her soul on something tangible, for a time when her life with Harry had been a better, happier one and when they too had been a family instead of three different people living in the same house.

David came back to see Peggy the next day. He managed to catch her as she was leaving the place in which she worked and going for her lunch break. The previous evening he'd told his friend Frankie what he'd done and the reception had not been favourable. Frankie was not sympathetic where David and Peggy were concerned, and his only advice to David was to leave well alone. But David needed something to hang on to, he needed a security and he needed to prove that somehow he was not all bad. He wanted to know that he could love someone and that they too would love him.

He was walking along a little lane with Peggy. At first she had just told him to go away and not to bother her, but he had managed to persuade her at least to listen to what he had to say.

They stopped under a tree. David leant against it and tried to pull Peggy towards him, but her body stiffened and she stood out of his reach.

'Give me a chance, Peggy,' he said, 'let me say what it is that I've come to say.'

He paused. A million thoughts were rolling about his mind. Suddenly he wanted the kind of love he knew that she could give him. He wanted her warmth.

'I want to marry you, Peg,' he said.

David could hardly believe that he was saying this. In a way it was true. He wanted to prove that there was some good in him, that he could do the right thing, and that he could be responsible.

She was amazed. Disbelief flashed across her face, and David saw the anger there. He knew that she was furious because he was seeking to open up old affections that she had spent the last few years trying to hide and to get rid of.

After a while she smiled.

'What's happened to your wife then?' she asked.

David explained that she had left him for another man. There was some sympathy in the way she looked at him, but it was tinged with sorrow and with pain.

'Let me tell you something, David,' she said, 'when I lay in that hospital having your baby. When I was on my own with no father for my child, with no one to help me bring her up, I wanted you more than anything in the world. You were everything I ever wanted. And now you come back after all this time. You're sorry for the things you do when you behave badly and afterwards you want to behave better. But it's too late David.'

'I came to tell you I want to marry you.'

'Or is it just that you want someone to fill in the gap?'

She paused and looked at him, feeling again the old attraction that she had always had for him. There was something there between them and at this moment, they both felt it. It was in the air that separated them, and David leaned out again to touch her. She drew back.

'I don't think about this chap I'm going to marry like I used to think about you, David. I don't go to sleep with a smile over my face at the thought of him, but what I do feel is contentment. He's not like you David,' she looked away, thinking, 'you're a luxury a woman can't afford.'

This was too near the truth for him, it was too close to what he knew about himself and David felt an urgent desire to justify himself, to prove people who thought that of him, wrong.

'I can't afford you, David, I can't,' she said.

He reached out and grasped her firmly by the arm. His voice was hard and pleading. He had to prove something to himself and he wanted to know that the mistakes of the past could be rectified.

'Give me a chance, Peggy,' he said, 'just give me a chance.'

'It won't make any difference, David.'

She turned and walked off down the road and David remained, leaning up against the tree.

He looked about him and saw the spring everywhere in the ground and in the trees.

Like the seasons, he wanted the chance to start afresh, to prove to himself that there was something he could succeed at. The past was murky, like an untended pond and David wanted to clear it. He wanted everything to be fresh and new.

He had to prove that the mistakes of the past could be undone and that they wouldn't go on repeating themselves, he had to know that life and the people in it would change and that once more he could be new.

He would come back the next day, he thought, and show Peggy that he meant what he had said. He would make things all right for her.

It was something that had to be.

It was getting on in the afternoon and Margaret still hadn't returned. Everyone could feel the tension and their voices were strained with the waiting. Mrs Porter looked up nervously every time the front door opened.

'It must be something very important to keep her from seeing John,' she said to Jean as they sat in the kitchen.

There was an accusing note in her voice and Jean explained that Margaret often stayed out all night when she went to see a friend of hers. She found it hard to lie like this and couldn't believe that her voice sounded particularly convincing.

'She always liked going out, didn't she?' said Mrs Porter.

Jean tried to change the subject. She didn't like talking about it as she was in constant fear of making a slip, or saying something that might give John's mother the idea that there was something wrong.

'I've done a terrible thing,' she said to Jean. Jean jumped at the suddenness with which she spoke.

'You see, I didn't tell Harry that I was going to meet John.'

Jean was surprised. To not tell your husband something like that implied so much deceit and misunderstanding that it made her feel sad. She knew that Mrs Porter was an odd, close woman, but she would have thought that this kind of event was something that a married couple would share.

Then she thought of herself and Edwin. There were things he had hidden from her, there were times when he had done things without telling her. She resented it and in a way she felt sympathetic to John's mother. She began to almost associate with her.

'I just didn't tell him,' went on Mrs Porter, 'you see, he never told me about the telegram when it first came. He kept it to himself for days. He didn't tell me that John was missing.'

'Perhaps he was trying to protect you?'

Jean heard herself repeating almost the exact words that Edwin had once spoken to her.

'You could ring him at home tonight, and tell him that you didn't get our telegram until after he had gone to work.'

Mrs Porter looked up. She was turning the cup of tea around in her hands. When she spoke, her voice was high and strained. Jean looked at the lost expression in her eyes. She could see herself in that woman's position, she could sympathise with the tension in her voice and the highly strung nerves which seemed to jangle from her fingertips.

'I envy you sometimes, Mrs Ashton, you're so much stronger than I am. You can cope with everything so much better than I can.'

For probably the very first time in her life, Jean actually felt close to the woman. She could understand her behaviour. She realised that, if she let herself get out of control, she too would be like that. She too would be unable to control her tears, and be unable to keep her hands still. She would walk about as if she were in a dream and would smother the small shreds that tied her to reality with overbearing affection. She would constantly look to the past for a picture of how their lives should be.

But she wasn't like that and she knew she had to look to the future however painful it was going to be. It was difficult, but it had to be faced. There was no point in looking away.

The door opened, and Margaret hurried in. She hung up her coat and hat and went into the living-room.

John.

He had his back to her and was playing with their son on the carpet. Suddenly, Margaret felt weak and undecided. He was the same as he had been when she last saw him. The same face, the same eyes, the same back. Somehow she had expected something different.

In front of her was her husband. He was playing with her child. There was something so right about the situation as if he had never been away. If he had been there always, then this would be how it was. But it wasn't like this. Things had changed.

In front of her, her husband, playing on the ground with their child.

And behind her was her lover, the man she had just come from.

Margaret was caught between the two and she felt her knees weaken. Her whole body, the fabric of her life began to fall about her.

She wondered how she would ever bring herself to do what she knew she had to do. It seemed a mammoth and impossibly cruel task.

She wished that she were somewhere else and that she didn't have to face the future.

John turned to face her.

'John,' she said, the name sounding at once strange and at the same time familiar to her lips.

'Margaret,' he said.

They looked at each other for a moment and then she smiled.

Things that she didn't want to see played in front of her eyes and she wondered if Michael had been right. Perhaps she should never have come back.

Or perhaps she should never have left in the first place. She didn't know. Right and wrong no longer existed, there were only alternatives to choose from and the one she chose was her own affair. It was in the choosing that the pain lay, and it was the final choice which brought on the suffering.

A cry.

She looked down and noticed that her son was crying.

As if they were one person both she and John leant down to comfort him.

It was an instinctive reaction that belonged to them both.

It will be in the final choice and the execution of it that the suffering will come, she thought.

She wondered who would suffer most.

Herself, or John, or their child.

'Michael and I love each other. We can't sacrifice two lives for one, you know,' said Margaret to her mother later on that day as they finished off the washing up in the kitchen.

'But he needs security, love,' Jean paused and wondered if there was anything that she could say which would make Margaret change her mind, 'he went out to fight, for you and for me as well as for everyone else. Don't you think you owe it to him?'

'I know it sounds cruel. I don't like it and nor does Michael, but life is cruel, Mum. I think it's more cruel than the war.'

Jean put down a plate on the table. She turned and looked at her daughter,

'And the baby?' she said, 'what's to become of the baby?'

Margaret looked up. There was something in her mother's voice that she didn't like. It was as if the fight had already begun in earnest.

'What about the baby,' she asked, 'a baby stays with its mother.'

'Are you sure you can count on that in the circumstances? You see, I know that we've all got to face the facts of the situation, but then so have you Margaret.'

Margaret knew that it had all begun now. There would be the constant arguments and the pressures that everyone, in their own different way would try to bring to bear on her. She hadn't expected such hard implications as the ones that were in her mother's previous words, but the more that she was threatened, the more that they forced her to justify her position and the more that they all tried to blackmail her into changing her mind, the more Margaret knew she would fight it. Her resolution hardened. There were weak links in that chain, she had felt them when she had first seen John that afternoon, but as she faced her family, they became cemented over again.

She went out of the kitchen and as she passed through the hall she met John. He was just about to take the child out for a walk in its pram. She offered to go instead, but he wouldn't hear of it. Suddenly, Margaret wanted to grab John George in her arms and take him away with her too. There was a fear that she might lose the son she loved so much. It was something she wouldn't be able to bear.

She heard a voice from behind her.

'Well, Margaret, we've got him back now,' said Mrs Porter from the door of the living-room, and if you'd missed him as much as I have, but then, I've never doubted he'd come back.'

Margaret turned round. She had been trying to avoid talking to John's mother ever since she came back.

Margaret felt as if the world was conspiring against her and the last thing she wanted now was to hear that neurotic voice pouring out its troubles into her supposedly sympathetic ear.

She made an excuse and went upstairs. She wanted to be away from them all, and she found it difficult to stifle the desire to run out of the house back to Michael.

That evening, David met Peggy in his local pub. He was there with all his own mates and was glad when she turned up as they hadn't believed she would come. They spent a pleasant few hours. It was just like old times. The same people and the same place. David wondered if things could have been different between him and Peggy. She seemed receptive to him as they sat there and passed away the hours.

On the way home, he kissed her and she responded to his embrace.

He picked up the photograph of his daughter which was on the mantelpiece of Peggy's home and looked at it.

'She looks more like you than me,' he said.

Peggy's face hardened and David wondered if he had said the wrong thing.

'Yes, perhaps that's just as well,' she replied, sharply.

'How do you mean?'

'You think you're winning me round, don't you David? You've been trying very hard to do that? There was a time when all I wanted to hear were the things you said this evening when you kissed me, but that time's passed now.'

David thought that he had succeeded and he moved towards her. She looked soft and loving. The slight lisp to her voice sounded welcoming to his ear and he came across the room towards her. For a moment, she rested in his arms. Then suddenly she pushed him away.

'Don't touch me David,' she said, 'I don't want you to touch me. You see, you don't mean anything to me now, and because I've seen you I can put you out of my mind and marry Tom without thinking I'm cheating him. If I hadn't seen you then I might have had to live with your memory for the rest of my life. Now I don't.'

David felt desperate when she said this, but in his own mind he knew she was right. You couldn't go back to the past and think that it would be the same as it was when you left it.

'I need you Peggy,' he said, but he knew now that he was lying, that he was doing no more than keeping up appearances.

'I needed you once. So if you really need me, I feel sorry for you because I know how it feels, David.'

David walked home, back to his room at the station. He felt hurt and sad. It hadn't been nice for him to be led on and then told what she had told him a few moments before.

He looked up and heard the noise of the bombers going overhead. They were his friends, his pals and he knew that some of them wouldn't come back the next morning.

There was no past to go back to, and no future to look forward to. In a way it seemed the best thing, for when you were up over Germany, dropping your bombs, you were wiping out the past of a million other people's lives and you were destroying the future as well.

He thought of Peggy and wished her luck. She had changed and become a harder person. He had changed too. Things didn't matter so much now, especially if you didn't think about them too much.

Nothing mattered very much he told himself half heartedly.

He wished it was true but he knew it wasn't. He wanted something to matter.

Margaret sat with John by the fire. It was getting late and he had said hardly a word. He looked tired. He looked up at her.

'I shall be all right you know,' he said, 'after a time they said I'd be all right and then I'd be able to earn a living and things. You see, you miss people being kind to you. When people are kind to you it makes you want to cry. I'm sorry . . . I'm such a mess you see, such a mess.'

He stood up, but almost immediately sat down again. It was as if the effort of even walking was too much for him. Margaret went over and put her arms under his. She supported him. He was like a baby.

'I took my pills, you see, to help me sleep. I have trouble sleeping.'

It was all he wanted. Just to sleep and to forget.

His voice was blurred and his thoughts incoherent. Margaret lay back in bed beside him and listened to his words. He rambled about Belgium and the cellar they had locked him in. Then he was silent.

They both lay there, both awake, both unable to sleep, and both unable to say the things to each other that needed to be said. John was completely exhausted. Margaret thought she had never seen someone so completely washed out and drained before.

There were other fears in her mind too. Mrs Porter had made some veiled hints that Margaret hadn't quite understood. She wondered whether she knew about Michael. Then she thought of the future, and she realised that if she didn't tell John what had happened, someone else would. It was something she had to do.

Freda had received the news that she'd been accepted by the hospital that afternoon, and had told Margaret that at some point in the future she would be moving out.

Everyone seemed to be leaving. Everything seemed to be breaking up. Even her parents hardly spoke to each other.

It seemed that there was so little left of the household that had once been such a close knit family.

Margaret turned over and lay on her back. In the darkness she thought of Michael and wished she could be with him.

The next day she went round to his flat. Michael was waiting for her, furious that she was late and furious that she hadn't come the night before as she'd promised.

'I'm sorry,' she said, 'but it was so difficult . . . still, I'm here now.'

He grabbed her as if his life depended on it and they kissed. After a few silent moments, Michael went out into the kitchen to make some tea. Margaret watched him through the doorway.

'I had to wait at Pier Head,' she said, 'there was some kind of hold up. I don't think I've ever seen the water look so grey. I saw a troopship leaving Prince's landing and they were all up on deck, waving. You forget, now that the bombing seems to have stopped, you forget that it's still going out out there, for people like David and Philip. And then there's Robert too . . .

She stopped herself. If she went on she knew that she would get too morbid, and anyway she didn't have long with Michael. He came back through the door with the tea.

'You haven't told him, have you?' he said, as if he knew she hadn't before he asked the question.

'He's ill, Michael. It's in his mind, he doesn't even seem to be able to string two sentences together. I couldn't tell him.'

'Even if you wanted to? Was that what you were going to say?'

'He needs time. We can afford to give him that can't we? We can afford a little more time.'

She wondered how long it would be before John was strong again and before she could look him straight in the eyes and say to him without a quaver in her voice or a shaking in her knees or even a shadow of doubt in her mind that she was leaving him.

She wondered just how long that would be.

CHAPTER EIGHT

July 1942

June passed. The sun came out and shone down on the parks of Liverpool. The light was new and John often just sat on a bench and looked around him. Sometimes he had to screw up his eyes because the sun was too bright for them, and occasionally when he turned to see that John George was all right, the rays of the sun would reflect so brightly from the pram that it would physically hurt him.

He had lived in the dark for over a year, in a small cellar in Belgium and the sight of the sun, the trees, and even other people confused him. He found it difficult to take it all in.

Sometimes he would stay out for the whole afternoon and not notice the time pass, or the people walk past him.

Margaret followed him once and watched him from a distance. She was amazed that someone could sit so still for so long. A leaf fluttered down and settled on his head, but he didn't even notice it. Margaret wanted to go to him and take it from his hair. But she didn't. She turned and walked home sadly.

He talked more nowadays, but often when he was speaking, the words became incoherent. It seemed as if there was a link missing in the chain of his thoughts. At night he would sit in the living-room and stare at the empty firegrate.

When the time came for them all to go to bed he would go on sitting there, sometimes for an hour or so. Then, when Margaret came down to see if he was all right, he would be too tired even to walk up the stairs, and she would have to help him. Help him drag his lazy feet upwards, step by step, and help him into bed.

Slowly she began to realise how dependent he was on her and it became more difficult to imagine telling him about Michael. The whole situation became more difficult and she felt a wedge being driven between her and Michael.

It was difficult to get away sometimes, and never could she escape from the accusing looks of her mother and of Freda. These two especially seemed to hold her actions against her and she felt the guilt whenever she said she was going out of the house for the afternoon.

Freda was hardly at home these days. She'd begun her nursing training and was living out at the hospital. Occasionally she came back for the odd night, but it seemed that it was something she did as infrequently as possible.

In a way it was a relief for Margaret when her younger sister wasn't in the home. She had had no idea how mean she could be, how little understanding and sympathy, it was possible for Freda to show. But when she wasn't there, it brought her into closer contact with her mother and father. She felt them looking at her all the time, waiting and watching for her to make some move. Either to stop seeing Michael or to tell John.

It was all so close, so claustrophobic that it made her want to scream. She wanted to forget it all and to run to Michael, but there was something stopping her.

It was the helpless look in her husband's face and his obvious need for aid.

It suffocated her, this closeness, it seemed that she could do nothing without being seen.

One night she and Michael had gone out together to the cinema. That evening Margaret had felt uneasy and at the end of the film, she had realised why. Behind her, about two or three rows back were Freda and Sheila.

Later that night, as she walked down the hall she'd heard voices coming from the living-room. It was Sheila talking to Edwin and Margaret had stopped to listen for a moment. She heard Sheila saying that they'd seen her and Michael at the cinema.

She felt sorry for Sheila. She sympathised with her situation and the way that David treated her. But she wondered how she had the nerve to talk like that when she was carrying on with another man.

Margaret had seen Colin coming out of Sheila's home a couple of times. She didn't know for certain if there was anything in it, but she suspected.

She wanted them all to go away and leave her in peace. She wished that people would keep to themselves and not bother trying to organise and pry into other people's affairs.

Margaret was feeding John George in his high chair, and

Jean was beside her cutting up some sandwiches. They were both silent. Jean piled the bread and sliced it through the middle.

'John was down in the night,' she said, 'I heard him and I couldn't sleep either so we had a cup of tea together. He says his tablets don't seem to work any more.'

'Yes,' replied Margaret, 'he is exhausted. That's probably why he's still in bed now.'

It was conversations like these that Margaret hated most. The constant undercurrents of recrimination as if it were her fault that John couldn't sleep, as if she could do something about it. Her mother seemed to try to be making her feel guilty just by the way she looked at her.

Margaret went to open the door when she heard the bell go. Anything was a welcome interruption to the tense atmosphere of the home.

She was shocked when she saw Michael standing in the porch.

'I want to talk to you,' he said and stepped inside without giving her the chance to invite him in.

She gritted her teeth and glanced at the stairs to see if John was there.

'You mustn't come here,' she said, 'go away and I'll meet you down the road or something.'

But he was persistent and she was forced to take him into the living-room.

He stood with his back to the mantelpiece and she noticed that his fists were clenched. There were rings under his eyes, his hair looked lifeless. The worry was digging furrows across his brow.

'Why didn't you come last night?' he asked.

'It was tonight, outside the Scala.'

They argued in whispers and Margaret hoped desperately that no one would come in. She strained to listen for footsteps coming down the stairs. It was just a misunderstanding as to when they said that they would meet, but in the atmosphere of the present situation it became magnified into something bigger and more sinister.

'It's been two months now,' he said, 'and you still haven't told him.'

She tried again to explain that it was impossible to tell him while he was as ill as he was. The more she said it, the less she believed it. As time went by, it just became more and more difficult, but she was sure that there would be a time when it would be possible.

'I just can't see any end to it, that's all,' he said.

The hatch opened and Jean saw who it was that she was talking to. Horror passed over her face and she closed it again without speaking.

'Please go, Michael,' said Margaret imploringly.

Jean sat down in the kitchen, fearful of what might happen if John came down. She was angry at the presumption of Michael's coming to the house and made up her mind to go and tell him to leave. She hesitated by the living-room door, listening. She heard footsteps coming down the stairs.

John stood at the bottom of the staircase, holding on to the banister with one hand to steady himself. His eyes were drooping with fatigue and his hair was dishevelled. He looked wild, at his wit's end for sleep.

'Where's Margaret?' he said.

Jean tried to stop him from going into the living-room, but he seemed intent on talking to Margaret. He opened the door.

'John,' she said.

He didn't seem to notice Michael standing there, and Margaret didn't introduce him. John had forgotten to put on his glasses and he fumbled about the room looking for his tablets. Margaret told him that they were in the kitchen out of reach of the baby. At one moment, he came face to face with Michael, but didn't seem to notice him. There was only a strange puzzled look that passed over his face briefly as he looked into Michael's eyes.

Slowly he shuffled round the room and then out again into the kitchen.

'Don't you think you ought to go now?' said Margaret to Michael.

She wondered whether the sight of her husband and the state he was in would help Michael understand her position. John was so ill, so helpless that it was impossible to feel anything but sorry for him. It was too cruel to add to his troubles and Margaret hoped that Michael would understand that now.

John found the tablets. All the time, Jean heard him muttering that he couldn't sleep, that all he wanted was to have peace and rest. After Michael had gone, Margaret came in and took him off to bed. As she led him out of the room her eyes met those of her mother. It was almost hatred that Margaret saw in Jean's glance.

She did feel guilty, especially when the two strands of her life came so close together but there was nothing she could do about it except to carry on and hope that, in the end it would all work out.

John spent the rest of the afternoon wandering around in a dazed sort of fashion. He would sit down in the living-room and pick up the newspaper, but Margaret could see he wasn't reading it. If she spoke to him, he would hardly answer. At about five o'clock, she left saying that she was going to see Marjorie.

They all knew where she'd gone except for John, that is.

Freda was just off to the hospital when John came into the kitchen and asked for his tablets. He said that he was going to bed. It was now about six o'clock. He picked up the bottle and sat down at the kitchen table staring at it.

'He seems a bit better, don't you think,' said Freda to her mother as she stood by the door in the hall waiting to go out.

'He doesn't sleep very well, and the tablets don't seem to work for him as well as they did when he first got back.'

Freda paused, fiddling with the strap of her bag.

'Margaret's still out I suppose?' she said.

'Yes, but we've got to the point where we don't talk about it any more. She just says she's going to Marjorie's and off she goes. I find it more and more difficult to look John in the eyes as time goes on.'

Freda leaned forward and kissed her mother on the cheek. It was an affectionate peck, but to Jean it was like a beautiful gift. It wasn't often these days that there was any spontaneous affection from one member of the family to another. She fingered the place where Freda had kissed her and then turned to go back into the kitchen. She felt lonely, as if they were all deserting her.

Edwin too. He was no more than a stranger to her. The days had gone when they would talk and try to understand each other's problems.

When Jean got back to the kitchen after fetching the empty cups from the living-room, she found that John had already gone up to bed. Jean looked around for the bottle of pills, but he'd taken them with him.

Later on, Margaret and Michael lay beside each other on the bed in his small flat. Michael leaned over and touched her, turning her face so that he could look at it, making sure that she would still look him straight in the eyes.

'Something's happened hasn't it,' he said, 'when I touch you, you seem to go away from me.'

'It's just a part of me, Michael, the part that was there before I met you.'

She looked at him and saw the tenderness and the desire to understand in his face. She wanted him too, but it was just so difficult and so confusing.

'Did it help you to understand, coming round to the house this morning? You see, when I first met John he was all I'd ever wanted. I suppose I wanted to be like Mum and Dad with a house and children.'

'And now?'

Margaret struggled with the words, but they wouldn't come easily. She wanted to tell him that she was frightened of what the future held. That she was scared of all the pain and of being torn this way and that. She wondered whether everything they had gone through might in the end turn out to be nothing. She suddenly had a vision of being older and of having no one by her side and of looking back over the years with Michael and them seeming unreal, as if they had never happened.

She thought of the baby that they had never had, and wondered whether that was the key to the way she felt. John George was so real, he was there, he laughed and he cried and the other baby. It was there too, but it wasn't real, you couldn't hang on to it.

'It's there,' she said, 'but at the same time it's not there. It's a ghost, Michael and it'll walk between us for the rest of our lives.'

She wanted to be happy and in the moment, she turned and pulled Michael to her. She dug her fingers into the back of his neck and forced his mouth down on to hers. She wanted what was real, the things she could hold on to, the things that would support her.

They struggled madly on the bed for a while and then they lay back. Margaret was exhausted. Making love became more difficult for her now. It was not the same as it had been.

She thought she heard a baby cry, and it was John George.

And then another cry.

The baby that did not exist. The ghost that was all that existed between her and Michael.

It would walk with her for the rest of her life, but it would never be there to touch.

There would never be any proof of it.

Margaret felt her will weaken again, but she pushed the fears and the doubts to the back of her mind. She pushed them down and away to the bottom of her soul and then she looked at Michael and wanted him again.

'Please,' she said, 'tell me I can be happy.'

It was quite late when Edwin got back that night. He had been at Sefton's club in the middle of town and they had had an evening out together. It was refreshing sometimes for Edwin to spend the evening away and it was something he did more often these days. He went into the living-room and found John sitting there in the dark. Edwin turned on the light.

'Should you be in bed?' he said.

'I have been. Woke up though. It's difficult to get to sleep.'

John paused and looked up at Edwin.

'Margaret's gone to see this woman again. Marjorie, she said, Marjorie.'

He rolled the name round his tongue, as if he was tasting it.

'I suppose she might be staying the night again,' he went on, 'mind you, I don't blame her. After all, I'm not that much to come back to am I? It's not as if I'm the world's most exciting company, what with being tired all the time and not talking all that much.'

It was the first time Edwin had seen John like this since he'd come back. The words came rolling out and Edwin wondered what had happened to make him feel so depressed and sad.

The thought crossed Edwin's mind that perhaps he had found out something about Michael, but he knew it would only give the game away if he asked him. The time passed and finally they both realised that Margaret wouldn't be back that night. It was too late for the last bus.

Edwin went to bed and left John alone in the living-room. There was nothing else he could do.

'I've missed the last bus,' said Margaret, 'you should have reminded me you know. I mean supposing they telephoned

Marjorie or something. It'd all come out then wouldn't it?'

'Yes, and perhaps it wouldn't be a bad thing,' replied Michael.

'You saw what he was like, you must see what it would do to him. Don't you understand how I feel, Michael?'

He got up from the bed and walked around the room. Margaret followed him with her eyes, wondering what he was thinking. It was difficult for both of them, and she felt that it was coming between them, separating them from each other. He turned and looked at her.

'What can I say. It's all ashes isn't it?' he said.

Things were getting out of control for Margaret. She couldn't tell John and as time went on she became more and more unsure of whether she should. And yet at the same time she wanted Michael more than anything else. It hurt her to hear him say things like that, and to see the despairing look on his face.

She wanted to fight against the inevitable process that seemed to be leading her back to John. It was not a decision she was taking, but it seemed to be happening more by default than anything else.

Soon she knew that she would have to make a decision and the one she wanted to take was the most difficult.

Was it always like this, she wondered, was it always that the things you wanted were the most difficult?

In her heart, she wanted to fight the forces that were leading her away from Michael, and yet she felt herself being carried along by them.

The current was becoming too strong, and it wouldn't require much more to take her under, to drown the final vestiges of strength that were left to her.

John sat on the edge of the bed. In one hand he had a glass of water and in the other was the bottle of pills.

He needed sleep and rest and peace. That was all he wanted and it didn't seem much to ask. His strength had been sapped. It was all gone.

He took a couple of the pills and swallowed them.

To be away. To rest. To sleep and to get rid of the awful weariness that had overcome him. He wanted to sink into oblivion and to be taken away from having to act, from having to get up in the morning, and from having to speak to other people.

He took two more pills and then he swallowed them too.

His hand crept out across the bed and he wanted to feel Margaret there, but she had gone.

He wasn't much to come back to. He heard his voice echoing across the room. He didn't blame Margaret for staying away.

Wherever she was.

He took two more pills and swallowed them as well.

He was surprised when they didn't work immediately, so he lay down and put his head on the pillow.

Minutes passed, and he was still awake.

There were only two more pills left in the bottle so he took them.

To rest, to sleep, to be somewhere where nothing mattered and where there were only white walls about him. Nothing to distract his eye. He wanted to be quite still. Never to have to move again.

After a time his head span and he felt himself going into a restful white room.

Then he closed his eyes and a terrible stillness came over him.

For a moment he was frightened, and then he was glad.

At last he could sleep.

He slept.

'He just needed some sleep,' said Edwin to Jean the next day after the doctor had gone.

Jean had gone into John's room early in the morning and seen the empty bottle on the floor.

'He was desperate for it and he didn't know how many he'd taken. For heaven's sake don't go and tell Margaret.'

Edwin was pleading with his wife. He wanted to avoid what they were all thinking and he didn't want it to be told to Margaret.

'I am going to tell her what I'm thinking,' she replied, 'because it could just be the truth.'

'But he wouldn't take them for that. Not to try to influence Margaret because he doesn't know.'

'Doesn't he?' said Jean, 'no one's told him and yet I think he feels it. You see, people have an instinct about being not wanted, Edwin.'

They both heard the door open. It was Margaret.

'I am going to tell her,' said Jean before she came into the room.

Jean told Margaret what had happened, and as she spoke, Edwin tried to explain the way he saw it.

Margaret just stood still and listened to them both.

'You see,' said Jean, 'it's no good any more. No one's told him, but yet he knows because you can't hide the way you feel. You've got to decide, Margaret and it's no good deciding tomorrow or the next day, because it's got to be now.'

There was a pause and Margaret looked at them both. Suddenly she felt sad and tired. Weary of all the pressure, weary of the fight to keep something she wanted when the odds and the circumstances were all against her.

'I have decided, Mum,' she said, 'I decided on the way home.'

What she had just said wasn't quite true. Her mind had only just been made up. The last vestige of her strength was now drowned and the current was taking her with it.

She turned and left the room.

Edwin and Jean looked at each other and wondered what exactly it was that she had decided.

That night, Margaret looked out of the window into the darkness. In the bed just behind her was her husband and he was sleeping. Now, he would never know what she had been through. Or at least not until they were both well enough and distanced enough for her to summon up the courage to tell him.

In the next room was her son.

She was sad.

Probably it was the only decision that she could have made, this one to stay where her duty told her she should.

It was such a pity.

She had been dragged in by the vortex of her family, the whirlpool of their feelings had taken her down into the heart of these people, and she felt their claws clutching at her, ripping her soul open to the sky.

She was going to give up the love and warmth she felt for another man because she was scared of what the future might bring.

The ties of her feelings for her husband and the desire to help him were so strong that that had pulled her back in. It required such strength to reject them and yet it required another sort of strength to refuse them.

She looked to the future and wondered what she would think of this moment when she had looked out into the night in the years to come.

Would she regret it?

Or would she know that she had done the right thing?

She knew that she would never be able to tell, and that when she knew the answer it would be too late.

Everything was too late.

She had taken a decision and that had been hard. Harder than anything she had ever done before.

But the pain of that decision was nothing, absolutely nothing to the pain that was going to come from the enactment of its consequences.

If only things could be simple.

They weren't and they never would be.

She looked down at John and thought of the future that they were going to share, and then she thought of Michael and the past that they had shared together.

She looked out of the window and saw that it was dark, dark as her soul, and frightening as the people in it.

CHAPTER NINE

July 1942

The last week in July was beautiful, and the sun shone so much that the family spent a lot of its time out in the little garden behind the house. There was only a small patch of lawn there, but it was enough for John George to play on.

John had been noticeably better over the preceding few weeks, and took his place in the family life with less and less allowances having to be made for him.

Margaret began to notice that he read more and that when he applied his mind to various tasks, he managed to follow them through to the end instead of leaving them half-finished as he would have done when he first got back. She began too to feel more affectionate towards him and she felt the pity that had been her reaction when she first saw him begin to turn into at least a semblance of what she had felt before he went away.

Margaret and Jean sat in the garden. Jean was doing some darning and Margaret kept an eye on her son. They basked in the unexpected warmth of the sun.

Margaret was telling her mother that the final notice of John's discharge from the army had come that morning. She was thinking to herself as she spoke that there was now no chance of avoiding the final split with Michael.

She had been seeing less and less of him over the previous weeks. It was difficult for her to bring the affair to a definite halt and she was trying to wean herself away from it, away from something that had meant so much to her.

Both she and Michael realised what was happening, and the more they drifted apart, the less they talked about it. It was like watching a ship sinking from a distance. They looked on at themselves in silence, waiting for the final explosion when they would both know that there was nothing left.

'When are we going to get our spare room back?' asked Jean.

'It was John's idea, you know, that we should sleep in separate rooms until he was better. I could have stuck it, sleeping with two men at the same time.'

Jean looked pained. She didn't like being reminded of the realities of the situation. Margaret saw the way she looked away, pretending to notice something at the end of the garden.

'I'm sorry,' she said, 'I know it hurts you when I say things like that, but I have to say how I feel. You see, it's like walking on a tightrope, balancing, and if anybody shouts at me, then I know I'm going to fall off.'

That was indeed how she felt, and she knew she was coming near the end. In sight was a secure footing where she could rest in peace and know that her balance wouldn't be upset any more, but it was negotiating the last few vital steps that was going to be difficult.

She stood up and gathered the things she had about her into a small bag. She walked back into the house. As she went she could feel her mother's eyes boring into her back. Margaret went into the kitchen. She put her bag down on the table and then, hearing a sound come from the living-room, she opened the door.

John was seated on the floor with the radio in bits. He was trying to mend it and it made Margaret happy to see him engaged on a task that so obviously absorbed him. He looked up at her.

'I spent a year doing this sort of thing in a little cellar in Antwerp,' he said mildly.

'Aren't you going to tell me some more about it?' asked Margaret.

John looked up at her and his face clouded at the memory.

'Perhaps sometime I will,' he said.

Margaret had an obvious fascination to know what her husband had gone through in the months that he had been a prisoner of the Belgium resistance. She wanted to know what it was that could happen to a man and which could change him so much. She wanted to know why he wouldn't talk about it and why it kept him awake at night.

She heard him sometimes through the wall, talking to himself, moaning in his sleep. The memory was so obviously painful. She was beginning to want to share it and see if she could take some of the burden from his mind.

'I met your old headmistress in the park the other day,' said John, 'and she wanted to know when you were going to come back to teaching.'

Margaret thought for a moment. It was a good idea and it would help take her mind off things. It would help her to make those last few steps to safety.

'Would you mind?' she said.

'It would be convenient. It's close and your mother could look after John George.'

'We've a lot of leeway to catch up on, haven't we?' said Margaret.

John stopped and carefully placed a part from the radio on the carpet. He turned one of the knobs round as if it brought back a memory.

'We are going to be all right, aren't we?' he said.

Margaret wondered how much he knew about what she had been doing. He couldn't know anything for certain, but he must have sensed her frame of mind. He must have seen that she went out less recently, and he must have noticed that they got on better since she spent more time at home. It was difficult to hide these things, difficult to pretend and somewhere deep down in his mind he must suspect something of what had been going on.

That morning, Sheila had visited the Ashton's home to see if anyone had found her ration book. No one had and she was now at home searching through her house for the second time. She didn't go round there much these days and when she did, she stayed for as short a time as was possible. The atmosphere had changed over the last year, and she noticed it especially over the last two or three months since they had got the news of John's return.

Sheila got the impression that no one in the household talked to anyone else any more, that vast areas of silence existed between them all as if they were scared to cross the dividing line that separated them, one from the other. She preferred the silence and loneliness of living alone in her little house than the silence of living alone among a group of other people.

She was getting so frantic in the search for her book that she didn't notice Colin come in the room. She was even talking to herself trying to calm down and search logically.

'First signs that,' he said, 'talking to yourself.'

She jumped, and then smiled at him. He was a very reassuring person to have around the house and she liked it when he came there, unannounced. There was little fear these days that

David would be around. Sheila knew that everyone thought she was having an affair with Colin and she was pleased that they were all wrong. Somehow the promise that was between them had never come to fruition, but there was always a hint of it there. One day, she thought, the moment will be right. When she had forgotten David completely and had escaped from the hold he had over her, the hold that still lingered strongly in her memory, when that had all gone she would be free to do as she wished.

'You left the door open,' he said.

'It's because of the heat.'

She explained that she had lost the ration book and he helped her look for a moment then went off to make a cup of tea. He came back out of the kitchen holding his nose.

'It stinks in there,' he said, 'you've got your drains all blocked up.'

'I know, but I can't get anybody to come and do them,' she said.

Sheila stood up from the floor where she was going through a box of old papers to see if the book had slipped in there. She watched Colin while he rolled up his sleeves and started to work on the drain.

She thought how nice it was to have a man around who would do this sort of thing for her. A smile crept across her face and he smiled back at her, almost relishing the helpless way she stood there. Colin found it difficult to hide his true feelings for her sometimes. He was more than just fond of her, but he knew that it was no good pushing things. He would just have to wait and wait, to hang on until the right moment arrived.

Then he would tell her how he really felt. It was a moment he looked forward to and which he hoped would not be too long in coming.

Margaret was furious when she heard that Mrs Porter was in Liverpool and was coming to see them. It was what she hated most about John for a husband. The neurotic stupid woman who would come into their lives every so often and upset things. Besides, she had arranged to meet Michael, and now she knew that she would have to cancel it.

Often, as she lay in bed or looked out into the garden, her sense of duty rebelled. She imagined running off to Michael and telling him to take her away from this stifling family with its loyalties and ties, asking him to take her to some far-off place where she wouldn't have to see any of them any more. She knew that, in her heart of hearts, she had made up her mind, but it wouldn't take much to upset that decision. Sometimes, when she was honest with herself, she knew that the reason she hadn't finally told Michael that she would stay with John was because she wanted to keep her options open. She wanted to have the escape valve to run into.

She knew she was being dragged into the only real option that was open to her in the circumstances, and yet she often prayed for the courage to escape from it, to run back over the tightrope she had been balancing on, to run back to something that was really important. She wanted the smell of danger and the feel of real passion. She wanted to escape from the half-baked sense of loyalty and duty that she was stepping slowly into.

Her mind still foamed with the alternatives, and she felt herself being pulled this way and that. Sometimes she felt that things were settled and then there were the times when she knew they weren't. Whatever decision it was that she took, she would always regret it for the rest of her life.

The promise of things unfulfilled is always so much more alluring than the reality.

Freda was wiping John George's mouth. He gurgled in pleasure.

'That woman gives me the pip,' she said, and then paused, eyeing Margaret, 'I supposed you've arranged to meet Michael this evening?'

'Yes.'

Margaret looked back at her sister and wondered whether she had any sympathy at all or whether the hard tone in her voice was the real Freda. She hoped it wasn't.

'I was meaning it to be the last time,' she said.

It was true. At some point during the day, she had felt the strength inside her to to break off her friendship with Michael. She had felt the ship sinking and suddenly she had wanted to jump and be free of the terrible burden. As the moment drew nearer she felt her will weaken, and the doubts crowded in again. It would never be possible to be free of those doubts.

'Would you like me to go and explain?' said Freda suddenly.

Margaret was surprised at her sister's offer, but it was the only alternative. She couldn't risk the chance that Michael might come round to the Ashton's if she didn't turn up to see him.

'What shall I tell him?' asked Freda, 'that you won't be seeing him again, or that you'll be seeing him once more?'

Margaret felt pushed, the old pressures flooding back in on her. Freda was so cruel sometimes. Margaret didn't understand it.

'Why are you so cruel?' she asked.

'I'm sorry,' said Freda, 'but it's hanging over us all isn't it?'

Freda walked to the bus, and the afternoon sun brought out little beads of sweat on her forehead. She felt herself trembling. For the first time in her life she was going to be alone with Michael.

She wondered what she would say. It would be difficult to control herself from telling him exactly what she thought Margaret was thinking.

Freda's feelings to Michael were ambiguous. On the one hand she felt a certain deep hatred for him. For a man who had caused so much pain in the family, so much disruption and who had come between a man and a wife at a time when the need for them to be together was so great.

And yet she couldn't hate him. She couldn't keep from herself the knowledge of her own feelings for him. She wondered, and it was something that quite occupied her mind, she wondered if the time had been different, and the place had been somewhere else, whether she and Michael would have felt differently to one another.

It was just a dream she had and she wondered why she should have picked on a man like Michael. Her sister's lover.

She knew it would remain, for the rest of her life, as just a dream.

'It's very simple really,' he said, 'I love her, I need her and at the moment I see her, quite plainly, slipping away from me.'

'I'm sorry, I don't want to see you hurt,' Freda replied.

She had gone too far and he had understood from the way she was speaking what was going on. There had been hints in the things that Freda said which had given him the feeling there was not much longer for him and Margaret.

'I get a touch of paranoia, you see, when I think of her back there with all of you lot, all trying to persuade her to do the right thing, whatever that is. And with me here, what is there I can do about it?'

Freda looked at him as he paced up and down the room, like a caged animal. She felt sorry and understood the way he must be feeling. In a way she felt it herself. There had been a time when she had felt it very strongly, when she had had no one to talk to and when she had been cooped up at home with all the closeness and tension in the air about her. He turned round suddenly.

'It was good of you to come,' he said, 'but I'd like to know what you are telling me. Are you telling me there's nothing to hope for? Is there something you know that I don't? You see when my wife was dying I hoped because there was nothing else you could do. There's a sort of threshold of pain and once you go beyond it you just feel numb. I thought I would never care for anyone again, but here I am now, caring for someone. You see, the minute you start caring for someone, for something, even if it's only a dog, you know there's going to be the pain at the end of it.'

There was nothing else that Freda could say. She had said very little but she knew that what she had said had implied a lot, perhaps even too much.

As she walked away, his words stuck with her. She felt sorry that things had to come to this, and she wondered whether there would always be the pain at the end, whether once you cared for someone it always ended with you or the other person being hurt. She hoped it would not always be like that, for herself, or for Margaret, or for Michael even. In her heart, though, she knew he had spoken the truth.

Jean sat on the edge of Margaret's bed. She had just finished tidying the room up.

Edwin sat opposite her. The heat of the day had passed and the beginnings of the slanting evening sun were showing through the trees lighting the leaves from behind. Jean stared out of the window.

'When's Mrs Porter coming?' asked Edwin. His voice disturbed the silence and the calm of the day.

'In about an hour, maybe before,' replied Jean, 'you know she'll have to tell him about it, I mean tell John about Michael. She'll have to tell him soon.'

'Give her time, Jean. The main thing is that she's going to stick by him. We'll all have to give the lad time to get back on his feet before she can tell him everything. He can only cope with so much.'

Edwin looked out of the window as well and watched the rays of the sun shine through the glass refracted by the dust. It was so quiet out there, so still, and he wished that it was like that inside his soul.

There was so much going on in him that it was difficult to forget, to just look peacefully out of the window and enjoy the sun. He remembered times when it had seemed possible to enjoy simple things like that.

He looked at Jean. She had been strange recently, oddly reticent and distanced from them all. This afternoon, when the phone had rung, she had been standing right by it and yet hardly noticed it ringing by her hand. She'd looked away and ignored it.

It was as if she was escaping into herself, and trying to withdraw from life.

It was true, he thought, a human being can only cope with so much pain, and he wondered if Jean had had her share. She no longer seemed to be able to take things in properly, she didn't react to him or the others in the house.

Somehow, she was miles away from them all, disappearing into a little world of her own.

Downstairs he heard the doorbell ring and someone go to answer it. The strains of Mrs Porter's voice echoed through the house as she greeted her son.

There was another one who could no longer cope, thought Edwin, it was as if everyone was going under, being dragged down until the pressures of life engulfed them all.

He too felt weary.

Margaret watched Mrs Porter kiss John when he opened the door. She fussed round him like an old bee. She touched his cheek and asked him if he was wearing the right clothes, whether he was warm enough. Suddenly, Margaret felt a revulsion come over her. The cloying, clasping affection of this woman was too much for her to bear and she turned and went back into the living-room.

If this was what she would have to put up with for the rest of her life, then it was something she didn't want.

It was seeing her husband being so remorselessly overborne

by his mother that made her resent the woman most. She seemed to want to keep John from being free, from being a man and from being himself.

When they came into the living-room from the hall, Margaret made an excuse and left. On her way she glanced at John and tried to catch his eye. She wanted to tell him what she was feeling, that she wanted his mother to go away, that if anything was going to destroy the first feelings, the first tentative reconstruction of their marriage, then it would be her.

After Margaret had left the room, John and his mother sat for a while listening to the radio. Its sterile tones were punctuated by her insistent questions. John began to fidget and his mother noticed that he wasn't really listening to her. John mentioned David's name, and his mother jumped at it.

'Another broken marriage,' she said, 'this family's full of them, but still anyone could have seen that that one wouldn't work from the start.'

'It's the war, Mum,' he said.

'I daresay that's what a lot of people would say, to excuse themselves.'

John noticed his mother looking at him strangely, out of the corner of her eyes as if she was calculating something, waiting for the best moment to say what it was she was leading up to.

'I mean, while the cat's away, the mice will play,' she said, and then paused as if she was about to try to sow some destructive seed, 'but then, it's just as well Margaret's such a nice girl isn't it?'

There was a note in her voice that John didn't like. She seemed to be implying that Margaret was like Sheila, and was flighty like Freda.

John sat up. Suddenly he was alert.

Down inside him, old fears came to the surface, the moments he had woken in the night and felt that Margaret wasn't there. When he had known she was spending the night away.

He tried to dismiss them.

After going through so much, so many harrowing months, so much torture and so many dreams of his home, he knew there could be no doubt.

There had to be no doubt. Whenever they came to his mind, these doubts that he felt, he pushed them away.

To entertain them was to lose belief and without that firm

belief, then his life would ebb away from him and flow out somewhere to the beyond. The beyond where it would no longer exist. His links with sanity, with reality were loose and insecure enough already. He didn't want them snapped.

'We can be tempted, you see,' went on his mother, 'all of us can be tempted.'

John got up. Without a word he left the room. He felt that his mother was trying to drive the wedge, was trying to instil the doubts that he wanted to forget. As he left the room, he heard her voice following him.

'I'll sit here,' she was saying, 'I'll sit here and wait for you. I'll always be here, waiting for you.'

He felt her claws closing round his throat, dragging back to the moments of his youth when he had run from the house in sheer desperation.

Run from the claustrophobic clamps of her affection, his arms flailing the wind, desperate for air.

He almost ran straight into Edwin. John looked up into the trustworthy eyes of his father-in-law. He would ask him, he thought, and then he would know.

Upstairs, Sheila, who had come round a few minutes before was helping Margaret make the beds.

She was thinking back to the afternoon when Colin had tried to kiss her.

It was a moment that she had been waiting for, in a way looking forward to it and in a way dreading it. It was a test of her strength and a test of how far she was away from David. There had been times before when the moment had almost come, but somehow she had avoided it, almost unconsciously, backing away from him.

As he had come close to her and she had sensed what was in his mind. The hot air of the afternoon and the sweat on his back after the effort of draining her sink and cleaning out the pipes had changed him. He was usually so neat and tidy, but as he stood there in front of her with his shirt off and the smell of his body close to her nostrils, he had become something else. Sheila had waited, not knowing how she would feel, not knowing what her reactions would be.

And then the moment when he grabbed her had been so sudden. She was prepared and yet it surprised her all the same.

The sudden panic overtook her. The memory of David and

Colin's face had become David's. She had wanted to grab him and pull him down on her, but at the same time she had pushed him away, realising that it was not her husband.

She cursed herself. There was nothing she wanted more than to be able to accept him softly and tenderly. She liked him, but it was not enough. There was not the same shaking in her knees as when David touched her, the same fluttering at her nerve ends and the same desire.

Somewhere, still although she had not seen him for almost two months David still held some kind of key to her feelings. She felt bound by him.

Hating him for the way he treated her.

And wanting him so much that it hurt her to think of him.

'It's difficult isn't it, Margaret? For you I mean, not knowing what to do and being married?'

Sheila associated with Margaret, she sympathised with her position. She would have liked to help her.

Sheila wondered whether, like her, Margaret just wanted to escape. She admired her braveness in facing up to the facts of her situation. Colin had said that he would come back the next day after his work had finished.

'I'm thinking of going off to Wales to get the kids back tomorrow,' she said. She couldn't face seeing Colin again so soon after the feeling that she had had that afternoon had engulfed her. She needed time to think, time to clear her mind.

'It would keep me on the straight and narrow you see,' she went on.

Margaret looked up.

'Are you off it then?' she asked.

'No, but tempted.'

'Don't be,' said Margaret with unusual vehemence in her voice. She was thinking of the play it made on your nerves. She had been tempted and she had given in. In a way she was glad, but the aftermath of sorting it out was what frightened her. She looked at Sheila and a common bond joined them together. Their eyes met and spoke to each other. There was no need for words, for they were just two women caught in a trap, their loyalties divided, and their feelings torn.

'Maybe it is running away,' she said, 'but then we all do that. When you're in the middle of things, it's impossible to think.

At least it is for me.'

Sheila stood up suddenly as if Margaret had helped her make her mind up about something. As she left the room, she passed Edwin on the stairs.

'Where's John?' asked Margaret as her father came in, 'he'll need a rest if he's been talking to that mother of his.'

'Yes.'

Edwin looked at Margaret and wondered whether or not to tell her what Mrs Porter had been saying to John. He had managed to reassure the boy that there was nothing in what had been said to him, that he shouldn't have any doubts, but Edwin was scared lest his mother said anything else. It was impossible to know whether she was just guessing or whether she actually knew something definite.

'She's been talking to him, Margaret. Saying things about temptation and something like when the cat's away the mice will play.'

'Oh God.'

Margaret sat down on the bed with her head in her hands. She felt near to tears.

'He doesn't believe her does he?' she asked.

Edwin told her that he thought he had persuaded John that there was nothing in what his mother had said.

'I lied very adequately, I think,' he said.

Suddenly Margaret realised the strain that she was putting on the rest of her family.

All the lies and deceits that they had to go through to support her.

She was tired of it all and she needed rest. The thoughts in her brain whirled round and she shook her head as if to get rid of the little biting jabs that came to her and pricked her mind and her conscience. It was like having a crowd of mites and bees around her ears. She felt herself caving in under the strain.

'I'm sorry Dad,' she said, 'I've put you all in a terrible position haven't I?'

She thought for a moment.

'If only I could tell him.'

'John, or Michael?'

Either was so difficult for her. To tell John about Michael would destroy the fragile, shallow foundations that he had so carefully built since he came back, and to tell Michael was going to make such a hole in her life that she didn't know whether or not she would be able to stand up after it.

She would be deprived of something she had thought, once upon a time might be the most important thing in her life.

She would be left empty again and then there would begin the long laborious process inside her of making her life with her husband a real life, one that was equal and in which they both helped each other.

At the moment there was no one to help her, no one to tell her what to do.

So many feelings assailed her. So many different choices and so much depending on each step.

That evening, Margaret got the chance to go and see Michael. John's mother took her son out to see some old friends and Margaret was left with a good two hours to spend with Michael.

As she left, she sensed that they all knew where she was going. Her mother and father at least pretended to ignore the fact that she was going out and treated it for once as the most normal thing in the world.

They made no jibes, no sly allusions; no passing darts came from them, and it was from this very silence that Margaret sensed they thought she was going to make the final split with Michael.

Indeed that was what was in her mind.

Finally, she had had enough of the tension and the suspicion, the constant jangling on her nerves while she waited.

Waited for John to find out, waited for mother to crack and tell him, or indeed waited for her own nerves to snap.

When she looked at him she knew that she herself would never tell him. The compassion in her heart was too great and the vulnerability in the stoop of his shoulders was too painful.

She walked away from Michael's house.

It was not yet dark. These days the light seemed to linger way into the time when it should be black.

She had talked to Michael and told him a lot of things, he had talked to her as well.

They had talked of anything but John, of anything but themselves, and Margaret felt they were still waiting, still knowing that their ship was sinking, but still standing and looking on in fascination.

They were paralysed by it.

Margaret knew that something would have to happen to her, that something would have to precipitate her decision.

She knew she couldn't act alone; a vast sense of weakness and of failure came over her, sinking her, engulfing her, rendering her emotionless and without the ability to move.

She was still. Waiting. As was Michael.

The next day, she spoke to Freda who was leaving on the way to the hospital.

'Did you get a chance to see Michael?' her sister asked.

'Yes. John's mother took him out for the evening. I saw Michael.'

'Did you tell him?'

'No. I wanted him to ask, but he never does these days. He just seems to be waiting. We both do in a way.'

Margaret and Freda sat in silence for a moment, and Margaret noticed a look on Freda's face that seemed to say she was beginning to understand.

The next morning, John sat in the living-room, reading the paper. His mother sat opposite him, watching his every move. It was beginning to get on John's nerves, this never ending sense of scrutiny, and he felt himself twitching, wishing that she would go away.

Her continual attentions were closing in on him and somewhere down his guts he felt a stirring. There was something there that he knew was about to break out. An explosion gaining momentum, some hidden previous strength coming back to him. It was a part of his old self that was finding its place again.

He felt that he was knitting together, that his tenuous links with the world were growing stronger.

'You're asking too much of me, Mum,' he said after a pause.

His mother had been badgering him as only she could, had been playing on his nerves, had been trying to force him to promise that he would leave the Ashton's and come back with her to Chorley.

'It'll be too late,' she said, 'if you don't come now, it'll be too late. The last years of my life will have passed.'

John wondered why she said such ludicrous things sometimes. She went on.

'You see they don't need you here. They don't need you as

much as I do.'

'Stop saying that. They need me more,' he said, 'one's dead and two are fighting. They need me.'

John felt his temper going, but he felt more than that. He felt a break working itself up inside him as if he was about to sever some old chain that had tied him down for the best part of his life. He heard his mother's voice rattling on incessantly.

'You fought. You, my son, and you'll come to live with us. You and Margaret and the baby. You'll be able to persuade her to come with you and then we can find you a house nearby. She'll come if you persuade her. She'll do anything you ask.'

John felt the world spinning round and his mother's words became arrows, her voice the stinging of a bee rushing about his ears, pricking his mind.

'Stop it, stop it,' he said.

But she didn't stop.

'You see you aren't better yet. You can even shout at your own mother. You need so much care, John, we all need care and we need you more than they do.'

John felt hysteria gripping him and he stood up. He began to pace around the room, and still she watched him, she went on speaking her whining voice.

John thought back to his childhood and wondered why he had never realised the extent of her selfishness, the extent of her hold on him. He wondered why he had never really tried to throw her off before. He began to shout back at her and tell her all these things, tell her that he cared for Margaret more than her, tell her that he was staying in Liverpool.

Suddenly he remembered something that had for ever burned a hole in his mind and that he never, never would forget. He had thought about it often when he was away.

He turned to her.

'Mum,' he said, 'when I was away, with no you, no Margaret, with nothing, I thought about things. I began to see that I had never understood before. I began to see things in a different way. In a way that I had never seen them before.'

The words came awkwardly at first and then faster, rattling like shingle on the beach, faster coherently, but always faster.

'I realised that it was you who had made me different. That it was you who had made me different from the other kids. When I was twenty-four I talked to my father for the first time in my life and I understood that he was unhappy, that it was you who had made him unhappy. I'd never cared before, because I'd never understood, and I hadn't understood because you hadn't let me.'

He paused. She sat silent.

'Do you know when that was? It was before I went away for the last time. To France. And I came home and wanted to see my wife, to see Margaret. I was going away and I wanted to see my wife. You knew where she was, but you lied to me. You didn't tell me where she was although you knew. It was important to me and you lied because you wanted me for yourself.'

He was shouting. The thoughts were emptying out of his mind so fast that he couldn't control them. The words repeated themselves in a hysterical flow. He shouted at his mother and it was as if he was hearing himself talk to her for the first time, and as if he was seeing her for the first time too.

He shouted.

'You lied!!!'

The words echoed across the room and out of the windows. He was shouting it from the rooftops and he wanted the whole world to hear.

Edwin was listening at the door.

He heard every word.

John sat down, and leant his head on his knees.

'I didn't know,' she said to him, 'she didn't tell me where she was so how could I know. I wanted to be with you, with my own flesh and blood. You don't know how terrible it is, a mother's love.'

John looked up at her and realised something.

He knew that he had broken a tie, that he had thrown off something that had been with him for the whole of his life. A link had been destroyed.

There was a part of him that now felt new, that felt as if it had been rebuilt.

The feeling came to him that he had been cruel and done something terrible.

And he was glad.

John got up. Slowly he walked out of the room. He didn't look at his mother for fear that she would drag him back into her clutches.

He felt her watching him. He heard a small voice calling his name.

But that voice was a million miles away. It was back in the sun of his youth.

It was no more than a small echo and he was free of it now. It could never touch him again.

Miles and miles away he heard it ever so faintly, and when he shut the door behind him he could no longer hear it.

It was gone.

Margaret was crying. Her head on the kitchen table and her father leaning over her. It was later in the day and John was upstairs asleep. Margaret knew that something had happened because she had gone up to see him. She knew that he had been awake when she walked in the room, but he wouldn't speak to her, he wouldn't say a word.

Edwin put his hand on her shoulder.

'How much longer can you go on,' he asked, 'it's getting too much for you Margaret. Let me tell you something about John, for what it's worth. I heard him shouting at his mother this morning and from what he was saying I could tell that things would never be the same between him and her again. He destroyed something very big in his life today because he could see it was going to come between you. He could see that Celia, if she got her way, would destroy what he had with you.'

Edwin paused, and then the phrase came to him as if from out of the blue.

'He's burnt his bridges, Margaret.'

She looked up at her father and saw the sincerity and the pity, she saw the pain and the suffering and she knew he was telling the truth.

Suddenly, she was peaceful. Far away she saw the debris of a ship floating on the water and she knew that, while she had been paralysed into inaction, the ship had gone, sinking beneath the waves without a trace.

She had had her back turned and the ship had sunk.

Now, she was free. Free to move and free to breathe again. The final jolt had come, and the tightrope that she had been walking was over. It had passed away and she was free, safe on a little platform of her own building.

If he, her husband, could burn his bridges and destroy something that was important to him for her sake, then she could do it too. She was strong enough now.

And then she knew.

There were no bridges to burn.

They had gone, sunk without a trace.

No bridges to burn, and all that was left were a few ashes, the odd piece of flotsam floating in the water, nothing to pick up, nothing to save.

She could turn her back now and walk away.

And it was sad.

But it wasn't like that for Sheila, however hard she tried and however much she wished they would go away, there were always the chains that tied her to her past.

When Colin had come round to see her, he had arrived to find her packing her cases. Understandably, he had been hurt and he had explained his feelings in such a way that hope had again stirred in Sheila's mind. She forgot the moment of the previous day when he had made a pass at her and they were friends again.

They had travelled to Wales together. The day had been beautiful, she had seen her children and on the way back a feeling of contentment came over her. She leaned against his chest and slept.

He was firm, secure and comfortable and she had wished she could cut the chains that held her to her past and she wished that she could love him.

They were sitting on the floor of her kitchen. She felt close to him and liked the feel of his arm around her shoulders. Outside the air was warm and still, the evening seemed to be waiting for something to happen.

'I don't know why we're sitting on the floor,' said Sheila. It seemed ludicrous to sit hunched up against the leg of the table.

'You could invite me upstairs,' said Colin, 'it'd be more comfortable there.'

Sheila froze. Her mind buzzed, and she prepared herself for the moment, and yet she didn't know how to prepare herself for she didn't know what she was thinking. She sat in silence.

'You still there?' he said.

'Yes.'

Her voice was small, waiting.

'I don't want to upset you, you know.'

She felt his hand caressing her shoulder and her body grew more and more tense. She sat still and felt him turn his face round and press himself against her. He kissed her. The hands wrapped themselves in her long hair.

She tried hard to like it, and she tried to respond. She knew what he was thinking and she knew that her behaviour when they were in Wales had led up to this.

In a way she had wanted it too. She wanted some sort of final test.

He was kissing her and she felt the urgency rising in him.

She tried to respond likewise, but somewhere there was a link missing, a feeling that didn't exist, there was a block that stopped her from feeling as he did and from being able to summon up the same kind of desire.

She sat up and pushed him away.

'I can't,' she said, 'I'm sorry.'

'Sorry? What are you doing? We went to Wales and you asked me back, why not? What is it that stops you?'

'I don't know. It's just that I can't,' she looked at him, 'please don't force me, Colin.'

'No, I won't force you.'

He stood up and put his coat on. Then, without saying another word, he left the room.

Sheila felt the front door slam, and then she heard the silence descend.

Across the room, she saw the photo of her husband staring at her out of its frame. The face was set in a perpetual smile. It was as if he knew what was going on and Sheila cursed him for it.

There were things she wanted to break, things she wanted to force herself out of and yet she couldn't. Something held her in, and she felt David's hands round her heart, pulling her towards him.

That was all she had.

A photograph, smiling at her from its frame, flat and unreal, and yet always with her.

She smiled at it and nodded.

Yes, she thought, you know what it is that keeps us together and you know it will always keep us together.

Or will it? she asked herself.

And then she wanted to curse that fleshless smile.

Margaret looked at John lying on the bed and smiled at him. She wondered if he was asleep. Slowly, gradually aware of his wife's presence, he opened an eye.

'Margaret?'

'I'm sorry I wasn't here. Dad told me about your mother.'

'What did he say?'

'That you'd burned your bridges.'

John nodded. The atmosphere between them was quiet and still.

'He had to help me to bed,' he paused, 'I'm sorry that you're seeing me like this.'

'You've been shut in. You haven't come to me. You've turned to the baby.'

She sat down and put her hand on his and then leant her head on his chest. They lay there for a moment.

'You see, I can't remember,' he said, 'what it was like before I went away. I know it was different from this though.'

'I'm sorry, I'm sorry,' she said, 'but it's going to be different now.'

He smiled and she leant over and kissed him. For the first time since he had come back, she felt that this kiss meant something and for the first time, the old desire moved inside her.

Margaret knew now that it was going to be all right between her and her husband.

Outside the wind stirred in the trees and they could hear the leaves rustling, waving on their branches. It was still light, and the deathly hush of the day was turning into a gentle murmur of life. The heat was going back to the sun from where it came, and from the depths of the night a life was appearing.

Their fingers touched and Margaret felt calm.

Most important, she felt no longer alone. She felt that, at last, she had found a resting place.

A long long time ago, she had hoped that Michael would be a harbour for her to shelter in, and when she had lost the baby, she had felt the water draining out. The feeling had lain dormant in her mind, and the harbour had remained dry and arid.

Now she had a different harbour. It would be a difficult one to live in, but it was one she didn't want to leave. It was quiet, protected, and the water was calm.

And John?

For the first time in years, he slept.

There were no pills, no nightmares that night, he slipped gracefully into sleep, and contrary to the usual pattern of things, he didn't even dream.

When Margaret saw Michael the next day, they had little to say to each other. They sat, silently, miles apart on the bed in his flat.

She looked around and thought that this was the place that, at one time, might have been her home.

It was quite a nice little room but now there was something unreal about it. As if it didn't properly exist, as if it was made of cardboard instead of bricks and mortar.

'It's all right,' said Michael, 'I've known for some time that it was going to come to this. There were so many things that were pulling you away and I could see it happening. I still hoped, but I knew that at the end there was going to be the pain again. The same pain that there always has been, I suppose. It's going to be a rough time for me, Margaret.'

She looked at him, and for a moment wanted to touch the hard, stubbly skin of his face. She felt tender towards him, but perhaps it was just a feeling that was hiding her guilt.

'Don't try to get in touch with me, Michael,' she said, 'please leave me alone to work out the things I have to get sorted out.'

He nodded.

As she walked away, Margaret wondered why she felt so calm. She shouldn't. She had always imagined it to be different, she had always thought that moments like this raged inside you, but it wasn't like that.

She wondered whether the pain had passed or whether it was sitting round the corner, waiting for her.

Michael sat on the edge of his bed, thinking, feeling only one thing, feeling that he was alone.

He was empty, he was curiously reactionless. He had felt like this before and he knew what happened. For a day or two he would walk around, dazed and feelingless. And then he would want to get in touch with her again, but he would force himself to stop, hold himself back. Then it would hit him.

He thought that probably he would cry.

But for the moment there was only one thing on his mind.

She had gone. Gone for good and there was no hope left.

He had had a wife once, but she had died. You couldn't get in touch with the dead.

Michael thought perhaps it was better that way.

Margaret stopped on the corner and looked back at the house where his flat was.

She thought how well she knew this road and how much of her life lay there, stretched out in front of her.

She turned away, thinking that the decision, once made, must remain. You mustn't touch it however strongly the feeling comes over you, it must be left alone.

She felt empty too. Empty in a way she had felt before and sad and sorry. So she turned and walked back home where there was something waiting for her.

Perhaps that was the difference. She had a future to go to, something to hang on to.

He didn't.

He would walk around alone, with no one to share the future and he would think back and remember the child they never had; and sometimes in the night he would reach out and grasp a ghost that hovered out of reach.

The ghost that would have walked between them.

The child they never had.

Margaret opened the door of the house. For a moment she stood still in the hall as if she was listening for something.

Then she heard it.

It was her son, John George, crying upstairs, and then her husband appeared from the living-room.

'I'll see to him,' he said.

PART FOUR

'A TIME TO MOURN'

CHAPTER TEN

December 1942

Time slid by evenly. Summer ended and merged into the autumn. It got dark earlier and earlier, until Edwin found himself crossing the ferry in the dark, as he travelled back from work.

He would lean over the side and miss seeing the light dancing on the ripples. He would miss seeing the skyline and wish again for the slanting bars of light to shine through the buildings, to hit the water, and to be shattered this way and that.

He remembered them glinting and sparkling, and now all he saw was the dark.

It was dark inside him. He felt that the life had gone out of the day and out of the people with whom he passed that day.

Some months before he had noticed the forgetfulness and lassitude that seemed to hang over his wife. She was constantly tired and perpetually weary. The gleam had gone from her eyes and sometimes he would watch her in the kitchen. She would stand in front of the stove, or sit at the table and it looked as if she was suspended, as if she was somehow out of time. She would sit still, and when someone came in the room, she would start with the effort of speaking to them.

He was weary too, but he carried it on his shoulders and although they bent a little, and even though he felt his soul buckling under the strain, he tried to force himself along. He would close his eyes and try to forget the silences about him, try not to look when Jean caught his eye and try to ignore the blame he saw there.

He walked up the road to his house. The parcel under his arm slipped. He caught it and tucked it into a safer hold. It was a piece of ham, a gift from Sefton for their Christmas dinner.

Edwin narrowed his shoulders and pulled his coat collar up about his neck. It was cold and he felt the wind bite into his face. It got into the niches of his body and he shivered.

He wondered if it would snow the next day, and whether their Christmas would be a white one. For a moment he thought of postcard pictures where the earth looked pretty and the sun shone on the unmarked snow. Then he looked around him and peered into the night.

It was Christmas Eve and not a bit like some of the Christmases he remembered.

Things had changed and he wondered when it might be possible to be happy again.

Edwin went into the house and took off his hat and coat, hanging them in their usual place.

Jean heard him. She was in the kitchen.

'Do you think Philip will remember to bring his ration card with him when he gets back?' she asked, 'we're going to be very short of butter if he doesn't.'

'He won't be here until Boxing Day now,' replied Edwin, 'he rang me at the office and said that they were running a special train up here then.'

They had received the news a few days previously that Philip would be coming home. He'd returned the month before from Cairo where an eye injury had put him in hospital.

'What's that?' asked Jean, pointing at the parcel under his arm.

'It's Sefton's Christmas offering. He gave it to me this morning.'

'I suppose it's blackmarket?' she asked.

Edwin knew that Jean disapproved of Sefton dabbling in the blackmarket. It was something that Edwin had come to accept. The odd gift of a bottle of Scotch or some pork made life just that bit more pleasant.

'Of course it's blackmarket, Jean, but there's no need for us to know that.'

'I won't touch it. If we know, then we know and there's no good in ignoring the fact.'

She sat down and Edwin saw the emotion rising in her face. She was thinking of something that disturbed her.

'Food comes in ships, Edwin,' she said, 'it comes in ships with boys like our Robert sailing in them. You used to have principles about things like that, but you've sacrificed them. While I seem to have found mine, you seem to have lost yours.'

Edwin hadn't seen Jean like this for months. She had been silent, wary. She had passed through the time since Robert died showing less and less emotion, retreating farther and farther into herself.

'I sacrificed my principles the day I married into your family, the day I sold myself.'

'The day you married me, you mean?'

Edwin looked at Jean, and wondered why it was that man and wife should have to talk to each other like this. His anger passed and a desire to make amends came over him. He wanted them to be like they were when they first married. He wanted some comfort from her. Some love even.

'We mustn't talk to each other like this,' he said, 'you shouldn't push me into saying these things. You see, there's got to be some understanding between us ... some tolerance ... some compassion.'

'Tolerance, compassion. How can I be tolerant and compassionate? How can I forgive when there's the memory of the son I shall never see again? My son, my dear sweet son who has gone for ever.'

Edwin thought back to the moment when he had decided to sign the papers which would send Robert to sea. The boy had wanted it, had almost set his heart on it. His friends had all gone and it had seemed to Edwin that the cruelty lay in refusing him rather than letting him go.

All the same he knew that Jean still blamed him for what had happened subsequently. She blamed him for Robert's death and held him responsible for the sorrow it had caused.

It was in every word she said to him and it was in her eyes. It was in the way she moved when he was near her. It was there, always, that blame. It would never go away.

It was the first time they had talked about it for some time. Before, it had existed between them like a cancer, but now it was bursting out into the open.

'All these months, you've bottled it up inside you and kept it to yourself,' he paused, for at this moment he so much wanted to be close to her and to feel once again a sense of companionship. He wanted to share things with her.

'Don't turn away from me, please, stay with me and face

things together. Please, Jean, don't turn away from me.'

Edwin stretched out his hand and touched her shoulder, hoping she would allow him to draw her towards him. He wanted to feel the weight of her head on his chest, wanted to feel the comforting warmth of her body against him.

But that body was cold and hard.

She turned away, and froze flinching at the touch of his hand.

'Don't touch me,' she said, 'don't ever touch me again.'

There was such venom in her voice, such hatred that Edwin felt they were prisoners, locked together in hell instead of simply man and wife.

It was as if there had never been anything between them.

Upstairs, Margaret was making up two beds in the boy's room. As she folded back the blankets, she thought of the last time that one of John's parents had come to stay. She smiled, knowing that in a way, she owed it to Mrs Porter for her continuing life with John.

The door opened and he came in.

John looked preoccupied as he stood there watching her pat the blankets into place.

'I think I'd be best to go back to the Treasurer's don't you?' he said.

Margaret looked up, wondering what on earth it was that he was talking about.

'How do you mean?' she said.

'When I start work again. I'll have to soon. I've been sitting around doing nothing for too long now.'

Margaret was uncertain quite what to say. It was the first time he had talked like this since his return and she didn't want to spoil the moment. Not only was it a step in the right direction, not only was it progress for him, but he was sharing something with her. He was being open and she wanted to respond in the right way.

'You don't have to rush things,' she said, 'I mean, we don't even have to stay in Liverpool if you don't want to, and then we don't want you back where you started. Why don't you carry on giving Dad a hand at the works now and then and let it rest for a bit?'

John stumbled over his words. She could see him fighting to express his thoughts. She watched him and waited for him to finish.

'I think maybe I'd be best to go to the Treasurer's Department. I'd be happier there. It'd be safe. You see...' he hesitated, 'I don't have that much confidence Margaret. I never did have too much and now I seem to have less.'

It was going to be a slow process, thought Margaret and it needed patience, but every so often there were the rewards for that patience. This moment was one of those rewards, the gradual growth of their relationship back into something that meant a sharing of their feelings and both of them helping each other to grow back together. It gave her confidence too.

There was a pause and Margaret saw that John had said all he was going to say. She didn't want to force him.

'Do you think your mother and father will be all right in here?' she said, wondering what his reaction would be to the mention of his parents.

'Do you know, I'd almost forgotten that they were coming.'

He hesitated. He knew how he felt about his mother now, he knew how things were changed between them and he wondered what Margaret thought.

'Look Margaret. If it seems awkward, if she seems different and more strained than usual, you'll understand won't you?'

'Don't worry,' said Margaret, 'I'll cope.'

He smiled unexpectedly leaning forward and kissing her on the cheek. Then he left the room. They both seemed to understand more and more as time went on how they both felt. She fingered the place on her cheek where his lips had touched her briefly.

Margaret was more sure than ever that she had taken the right decision in staying with him and it was beginning, ever so slowly, to bring its own rewards.

And then she thought of Michael. The road with John was difficult. It was a long, hard journey she was travelling, but it was rewarding. Her instincts had told her once that she would look back on a decision to go with Michael and regret it in later life. She was sure now that those far off intangible feelings had been right.

'How's John?' said Freda.

Freda had just returned with Doris. They were in a hurry, loaded down with paper parcels. Edwin had met them in the hall when they came in and it had gladdened his heart to see the two grown up girls behaving like children. That was the way Christmas should be, and he heard their laughter cut across the silence in the house like a knife.

'He's fine,' said Margaret evasively.

She looked at Freda. They had become much firmer friends since the day that Freda had gone to see Michael in the summer. She seemed to understand more.

There was something that Margaret wanted to get off her mind.

'He keeps writing to me,' she said, 'of course, I don't write back, except once, that is and then only to tell him not to write again.'

Freda looked at her sister and felt sympathy. Working in the hospital had made her understand what the sorrow and pain of other people really meant. Until the day she had left home to go and work, she felt that she had been asleep. Even her first day at the hospital had wakened her and had brought home to her just what it was to suffer. There was no malice in her towards Margaret now, for when she saw the pain cross her face she remembered the faces that she saw every day in the wards and she began to understand.

'Would you like me to go and see him?' she said.

Relief flooded through Margaret. It wasn't that she was a coward. She still felt precarious and didn't want to go through anything else that might upset her carefully preserved, her hard gained balance.

She felt that even the sight of Michael, let alone the sound of his voice might send her spinning off again, spinning away from safety and back into confusion.

'Yes,' she said, 'if you would.'

'All right,' replied Freda, 'rather me than you and anyway we don't want to go through all that again do we?'

Freda remembered what she had felt for Michael, and what they had all been through. A little tremor went through her body.

Margaret went downstairs, leaving Freda to unpack all her parcels. On the way down she passed Doris who smiled brightly. It was nice to see someone who seemed so happy all the time. Margaret wondered whether Doris was always like that. She seemed to find life so simple, but then, thought Margaret, you never can tell.

'Your father's in the kitchen,' said Doris and rushed on up the stairs. Margaret paused for a moment and listened to the happy, childish glee of Doris and Freda as they sat in the bedroom and laughed over their life at the hospital.

Edwin was cleaning down the plates for supper. He expected the Porters at any minute.

'Happy Christmas,' said Margaret, inconsequentially.

Her father looked at her, and she noticed that he wasn't smiling. There was a long drawn look on his face and his eyes were tired.

'Where did it get to then,' asked Margaret, 'all the peace and goodwill that's meant to be with us at Christmas? It's all just long faces and silent meals. I suppose Mum's gone sour because of Philip not getting back till tomorrow.'

'She's certainly disappointed,' said Edwin evasively.

They heard the doorbell go and Jean walk through the hall. The sound of strained greetings and Mrs Porter asking, the moment she stepped in the house, for her son. Margaret listened for a moment and looked at her father.

'Dad?' she said, 'if I ever get possessive about John George, will you drop a brick on my head or something?'

She smiled nervously and Edwin did likewise. It was one of those little good humoured remarks which conceal so much. They both knew that the presence of Mrs Porter over Christmas was going to be a strain on them all. A strain at a time when it was the last thing they needed.

'Sheila is coming round, isn't she?' asked Edwin, 'it's a long time since we last saw her, I miss her you know.'

'So do I. Freda said she saw her and that she was going to be here.'

'David's gone on leave in London.'

'He's a selfish hog then,' replied Margaret.

'I've got a number to ring him at. Some place he's staying with a friend. We'll ring when Sheila's here. After all, it is Christmas and even if nothing else, they've got two children to share. They're going to have to talk to each other some time, even if it is only as two civilised human beings.'

That was what Edwin longed for. The time when he had been able to talk to Jean in a civilised way without the recriminations and the lies, and the blame that gave a false weight to every word they spoke.

But that time had passed, and here they were, all of them hanging on to a thread. A small thread that was no more than a reminder of what things had been like before.

A long time ago.

Later that evening, after they had finished supper, John and his parents sat in the living-room. Jean listened to them from the corner. She had hardly said a word all evening. In fact the only person who really spoke at all was Mrs Porter and her endless stream of self pity washed over them all.

They were all tired of her, and sick of listening to how life treated her so badly.

John sat back. For once he did not feel the usual anger that he had felt so often when she talked like this. He remembered the argument he had had with her in the summer and he was glad that this was a part of his life with which he had broken.

Sometimes he smiled at his father and across the room they established a union that sprung from their understanding of the woman who had ruled their lives for so long. John felt that, in distancing himself at last from his mother, he had come close to his father. He understood what life must have been like for him all these years. In the same moment he felt sorrow and a certain admiration.

Mrs Porter got up to go to bed early. She said that the strain of the journey had been too much for her.

As she walked through the hall to the stairs her eye was caught by a pile of letters. Quickly she sifted through them, and found what she had suspected. A letter addressed to Margaret. Her hand quivered above it and she put it in her bag. There was something about the handwriting and the feel of it that made her suspicious. She looked around her to make sure no one was watching and then hurried on up the stairs.

That afternoon, Colin paid a visit to Sheila and brought her a present for Christmas. He had just been passing through and she hadn't the time to talk to him as Freda and Doris were there.

It was late and she finished her supper. Sitting there alone, in her small house she thought naturally of David and wondered where he was.

She didn't relish the prospect of spending her Christmas alone and she began to wish that Colin had stayed. She was still fond of him and wished that things could have turned out differently between them.

She looked up and saw her husband's photograph still sitting in its usual place and still staring at her with that half smile on its face.

The smile that brought so much back to her, that brought back the memories of what their marriage had once been. She remembered the stirring in her when he used to arrive home on a short pass and then the long string of second honeymoons.

Time was beginning to erase the memory of the arguments and rows that had happened between them. It was beginning to paint out the black periods of their life together.

She shook her head, not wanting to fall into melancholy yet again, but it was difficult being Christmas and sitting alone, not to wish that the past had been different and had led up to a happier time.

It all seemed a waste that things should drift by and away until they were no more than a foggy blur in her mind.

Again, she wondered where her husband was, and across the room, the photograph smiled at her.

Except that she thought she saw it sneer.

David woke up the next day and his hand stretched out across the bed, searching for the flesh that he remembered from the night before.

The bed was empty and as he sat up, his mind cleared and the haze of the previous evening began to waft away until he was left with a clear picture of what had happened.

He had arranged with a friend of his, Peter Gould, to spend the few days they both had off for Christmas at his flat in London. It was to be a bachelor day or two, but when they arrived, Peter found that his sister, Grace, was still there.

David remembered standing in the hall to the Kensington flat. It was like nothing he had ever seen before. Even his uncle Sefton's house, which David had always thought of as being a well appointed residence of a rich man was nothing like this.

There was something about the glitter of the place, not so much the size. The well stocked glass cocktail cabinet, the radiogram and the silver on the sideboard. David began to realise just what money meant, and what it could buy.

Later that night, they went out for a meal at a London hotel, or at least, Grace had taken David to what she called a small boozer down the road, Peter wasn't with them. He had a previous arrangement.

David had heard of the Savoy, but never seen it, indeed never been anywhere like it.

It had made him nervous walking in there. The war washed

off his back when he saw the people, throwing away money, desperately enjoying themselves.

And then there was Grace herself. She too was like nothing David had met before. He had dreamt that women like that existed. She was tall, beautiful and elegant. She spoke as if her voice had been smoothed down with velvet until there was not a rough edge left on it. Every movement was lazy and polished, smooth as silk, and in the way she draped herself over chairs David compared her to a piece of material that seemed to fit the contours of the furniture exactly.

David felt that she would never be ill at ease, that nothing could ever disturb the cultivated ease with which she walked and with which she talked.

It was so different from his home life and the people they talked to had none of the angular illease to which he was so accustomed. There was none of the roughness that he knew from his earlier days. Grace floated through life with the ease of a sailing ship in a calm sea. Tall and graceful, the world parted in front of her. The people he knew at home were like tramp steamers in comparison.

She made David feel like a child again.

Then after the meal, both having drunk too much they rolled back to her flat and went to bed.

There was no trouble, no conscience in it. It had been simple and straightforward. There was no guilt around the corner and David had enjoyed it. He had the feeling that Grace enjoyed it too. But she behaved as if there was no difference beween them going to bed and the wine they'd enjoyed with their meal.

'How'd you like the Savoy?' asked Grace. David looked up at her leaning in the doorway, dressed in a white long drape.

'I liked it,' he said, 'but that's what it's for isn't it? You're supposed to like it?'

Grace just smiled at him and David felt a bit small as he lay on her bed, naked under the sheets.

For a moment he wondered if he was anything more than an amusing toy to her.

And then he wondered whether it mattered.

'Hungry?' she said.

David nodded.

'I'll get you something. Believe it or not, I can cook as well, you know.'

She amazed him. In everything she said there seemed to be

the hint of sex. He had never met anyone like her before.

A moment later she came back with a cup of black coffee. She put it by him on the bed.

'Come on,' she said, 'wake up.'

But David didn't want to wake up. He was in a dream and wanted to stay there.

Harry Porter found the letter early that morning as he was looking through his wife's case for his shaving things. It was unopened and he sat there looking at it, wondering what on earth could have persuaded his wife to steal other people's mail.

He heard Edwin coming from the bathroom and hid the letter again under the blankets. Edwin knocked at the door before he entered.

'Morning Harry. I heard you were up and wondered whether you wanted a bath. As a matter of fact, I wondered whether you'd want to be coming to the pub this evening. I'm going down to have a drink with my brother-in-law.'

Edwin noticed the hesitation that passed over Harry's face, and understood what he was thinking. He knew that if Harry came then his wife would pick on it and turn it into some kind of slight against her. She always took these things personally.

'I'll need an excuse,' said Harry apologetically.

Both men had always felt a certain sympathy for each other. Ever since Margaret first introduced John to the family, Edwin looked forward to the occasional moment he had with Harry when they managed to get the chance to talk to each other. Now, even more than before, since the time when Jean had first started to withdraw from him Edwin felt a growing deeper sympathy towards the other man.

'You're not the only one that wonders about his marriage, you know,' he said, 'of course, there's not much point in wondering when you get to our age, but you do get to think that you've failed.'

Edwin remembered the moment of the previous day when Jean had told him never to touch her again. It was an odd situation for two people who had been married for over thirty years.

'I used to wonder about Margaret and John. He was always a quiet sort of lad. They were so young and I wondered whether they were getting married for the right reasons,' Harry paused, wondering whether Edwin understood what he was saying, 'I think they're going to be all right, don't you?'

Edwin reassured him but he didn't like talking about it and Harry couldn't fail but notice his reticence.

'Yes,' he said, 'we'll damn well go and have that drink.'

They smiled at each other, pleased at their own, very mild, little rebellion. Sometimes, thought Edwin, you have to do what you want, you can't be held in all the time.

There comes a moment for escape, however small it is.

It was sunny that Christmas day, cold but sunny, and Freda walked to the place she had arranged to meet Michael. She pulled her coat around her ears and let the frosty light bite into her cheeks.

The arches of the colonnade stretched out in front of her and as she ran up the steps she heard the beginning of the echo of her own feet.

Michael sat at the other end of the long passage on a small bench. He looked lost and cold. His figure appeared small against the scale of the large arches, and he didn't look up until she was quite close.

Freda stood in front of him and he looked up at her. Then as if it was an effort, he got up. He was much taller than her, and she saw a long, suffering, sadness in his eyes as he asked her why it was she who had come and not Margaret. It seemed that he had grown accustomed to the inequality of a situation in which he had lost a long and hard fought battle.

'I'm sorry,' said Freda, 'but I knew you wouldn't come if you knew it was me you were seeing and not her.'

'She might have come herself you know. The last time I saw her we only had about five minutes. It's difficult for me, after all that time, to be just pushed off. I've been something important in her life and now she won't even allow me five minutes of her time.'

'It's not that,' said Freda, 'I think if she saw you again, then she'd have to start over again ... start getting used to the fact that there was no hope for you both.'

Freda wanted to leave. It was painful for her to see a man whom she liked and whom she felt a lot for, being slowly destroyed, slowly falling to pieces just because of another human being. She didn't know what Margaret felt for Michael, and at this moment it didn't seem to matter very much. There was no hope left for him and the only thing she could do was to make it as easy as possible. Her words were empty and she wanted to bring some comfort to him, but there was none she could bring.

'Nothing's permanent,' said Freda, 'nothing can be permanent.'

And she felt the truth of her words running through her whole body for it was something she had been through. She liked Michael now. He could be a friend if things were different, but there had been a time when the sight of him would burn inside her.

'Permanent? So you should say that. There's a friend of mine over there and he's waiting for me. We were talking about something like that and I remember saying that in a billion years from now, the whole world's going to explode,' he paused and looked at Freda, 'no, nothing's permanent, but what does it matter? What difference should it make?'

Freda didn't know what to say. It seemed that there was no answer for her to make.

There was nothing more to say.

Michael had come into their lives, briefly and now it was time for him to leave them. It seemed cruel to think about it like that, but it was the fact of the matter. She wondered what he would do and whether, some day after the war was over, some day far from the present, Freda wondered whether they would meet again.

'Can I tell her you won't write again?' she said. It seemed best to be straightforward about it.

'Yes,' he said, 'you can tell her that.'

Impulsively, Freda leaned up against him and kissed his cheek. She wanted to show that she was sorry things were the way they were, she wanted to tell him that she wished they had turned out differently.

But she couldn't, so she turned and walked away.

For the second time her footsteps echoed on the hard stone and their sound bounced off somewhere into the cold still air. She paused and looked round at him.

He was standing there, looking down at the ground, his hand on the place where she had touched his cheek.

Anyone, standing up above, looking down at them from the roof would have seen only two people, sitting, talking, and then parting. Just two people, a man and a woman. They could have been anyone.

Celia read the letter to Harry as they sat in their room before going down to supper with the rest of the family. He had come back from the pub with Edwin and John. For a few minutes, the time it takes to drink one or two pints of beer, the three men had been in another country, far far away where they had felt free and enjoyed themselves. When they got back they were all a bit merry, but the look on Celia's face had cut the atmosphere dead.

He had begged her, implored her not to open it, but she had snatched it from him and torn it open. Now, as he leaned his head against the wall of the bedroom, he heard her voice read out the contents.

> '... and when you were in the hospital, and we thought you'd lost the baby because of your back ... would you have stayed with me if the child had lived? Would you have turned away from him then?'

Celia put the letter down and tried to leave the room, but she found Harry barring her way. She stared him in the eyes and he saw such a destructive hatred there that he was almost afraid, but his main fear was for what his demented, tortured wife would do with the knowledge that she had just acquired.

'So you see,' she said, her voice shaking with rage, 'that's what your precious Margaret will do. Another baby by another man. Your precious Margaret.'

'You say nothing to John, I tell you. If you do you'll destroy him. Do you understand, you'll destroy him.'

It was all Harry could think of. Somehow he had sensed that there was a story like this behind all the glances he saw pass between Edwin and his wife, between the rest of the family as they looked at each other behind John's back.

But he knew that the still tenuous links of his son's marriage would break open, would split apart if he knew what they both now knew.

The meal that evening was disastrous. They hardly even spoke and only Doris and Freda tried to lighten the atmosphere with a few jokes and comments. For the most part there was no conversation and the few words that they said were tense and loaded. It was as if they were all looking for the hidden meanings behind even the most simple remark.

They all seemed to be waiting for a storm to break and Jean

sat at one end of the table, morose and self-contained seeming to not even notice that it was unusual for a family to sit at their Christmas dinner and not say a word.

Finally, Edwin got up.

'I'll ring David,' he said.

Edwin was surprised to hear a woman's voice answer the phone, but he did his best to put it out of his mind. It was what he might have expected and there seemed no point in worrying about it.

Sheila and David had little to say to each other and they passed a few brief and painful minutes on the phone. There were long silences and they talked about the children. Sheila didn't dare ask him where he was, but in the background she thought she heard a whisper and the sound of a record playing.

She could guess that he was with someone, but she didn't really want to know. It seemed best to forget about it.

Finally, after a word with his mother, David put the phone down.

He had wished them all a merry Christmas. It seemed ironic to have to keep up such a pretence.

But it brought back something to him and as he looked around the smart room that he was in and saw the long elegant figure of Grace watching him from the doorway, he would have given anything to be able to begin over again.

He realised that he was homesick.

'You know,' he said, looking up at Grace, 'when I was a kid I remember seeing this film. It was Christmas and all the people were happy. Kids on sledges and things, they were all good people, nice people and they all looked happy. Nobody bitched there, it was a good world, Grace.'

She put the back of her hand to her mouth, disguising a yawn. David hated her when he saw that.

'It was a lovely world, Grace, where's it gone?'

'Shall we go?' she said after a respectful silence.

Grace wanted to have a good time. It seemed to her that that was all there was room for at the moment. She didn't want complications and she didn't want emotion.

David felt sorry that things were as they were.

As he got up from the bed, he thought maybe it was best to forget about them. After all, he had to go back to his base soon and maybe there wasn't much time left for him either.

Sheila left soon after the phone call. Edwin and John went out for a walk. Margaret went to the kitchen to do the washing up. As she washed the plates she felt the tensions of living in this family grow on her, until she was almost throwing the cutlery into the water in an attempt to get rid of the strain.

'Getting it out of your system are you?' said Harry from the door. He had been watching her for a few moments. He noticed the tension in her movement.

'Why don't you let me help you?' he said, taking a cloth down from the place where it hung on the wall and picking up a plate. As he dried it, he looked at her.

He wondered how she could have borne the tension in this already strained family; how she could have borne being under scrutiny all this time. He didn't blame her, instead he felt an admiration for her strength.

'It's all right is it? You and John?'

Margaret looked up. It was a question she was becoming tired of being asked. So many people, so many different voices had punched those words on her brain that she reeled from the blows.

'Everyone asks me that,' she said, 'and now you. It's like being put in a cage to mate and the people peeping in at you and wondering whether you're all right, whether it's working, and whether you're doing it.'

She hesitated, surprised at the force of her own words.

'I didn't mean to be inquisitive,' said Harry, 'and anyway, it's not me, it's Celia. You see, she's found out about this other man.'

The plate dropped from Margaret's hand, and inside her she felt a whole world crumbling and a carefully constructed edifice falling down about her head.

She felt faint for a moment as her mind went blank and her body weakened. The joints at her knees gave way. Her head reeled and then there came a split second blackout as she sank to the floor.

Harry watched all this happen in her face and he saw the muscles sag as she slid down.

They were silent for a moment and Margaret huddled in a corner of the room, cradling her arms about and rocking slowly back and forth.

She moaned slightly.

There had been so many months of strain, so many people

who had, in their own way, stood by her, and now the one person in the world whom she didn't want to know about it had found out.

There would be no end to the recriminations, the world would not let her forget about her past, and worst of all, she wondered if Mrs Porter would tell John.

After a moment she recovered and looked up into Harry's comforting, sympathetic eyes. They had always understood each other, Harry and Margaret, and they had often looked and smiled at each other behind Celia's back.

She began to speak, to explain what had happened and how she felt about it. At first the words came slowly and then it was easier. She felt her mind lighten as she talked about it. A burden lifted from her back.

'You see, I went the full term but then the child was stillborn. It was a year and three months ago yesterday. Sometimes when I go into see John George, I see two children, two of them lying there. The child I never had. I don't see the man any more and I haven't told John. Maybe one day when he's stronger, but he's not ready for it yet. It would be tragic if he found out.'

'Then I'll have to stop her telling him won't I?' said Harry.

He knelt beside her putting his arms round her shoulders. She felt warm there, and safe. She knew he would do his best to stop his wife telling John, and she just hoped that he would succeed.

'I'm not the person you think I am, you know,' she said.

'I don't believe that. I suppose we're all much more complicated than we seem. You'd be surprised what goes on under my rather tatty middle aged exterior.'

But Margaret wasn't surprised at anything now. So much had happened and so many people had behaved in a way that you would never have expected them to. She had learned it was impossible to judge anyone. It was impossible to predict. You just had to wait and see, and then, when the actions were completed and the thoughts expressed, it was the time to judge and comment. But not before.

Crash; and Sheila threw the photograph of her husband across the room. The Christmas present that Colin had given her was a bottle of sherry and she had drunk most of it. She was sitting in her nightshirt on the floor of her front room, and then, looking up through the mixed vision of her drunken eyes she had seen the smile move. It had laughed at her.

So she threw it across the room and it shattered against the wall. Then it lay in pieces on the floor. The cardboard bent in the frame. The glass lay in pieces over the floor. She stood above it, swaying slightly, and the smile was still there in front of her eyes. She trod on the wide mouth, wanting to crush it into the ground, to wipe away that memory.

She heard the door open, and quickly tried to straighten her hair, to push the stray strands into some semblance of order.

A voice she recognised came from behind her. It was Colin and she was glad that he had come. It was nice to have some company on Christmas Day.

She walked over to him, swaying slightly and as he unbuttoned his raincoat, she helped him in her anxiety to have him stay there. She needed someone.

'I'm glad you came, Colin,' she said, trying to control the slur in her voice, 'you see, I've been drinking your Christmas present.'

She was leaning up against him and she felt the warm safety of his body against her. She mumbled into his chest.

'It makes you see things differently, you know, all sorts of things, it makes you see things quite differently.'

The drink was giving her courage and made her strongly aware of the feel of this man against her. She felt the loss of David whom she had not seen for months. Her eyes closed and as they did, she leaned up and kissed Colin on the lips, drawing him at the same time time into the room.

Suddenly, drawing back from him, she looked at herself in the mirror. Then, making excuses, she went upstairs to tidy herself up.

'I'll only be a minute or two, if you want any sherry, then help yourself, it's on the table.'

Colin walked round the room, pausing at the smashed photograph of Sheila's husband. He bent down and picked up the remains, setting them on the table. Then he picked up the bottle.

It was empty.

Sheila came down after a few minutes. Colin went up to her and kissed her on the forehead.

'Goodnight, Sheila,' he said, 'I'm off now. If I stop here and it happens; what will happen with you in this state, then when

I come back tomorrow you'll only throw the kitchen sink at me. It's you I want, Sheila, not what a bottle of sherry does to you, not what the sherry kids you you want. If you feel the same in the morning then we can . . .' he hesitated, only just able to hold himself back. It was true, he did want Sheila more than anything else, but he knew that this wasn't the right time.

Colin turned and walked out of the room, and Sheila looked after him. When he had gone, she picked up the photograph which he had replaced on the table.

She put it close to her face until the two images merged into one.

'He was right, David Ashton, I would have done. Oh yes I would, if he'd given me the chance.'

She wanted the chains to break, and just when she had been ready to break them, drunk or sober, she had been unable to. It wasn't because she didn't want to, it was because someone else hadn't let her.

She would have done. After all these years, she would have finally made the step that had always eluded her.

But David was far away and had no such qualms.

He was with someone else, and in his own way he was quite happy there.

He couldn't hear her talking to his now crumpled photograph. He couldn't hear the words she was saying.

Philip arrived back late that night. He had managed to get on an early train. The bandage was still over one of his eyes, but he could see clearly out of the other one. His father opened the door and took him into the living-room. He walked to the centre of the room, and looked around it.

'It's just as I remember it, Dad. This is the moment all the lads dream about. The first time home and everything just as it was.'

The words made Edwin sad. He knew things weren't just as they had been.

So much was changed.

Upstairs, Jean was dreaming when the sound of Philip's arrival wakened her. She had dreamt of the time when she'd locked Robert in his room. It had been raining, and she remembered walking back and looking up at the house. The rain ran down the window panes and in her dream the tears of her son, as he looked out, had become those drops of rain.

The rain went on coming down and it was her tears too.

She was tired, weary, lost. She wanted her youngest son back again, and she wanted to see those tears, which were her own sorrow, go away and disappear into nothing.

Everything disappeared into nothing. There were no memories any more.

Nothing to hold on to.

She felt her heart cracking under the strain, and her body breaking. There was nothing to hold on to, she was loose and wandering with no ties to keep her down.

She felt that, round the corner, the end was not so far away.

And in her own manner she was glad of it.

'Mum!' said Philip as Jean entered the room in her dressing gown.

'Let me look at you,' she said, putting her arm around him, 'are you hungry?'

'Yes.'

'I'll get you something.'

As she left the room, she paused for a moment and looked at the son who had just returned.

In her mind he became confused with the tears running down the window pane; he became all her sons, all three of them standing in front of her smiling as it had been once upon a time.

It wasn't like that any more. It wasn't the same at all.

Then he was Robert, overcome by the waves and drowned by the tears.

'Look at your table,' she said, 'I've kept it nice and clean for you. Polished it, looked after it, and cleaned it every day.'

She left the room.

Philip looked at his father, concern in his eyes and a wish to understand his mother's words.

Edwin looked down.

'It's the one Robert brought her back after his first trip. You see, she seems to get a bit mixed up these days,' he said.

Philip wondered what had happened in his absence. Everything was not the same as he had imagined it would be. Not the same at all. He looked down at the table and then up at his father. His gaze turned across the room to the kitchen where he heard the sound of his mother as she made something to eat.

Outside a cold wind blew a chill through their hearts, and Edwin remembered a time when he had been on the ferry.

It had been Spring and he'd found himself wondering what the Winter was going to be like.

It was colder than he'd imagined. He was chilled to the bone and an odd kind of fear for the future came over him.

Something seemed to be stopping.

As if an era was about to come to an end. He wondered why he felt like this, and he wondered whether anything would be the same again.

He knew it wouldn't.

The wind howled. It was dark and seemed to be trying to tell him something.

He listened hard to the voices round his ears, to the wind outside the window, but he couldn't make out the words.

Nothing was clear, except the wind speaking to him.

Howling in agony.

CHAPTER ELEVEN

January 1943

January. A cold bitter month where the trees are bare and there's hardly even a leaf to add a bit of joy to the houses and the avenues you walk down.

The houses that Jean walked past, and the avenues that she walked down. She heard her own footsteps on the pavement, and, looking down, she recognised the paving stones. There were a lot of things she recognised, in these, the places around which she had lived her life for the past thirty years.

Memories came back to her and sometimes she would recognise her youngest son as he walked round a corner ahead of her.

'Robert,' she would almost shout.

Almost.

But the sound didn't come from her mouth. The lips opened and there was no sound.

She only heard the silence of her own voice, for her son would turn and then he would not be her son any more. Just another young lad in a uniform. There were so many of them about at that time. There was one who was missing and he was important.

He was her own son.

Sometimes a flash of memory and there she was with Edwin, walking hand in hand along the road, happy after the birth of their first child, and then always happy after the births of their other children. The children who mattered so much to her.

They were grown up now.

One of them was dead, and none of them had lived their lives as she would have wished.

All the joy having gone out of the family. There were no more small pleasures left to her. Only the long dark years that they had passed through, and in those years, the suffering that had been brought to her.

Edwin slowly retreating. Growing smaller as he meant less and less to her. Then there being nothing left. She could have immersed herself in her children, but now they were grown up and didn't need her care any more.

Sitting by the fire and hearing the silence of her husband's breathing. There was hardly a word they spoke to each other that still meant something.

He had signed the papers, that man who was her husband, signed the small meaningless document which had sent their youngest off to the sea.

There had been times when he'd come back, and then she'd seen him go, whistling as he walked down the road.

There was the time he hadn't come back.

The places and the people that had meant so much to her were empty now. Many had gone away and like her son had not returned.

She wondered as she walked down that road what remained. It seemed so little. There were so few who cared, she had only herself left to live in and only her own memories to nourish her.

Even they were empty now and left a sad rotten smell in her mouth.

She looked up at the sky. It was still light. Still. Light.

It closed in that still light sky until it pressed on her brain and became dark and heavy.

Clouded over and over crowded with voices from the past calling to her. She tried to look ahead but she saw nothing, only the long trail of the past repeating itself.

She wondered if Robert had thought of her as he lay dying, or as he sunk beneath the waves.

She was sinking too, and at the same time she was thinking of him.

'It was Robert's,' said Margaret, taking the little stool away from under Philip's feet.

'I know it was Robert's, but if we're not going to use it hadn't we better put it in a glass case or something?'

Philip paused, realising that he had said something to hurt his sister. In the past few weeks he had learned a lot of tact. It pained him to see the way his own family had withdrawn from each other into their own silent worlds.

His mother hardly spoke any more.

'All this tiptoeing around her, Mags, it doesn't do any good. Nor does all the nonsense about going to church twice every Sunday. I don't know what it's all coming to.'

'Nor do any of us, but what can we do?' Margaret shrugged her shoulders helplessly, 'we can't bring Robert back, and all this tiptoeing around her as you put it. It's the only thing to do. You see we've been here all the time and we've lived through it, watching her since Robert died.'

Philip saw that Margaret was speaking sense and he found himself doing some tiptoeing round his mother of his own accord. Little things like steering the subject away from the fact that he would have to go back to fight when his eye had cleared up. Jean seemed to be under the impression that his leave was indefinite. It seemed easier, the way things were, to let her go on thinking that.

Edwin came into the room brandishing a bottle in his hand. There was a false gaiety about him.

'It's for tomorrow night,' he said, putting the bottle down on the table, 'have you told your mother we're having a birthday party for you, Philip?'

'Yes,' said Philip, 'although it didn't seem to make much impression on her. Still, perhaps it'll do some good, you know, cheer her up a bit.'

Edwin sat down on the sofa. The gaiety went from his voice and his shoulders slumped forward. He took his handkerchief out of his pocket and wiped his brow.

'Yes, I'm hoping it will too,' he said, 'I'm hoping something'll do her a bit of good, son.'

They all looked at each other, knowing that however many parties they gave, however hard they tried to celebrate, it wouldn't make any difference. Nothing would bring Robert back and nothing would take them all to where they were before the war started.

It was dark now and Jean walked past an old house. A ruined, bombed out shell of a place. Once it had been a large house, with a gatepost and a drive. She stopped in front of it and then picked her way carefully over the rubble.

She felt her lips move and this time the words came out of them. Very gently, she muttered to herself. She was remembering the house, for she had lived there as a child and she looked back to the large airy rooms and the times he'd played with Sefton and her sister Helen in the drawing-room.

Large rooms. There had been nothing cramped about her childhood, none of the smallness and constrictions that she'd found with Edwin.

'Don't stop,' she said to herself, 'don't stop. It's just a heap of old ruins now and the floors have gone, the floors that once held you up and the walls that surrounded you, and the wallpaper on them. Mother never saw that wallpaper, it's a good thing. Pretend, pretend it isn't there.'

She walked past the old house, and tried to forget where her footsteps had taken her, but there was no forgetting the empty shell with its holes where the windows were for eyes. Its roof gone. The rain now coming in.

There was no forgetting that it was empty, that it told her of an empty past where her treasured memories were locked. It told her that they no longer existed.

She walked away and voices from the past started to echo through her brain. It was always voices from the past, never voices that gave her a hope for the future.

There was no future and the part of the past that mattered had gone anyway.

Edwin was in the hall when Jean came in. She was wet from the rain, and he thought he saw tears on her cheeks, but it was difficult to tell with the water running from her hair.

'Where've you been?' he asked as sympathetically as he could, 'I wouldn't have known you were out if John hadn't seen you go.'

'Out, I've been out seeing Sefton, only he wasn't there. I think I'll go straight up if you don't mind. Goodnight.'

She walked off up the stairs, and Edwin looked after her. It was still early in the evening.

'Goodnight,' he said after her.

Edwin turned to go back to the living-room. He'd been having a conversation with one of the doctors from the hospital who had come to collect Freda. He seemed a nice man and Edwin wondered, hoped, that there was something between him and Freda. She'd been so embarrassed when he had arrived that Edwin couldn't help but notice the blush on her face.

As he got to the door, he hesitated and looked back into the hall.

Jean hadn't even taken off her hat and coat. She had gone straight upstairs in her dripping clothes.

Edwin felt something inside him move, he was beginning to

get very worried about his wife, but he couldn't even ask her about it.

She rejected even the best meant solicitude.

The next day, after they had all had lunch Edwin went into the kitchen where Jean was doing the washing up. As he came in, he saw her finish the last plate.

Jean took off her apron and laid it on the table.

'You could have left that to me, you know,' he said.

'It's finished now. I'm going out to see Sefton, and I don't expect I'll be back for tea, so Margaret'll look after you all.'

Edwin had wanted to talk to her, but before he had the time to stop her she had walked past him and gone into the hall. He felt that she was purposely ignoring him.

Freda was coming down the stairs as Jean left the house.

'Bye, Mum,' she said cheerily, but there was no reply, just the door shutting and the sound of its bang on the empty hallway.

Freda went into the living-room. John was there, looking through some of his old accountancy books. He looked tremendously serious but Freda didn't feel in a serious mood. She felt lively. There was no time to be depressed or downhearted.

'Clark Gable's joined up, did you know?' she said.

John looked up and smiled. He liked Freda when she was happy.

'So that's why the Germans are bringing their reserves back from Stalingrad?'

They both laughed. Freda sat down and the moment of humour evaporated as they so often did these days.

'Freda?' said John, looking up from his books, 'you know after the telegram arrived about me. I mean saying I was missing ...'

He paused and Freda looked round to see if there was anything she could do to stop him going on. It was something she didn't want to talk about, that time after they had received the telegram, and she knew she wasn't too good at lying. She wondered if he suspected anything. At that moment, Edwin came in and Freda breathed a silent, private sigh of relief.

'Mum's gone out, did she tell you?' she said quickly.

'Yes.'

'By the way, I won't be able to be with you tonight at Philip's party. I have to go back to the hospital and Ian's picking me up at seven.'

Edwin thought he saw a little hint of the blush he had noticed before come to her cheeks, but it passed from his mind quickly as he remembered something odd that Jean had told him.

'Your mother said she wasn't going to be in for tea. It didn't strike me when she said it, but she must have forgotten about the party.'

They all looked at each other, knowing full well that the only real reason they were giving the party was to try to cheer her up. It wasn't like a mother to forget something like that.

'I'll ring her at Sefton's. She mentioned she was going there,' said Edwin.

Jean walked a lot of the way to her brother's house, and when she got there, she was glad to find him at home. She found it hard to walk into that house without feeling the tears come to her face. It was full of so many mementoes of her childhood. There were the photographs on the mantelpiece, pictures of her sister and of her parents. She felt close to Sefton, for he was her own blood. He was part of her past, the past that had died over the years, and which she would so much like to have back again.

'I want to see Dr Willy,' she said.

'Wouldn't you do better seeing someone else, Jean,' said Sefton, leaning back in his chair, 'no disrespect for old Willy, but you might as well ask for the plumber. He should have packed up years ago, and he knows it.'

Sefton eyed Jean. He knew his sister like the back of his hand, and watching her as she sat opposite him, silently crying, and yet not even seeming to notice the tears fall down her own cheeks, Sefton sensed that there was something very deeply wrong with her.

'I must see Willy,' she said, 'and please, Sefton, don't say anything about this to the rest of the family. I don't want them fussing round me. I don't seem to be able to stand their fussing these days.'

There was something about the way she said it that made Sefton instinctively respect her wishes.

'All right,' he said, 'if that's what you want then I'll keep it quiet for the time being.'

He got up to go over to the phone, and Jean looked after him as he walked across the room. She was fond of his funny shuffling gait.

'You're a good man, Sefton,' she said.

There was something about her insistence on seeing the old family doctor that gave Sefton the impression she was searching for the past. She seemed to be trying to regain a time, a set of memories and experience that she had lost. It was as if she was in a hurry to find them again.

Sefton shuddered slightly. Something she had said to him earlier came back, and he wondered whether she was trying to find those things before it was too late.

His hand was on the phone and it rang before he had the chance to pick it up. It was Edwin asking if Jean was there and telling Sefton to remind her that she was due home for tea.

'I'll tell her, Edwin. She's just this moment gone upstairs to look through some of mother's old photographs. She didn't tell me she had a party, but then we all get a bit forgetful in our old age, don't we?'

Sefton tried to ask Edwin, in as oblique a way as he could, whether he had noticed anything wrong with Jean lately. Edwin told him that she had been a bit vacant, and the two men left it at that. Secretly, Sefton was becoming more and more worried about her.

'I take it you don't mind if I come as well?' he said, 'seeing as it is a family occasion.'

'Yes, of course,' said Edwin, 'I was meaning to invite you.'

He put the phone down, and Sefton stood there for a moment. He wanted to go to the party because he felt the need to keep an eye on his sister. Somehow he felt she might need him.

In the middle of the afternoon, John and Philip sat in the living-room, talking. It wasn't often they talked. In fact, before John went away, he'd found there was very little he had to say to Philip, but their experiences seemed to have brought them together and Philip was genuinely interested in John's experiences in Belgium.

It was difficult ground though, and Philip recognised the blank look that passed over John's face when he mentioned the subject. It was a look that Philip had seen often enough on men's faces as they did their best to push things they had seen to the back of their minds.

Self protection, anything to forget what had happened, the mechanism of memory that brings on forgetfulness, and blurs the full pain, it was something Philip had known in the men he'd seen reduced to jelly at the sound of a gunshot.

There were limits that a man could endure and every man found his own level.

'You didn't come back until after they heard about Robert, did you? said Philip as he idly watched John place one of his shoes on a last and pick up the hammer.

'Yes, but I've seen what it's done to them all. Poor old Dad, he only did what a lot of others would have done in the same circumstances. Now she tries not to talk to him and he just sits there, trying to pretend it's not happening,' John paused, 'it really chews me up.'

Philip nodded. You didn't have to be a genius to notice the way things were between their parents. It was like being in the middle of a battlefield again, except without the noise.

The door opened and Freda came bouncing in. She had a handful of cutlery on a tray and she put it on the sideboard. It was for Philip's birthday meal, and in the present atmosphere, the prospect of a party seemed somewhat out of place.

'What time's the boyfriend calling for you,' asked Philip mischievously. He enjoyed teasing Freda. She took it so seriously.

'Say that again and I'll crown you,' she replied laughing, but they had all seen her behave like this before and knew there must be something there.

Edwin listened to them from the kitchen. He heard the light-hearted laughter and the frollicking about as Freda chased Philip round the room with a tea-cosy.

He remembered times when this had happened every day. Then, it had been the simple high spirits of a happy family, enjoying each other's company.

Now it had the frantic edge of people enjoying themselves in order to escape something that was painful, in order to fill in the gaps that fell so easily between the words.

He heard a trumpet sound in some far off time. A child's trumpet, Robert's trumpet that they had given him for his fifth birthday. He saw Jean standing, smiling in the corner of the room, looking on as her family played.

The trumpet blasted in his face, turning the smile to a frown. He was standing on the ferry, the wind whipping at his collar and the trumpet was no longer a trumpet, it was a ship's hooter, echoing across the sea.

Freda sat down, exhausted and John left the room, taking his shoes with him. It was obvious that he wouldn't get them mended in the midst of all that racket.

Philip and his sister sat there silently for a moment. When they spoke, it was with sympathy and understanding. Philip wanted to know more, he wanted to be able to understand why things were as they were.

'And what else happened while I was away, Freda?' asked Philip casually.

'Nothing really,' she replied, 'apart from Margaret's baby and all that business about . . .' Freda pulled herself up short. She felt the blood rising to her head. She wondered why she was such a fool.

'Freda!'

Philip stopped her as she tried to run from the room. For a moment he held her tightly in front of him, determined not to give her the chance to escape.

'How could she have had another baby? John wasn't here.'

It was too late. She had said it and now, Freda thought, she might as well tell the whole story. He was her brother after all.

'We weren't going to tell you. You see, we thought it would be nice to have someone in the house who could look John in the eye.'

Freda went over and closed the door. They spoke in whispers.

'She met this man, and then suddenly she started going out after months of staying at home. I think she made herself believe that John was dead. She doesn't see him now, but she had a baby by him. It was stillborn because of an injury to her back after a raid.'

'Was she keen on him then?'

'Yes, and don't you go throwing stones. We've had to live with it, and it's not been nice.'

It all came back to Freda. It wasn't any better in retrospect than it had been at the time.

'Now do you understand why Mum walks around like a ghost?' she said.

Philip understood. He was beginning to be able to put all the pieces together. All the little hints, the half-sentences and the moments of embarrassment, the glances when someone got too near to the truth.

Everything began to fall into place for Philip. He saw what it must have been like.

Things had changed. It wasn't the same happy family that every soldier dreamed of coming back to after being away. It was a different set of people, the only thing was that they all looked the same as he had left them, but underneath things had happened making it impossible for them to be the same ever again.

In a way they were ghosts, or at the least, shadows of what they had been before.

And he understood the tight-lipped look on his mother's face, and the dull sheen in the eyes that had once danced with life.

Jean had meant to go straight home after she left Sefton's house, but she walked, something the doctor had said made her mind drift off. She forgot about the time and direction.

Old Doctor Willy. He had been a young practitioner in her youth when he first came to Liverpool, and he had stayed with the family throughout the years.

After he'd given her a prescription and left Sefton's house, she had gone back upstairs to continue looking through the photographs.

Snapshots of times she hardly remembered, and pictures of moments she would never forget.

Willy had asked after David. He had said he remembered delivering him.

So long ago.

He should never have married her. Jean loved Sheila, but David should never have married her. He wasn't old enough at the time. He should have waited.

They should all have waited.

There were too many hasty decisions. They all needed time, she needed time to think, time to get over the memories.

Snapshots of long ago.

Her, her mother and her father, walking along the sand. She'd picked up one of the photos and glanced at it. There was something in it that made her look again. A small figure in the background, throwing a stone into the sea.

Edwin, only about a fraction high. Tiny as a pebble and she remembered the time when he had been only small in her mind. He had grown on her and the more her parents told her that she shouldn't marry him, the more she insisted, the firmer her resolve had become.

Her father had disliked Edwin so much he hardly spoke to him.

Other snapshots too.

Ones she preferred to forget, like the one of Robert sitting on the grass in the garden. He was just a little baby then as he sat, his legs tucked under him and his thumb stuck, obstinately, in his mouth.

There were many more, too many to remember.

There were too many memories and few of them seemed happy. The laughter and the good times receded to the back of her mind and the sense of the present became overpowering. The sense of the recent events clambered around her body, fought for prominence in her mind as she tried to shrug them off.

Where am I?

What is this funny building in front of me with the vaguely familiar gatepost and the empty windows, the black spaces where curtains once hung.

It's Philip's birthday and they're giving a party.

Should I go back? Do I want to? Where is back? Where is it that I should go?

Questions, questions crowding my brain; none of them clear, none of them understandable. Like birds flying above, floating gracefully around my brain. Out of reach, all the questions so far out of reach.

Jean turned her steps to the direction of her home where she knew they would all be waiting for her, but she didn't want them to wait. She wanted the time to be alone, the time to think for herself.

She didn't feel the need to return to them. She felt the duty, but not the need.

And if there is no need, if there is no point, then why obey? Why should she obey the regular signals that her brain was sending out, clear as clockwork.

She let her steps take her where they wanted. She gave her feet their own accord to wander as they willed.

'I mourn him too, you know, I mourn him.'

She turned quickly, but there was no one where the voice came from.

'I wanted to be with you, son, not for you to be with

strangers, I wanted to be with you.'

She turned again, startled by the sound of her own voice coming from behind.

Then, wandering across the park or along the waterfront, she looked down into the depths and wondered what it was she saw there.

A strange, familiar face, smiling up at her from the waves, merging with the memories.

The times that had passed, floating round her.

It was Robert's face hovering out of reach.

'They're not strangers, Mum, they're friends, mates.'

The ones who were with him at the end?

The ones who died with him, or had they deserted him, too intent on saving their own lives?

Jean, sitting alone on a bench, her headscarf surrounding the face and the eyes staring out, looking for something, looking for someone. The blank eyes with all the life sapped from them, dull eyes, tired eyes, weary eyes.

A stranger passed her by, a young man and as he glanced at her, he wondered who that strange, lonely looking woman might be and where she came from.

They all were sitting round, all the Ashton children, although they were grown up now, preparing for the evening meal. The occasional comment passed between them, and then suddenly Margaret looked up.

'You know, I don't think that this party's such a good idea,' she said.

'Yes, and I'll tell you what's wrong with it,' said Freda, 'Mum'll be sitting there like the rock of Gibraltar and it'll fall as flat as a pancake.'

'I don't understand it,' said Margaret, her thoughts going their own way, 'they've been married for over thirty years and it's always seemed sort of perfect to me.'

'Rosy coloured glasses, love,' said Philip, folding up the last paper napkin, 'it's a class difference in a way. What with Dad having to work for Uncle Sefton. I often wonder if the reason she sticks up for Dad against Uncle is because she's his wife, not because she wants to.'

'Rubbish,' said Margaret.

But they all knew it was true in a way. Margaret remembered something her mother had once said to her. She had said that she wondered what kind of life she would have had if things had been different. Margaret had never quite understood what she meant by different, but it was coming to her now, slowly.

Philip was pursuing his train of thought.

'I wonder if she ever thinks about the kind of life she would have had if she'd married into her own class. I'm not saying it would be any better, but when your life's not as you want it, then you would wonder about that sort of thing.'

'She's had a happy life,' Margaret said, only half believing it.

'Happy,' Freda stood up, 'you call Robert and David and Philip being away and John being missing, you call that happy. What with that and . . .'

She stopped herself, seeing John, sitting silently in the corner, she stopped herself just in time before she said what was on all their minds. The one other main cause of their mother's unhappiness and the only one they couldn't talk about among themselves.

Each one of them had their own private theories, and each one of them knew that they would never really understand.

John looked up.

'It's the war isn't it?' he said.

And none of them could think of anything better to say. It wasn't enough, but it was a reason that they could all understand.

It was some sort of excuse too, for their own behaviour. You could always blame it on the war. Perhaps, you could say, none of this would have happened without the war. That took the blame away from themselves; but it would probably have happened anyway, whatever the circumstances, wherever the place.

Edwin opened the door. He was whistling and he set an old photograph of himself down on the sideboard. It was him in uniform. He looked round.

'Your funny old Dad in the Great War,' he said, and they all laughed although the laughter was not far from the weeping.

Edwin took Philip off to the pub, and when Ian Mackenzie came to collect Freda, both John and Margaret left them alone in the living-room. Freda was embarrassed by their exaggerated tact.

Later on, Margaret sat with her husband playing cards. They were waiting for the rest of the family to return.

'We could start looking for a place of our own soon,' said John.

Margaret looked up.

'It's affecting you too, is it?' she said.

'People are usually better on their own. I'm sorry, but it's something about the house that gets on my nerves, and anyway, I want things to be as they should between you and me.'

'Yes,' said Margaret, 'I want that too.'

She stood up and went over to him, taking his head in her hands. She leant forward and kissed his forehead and then his lips. There was no passion in the movement, no desire, but that didn't matter because it was a good moment, it was quiet and peaceful.

It was the rest that Margaret had been seeking. The tender comfort that she had fought for inside herself and it was what she wanted.

A good quiet peaceful moment, that was all.

It was enough.

Sefton let himself in as the front door was open. They heard his voice as he stood in the hall and shouted for someone to come.

'Anyone at home?' he said.

Margaret went out and helped him off with his coat.

'Is your mother here?' he asked her.

She looked at him questioningly.

'Dad said she was with you, and that you'd both be coming here together.'

A frown passed over Sefton's face as if something was worrying him. He went over to the phone and dialled.

'I've made you a cup of tea, Uncle,' said Margaret, after Sefton had finished his call.

They were sitting in the living-room now and John had gone out. He never felt at ease when Sefton was around. They had so little in common.

'John's gone to the pub to tell Dad and Philip that you're here,' she said.

Sefton looked up. He was fingering his tea cup nervously.

Margaret wondered what was on his mind. It wasn't often that she saw her Uncle as distracted as this.

'What's it all in aid of, this party?' he asked.

Margaret explained that it was Philip's birthday, but that the real reason was to try and cheer Jean up a bit.

'You don't have to tell me about your mother. If I've seemed a bit irritable tonight, then it's mainly because I'm worried about her. You see, she came round to the house wanting to see Doctor Willy. She made me promise not to say anything, but she's been getting headaches. Said she felt as if she was slowing down. I wouldn't have thought twice about it except her behaviour was rather odd, and she kept saying that she wanted mother. Unusual thing to say, don't you think?'

They both looked at each other, thinking the same thing and wondering where it could be that Jean had gone.

The bar of the pub was crowded. Philip and his father sat, hidden away in one corner. Philip noticed that Edwin was drinking more than he usually did. His speech wasn't slurred or loose, but he was saying things that in more normal circumstances he would never have said.

'You see, you've been away, Philip and you've missed a few instalments. You know what your mother said to me at Christmas? She said she never wanted me to touch her again. I've given thirty odd years of my life to what you call home and what am I supposed to do now? Start again? There are other things she's said to me. When I told her she made me feel a failure she said I was a good man. But it was said with less affection than you'd give a dog.'

To hear his father talk like this embarrassed Philip. It wasn't so much that he didn't want to hear these things, but that he knew there was nothing he could do about them. He could give sympathy and in so far as that helped, then it was a good thing, but he could never help his father beyond that.

'Hadn't we better be getting back?' he said.

'Back?' repeated Edwin, 'I'm not so sure that I want to go back.'

He paused and looked up at the son who had been away for so long.

'Have we spoiled things for you?' he asked.

'No . . . but I've always thought of home as a happy place. It was one of the things that kept me going.'

'And I'm destroying it for you?'

'Yes.'

It was so simple. Just that one word and the nod of assent that went with it.

The noise of the bar all around them, and in the corner, the little huddle of father and son, talking as they had never talked before. That conversation and the things they admitted to each other changed them. It changed their relationship. Never again would they look at each as son to father, but now as man to man, and each seeing in the other something different, something that hadn't been there before.

Philip looked up and across the bar he saw John come in. In a way he was glad that the moment between his father and himself would disappear. It would never be forgotten, but they wouldn't talk about it again. It would always be there, for they knew so much more about each other now.

'Been sent to fetch us home?' asked Philip when John got to their corner.

'Well, a hint was dropped, but I've got permission to have a pint though.'

John sat down and looked about him. Edwin rose and went to the bar. John noticed the slight unsteadiness in his walk.

He glanced at Philip.

'It's going to be one of those nights isn't it?' he said.

Philip nodded.

'Yes,' he replied.

Jean left Sheila's home, disappointed. She had been there to try to talk to her, to tell her what the past meant, to try to make her understand. But Sheila hadn't really seemed to be interested in what she was saying.

There had been a man there too. It didn't worry Jean, for she was past noticing these small exigencies of human nature. Her family was splitting up, so why bother about it, she thought. It was just another link in the chain towards chaos.

She had told her daughter-in-law about her childhood, about the ideals she had treasured then, the hopes that she had carried about with her.

'I was a suffragette once, you know,' she said, 'about the time I met Edwin. I was young and politically advanced in those days, as he was. If it hadn't been for my mother, I think father would have turned his back on me for good when I married Edwin. Mother drew us all together again. Can you see it in me now? Can you see that young girl?'

There was a long silence and Sheila hadn't understood what she wanted, what she was trying to say.

Jean thought how she had been young once. How she had ideals in those days. Time had taken them away from her, stolen the beauty of her youth and the excitement of her life.

The overbearing pressure of her marriage came back to her, and the claustrophobic atmosphere of the home was all she could think about.

Her own home, when she was a child. So big, so light, and airy. She wanted it again, she wanted the rest and the happiness of the garden. Her mother too, so good to her, so calm and understanding.

She looked up and there, in front of her was the house. The shell of a life staring her in the face, seeming to speak, seeming to call from a time when things had been different.

She stood under the walls. Looking down she saw one of the window frames lying empty, no glass left.

So empty, such a poor stark replica of her life.

She sank to the ground, feeling weary, feeling the sleep come over her and her mind escaped once again into the dreams that had haunted her more and more over the past weeks. The weariness slipped from her shoulders as she sat in the mud, and a rest came to her mind.

A good man. Edwin is a good man. I've never been able to forgive easily. David, Margaret, you, although I know you mourn him as I do, but it is so hard to forgive. The children are dying all over the world, without mourning, without papers, and the mourners are dying too, and then mother, lying now like a vegetable in a home, unable to speak. We don't live for ever, none of us do, we're all dying.

A gatepost lying in the corner.

The tree that father planted for me, now bare, but still standing. Only a semblance of life in its dead branches.

Me, standing in the drawing-room looking out of the window and Edwin in the garden talking to father. Giving in to the pressure.

Oh yes.

It started long ago, this process.

Edwin beginning not to be Edwin any more, letting father beat him down and destroy him. 'If that's what you want,' he would say, 'if that's what you want.'

The submission. Not what we want, Edwin. We need to fight.

But the fighting's over now, and the end is in sight.

Just a shell.

A model, empty and staring, lifeless and dull, a model of what was meant to be.

It's not like that any more.

The children have left us, and now we, we are leaving too. They're all leaving us alone.

This is not what it was meant to be.

It should have been different, but the weight is now too heavy. It pushes us under as it has always done.

We should have fought, but we gave in and let ourselves be engulfed.

And the price.

The price is a heavy soul, and a weight on our minds that makes thinking impossible, which dulls the will to fight, and which, in the end, makes nothing of us all.

'Mrs Ashton, are you well?'

The voice standing over her of George Askew. The family solicitor, driving by, seeing the little figure leant against the old house.

Askew looking up at the house.

'Odd thing, blast ... I've seen odder things than that. He has a lot to answer for, our Mr Hitler. It was a good house.'

'Mrs Ashton?'

And Jean looking up at the face she had known for years. Askew. The man her sister had nearly married.

Blurring. Moving back and forth with the time, and the past, hazy, fogged to a picture of the window pane with rain, tears, rain, running down it.

The face of her son looking out.

The past all about her.

Father had liked Askew and would have been happy for Jo to marry him.

Things didn't happen like that. Her sister had gone off to Australia.

Oh yes, it all started a long time ago.

Mother liked Edwin, she had brought them back together again. There she was, like a cabbage lying in the hospital.

Jean let the big man who stood over her gather in his arms about her, and carry her off to his car.

She was being taken somewhere but she didn't care where it was any more for she herself was travelling elsewhere.

Going off.

Back to a time when it mattered.

What mattered?

Nothing really.

Or everything.

The same difference, for it had started so long ago.

The hospital was busy. There were nurses everywhere, and the sister bustled round in her efficient way.

'I've told Nurse Ashton to get the side ward ready. There's a patient coming up from casualty.'

The sister sent Doris off to help Freda prepare the ward. Freda was in high spirits after her lift to the hospital from Mr Mackenzie. Having a consultant take an interest in you was like being looked at by the Archangel Gabriel, or at least so said all the other nurses.

Freda wasn't that impressed but she enjoyed their jealousy.

They made the bed, and stretched the white sheets until they were tight as a drum. Freda opened the window, turning her back to the door as the patient was wheeled in.

She had become immune to this sort of thing now. Once, the suffering she saw on the faces had disturbed her, but now it was just one more in a long line.

She turned and looked at the face on the pillow. Its eyes were closed as if in sleep and Freda assumed that they had given it sedatives.

She looked again.

There was little point in crying.

She wasn't immune to this patient.

Her mouth opened and the world span round. Her hand up to her face.

No sound from her lips.

She knew those eyes, they had looked at her for years, they had fed her, touched her, loved her, supported her and she had smiled into them and she had shouted at them in anger, but now she realised how much she had loved them.

In her mother's eyes there was the dull lustre of the lights on the ceiling and there was a faint flicker of life. But it was so faint that you might have missed it.

Her own mother.

'You sent for me sister,' said Mr Mackenzie.

'Yes, I wondered if you would take Nurse Ashton home. I believe you do sometimes. It was quite a shock for her, but we've given her a sedative and she seems to have quietened down now.'

Ian looked across the corridor and saw Freda standing against the wall. He saw the shock in her eyes and he went up to her and put his arm about her, guiding her down the corridor out and away from the place where her mother lay.

Ian felt her skin under his hand. He often hoped for that feeling. He was more attached to Freda than he cared to admit to himself.

But if only it could have been in other circumstances.

Freda, wondering, thinking to herself why it had to be this way.

'Has anyone rung David?' said Margaret, 'we'd better, hadn't we?'

They were all off to the hospital, and John volunteered to ring his brother-in-law. They had a London number to ring.

'Life, my dear is far too short to worry about things like that,' said Grace, 'anyway my husband and I have an arrangement. I'm nice to him when he comes home, but we don't expect any more from each other than that.'

David wondered how she could be so cold, so collected and how she could compartmentalise her life so neatly. It was something he couldn't do. He often thought of Sheila and the children. However hard he tried, he could never forget them.

'I'm feeling reckless, you know. The more it looks as if we're going to win this war, the more I want to go on living. I'm off ops for a bit now, but when I go back I'm going to be terrified, scared out of my bloody skin. I want a good life, Grace, and the more I like it the more I'm scared I'll get the chop one day.'

He paused, looking up at the elegant figure of Grace, and he knew she was bored when he spoke like this.

'Isn't that what it's like for all of us,' she said lightly, 'life is a bit like some sort of op, isn't it?'

David laughed and tried to forget about the things that

mattered to him, but they wouldn't let him go.

The phone rang.

He listened to the voice at the other end of the phone and then, without a word, he picked up his jacket and left the flat.

There were things that mattered more than this woman and the good life she offered him.

Grace looked after him as he shot out of the room.

'I take it we're not going out,' she said, and David didn't answer.

She pursed her lips, and then, turning to her bag, she looked up a name in her address book.

There were others where he came from, she thought, others who were less trouble and who didn't constantly have to talk about their past as if trying to prove that it didn't matter.

Jean's brother and her husband sitting by the bed. It was late on into the night and she hadn't spoke or even blinked an eyelid for hours.

Outside the wind howled and Edwin listened to it. It was speaking to him again saying what it had tried to say before. Edwin understood now. He was being told about the pain, a warning of what had been happening while his wife walked around Liverpool.

He looked down and tried to think, tried to search out the mistakes of his past.

Jean opened her mouth and muttered something. They both leaned nearer trying to hear.

'Can I have a peach, Father?' she said.

She seemed to be reaching back into the past for something she had lost. That was where she is going, thought Edwin, back into the past and away from the present, away from me and the failures of our life together.

He wanted to call her back, but he did not know the words. He wanted, in this last instant to explain the truth to her, to tell her why it had all happened and what had gone wrong.

But it was too late.

He had lost her.

She was slipping away and now, it was only a question of time.

'Can I have a peach, Father,' she said again. But this time her eyes opened and the words were clear. She looked at

Sefton and then she looked at Edwin.

Her eyes met his, and then turned away. For a second they roamed the room as if they were roaming over the contours of her life, searching the geography of the places she had lived in and the people she had known.

Searching for the key.

But in that little room, she didn't find it, so she closed her eyes again. This time, it was so calm, so definite, the way her body relaxed. There was no doubt any more.

She slipped away to a place where she could search to her heart's content. Where it was quiet and restful.

Edwin looked up at Sefton. They both stood and left the room.

There was nothing to say.

The moment had passed long ago. The moment for speech had passed and Edwin wondered if the things they could have said would have made any difference.

He had always had the feeling that it was too late for them all to make amends, and now he knew.

There were no amends to be made with the dead.

CHAPTER TWELVE

There were no amends to be made with the dead, but there were still those who were living and with whom there was a life to be lived.

The coffin sat, traditionally, in the front room of the Ashton's house, surrounded by flowers.

Edwin looked at the beautiful blooms which almost obscured it from view.

They all came to pay their last respects. Mrs Porter, the family and old friends.

But what use, thought Edwin to pay such respects, and how much better it would have been to pay those respects when there was still life in her veins and still a breathing in her mouth. If the sentiments and outward show of love had come then, it might have altered the process of her dying.

But now they came and were little more than empty words, perhaps a salving of the occasional conscience and a tinge of regret, but they were words that might as well not have been spoken.

Her face looked rested and peaceful in its death and oddly, as Edwin dreamed, he felt jealous of her, jealous that she had deserted him without even so much as a word.

There were so many things they had left unsaid and now it was too late. All the missed opportunities crowded in on his brain, all the things he should have said, but it was too late. He would live now in a welter of regret and a slough of conscience wishing that time would turn back and give him one more chance.

It's always after the event, but then when the understanding came the time has always passed. The moment gone.

There is little point in regret at times like this. Edwin thought he should look forward and tell himself that he could learn from what had happened.

What was there to learn?

Even if you could learn, then what purpose would there be in those lessons?

It rained as they lowered the coffin into the ground. The droplets spattered on to the wood and the mist hung low. A sea fog closed in on them and far away a ship sounded its own private memorial.

Of its own accord, the fog gave forth the memories and harboured the reasons.

A ship's horn sounding said more than any word.

Margaret's hand crept down and held John's. He squeezed her fingers tight, telling her that he was still there.

They walked out of the graveyard among the headstones that peopled the place with their own kind of memory. The inscriptions meaning nothing except to those who had written them.

'I shall have to stay now,' she said, 'to look after Dad for a bit.'

'Of course,' he replied, 'it's not a good time to be getting a house anyway. If the raids started again, we could end up with a pile of bricks.'

He smiled at her, wanting to reassure her that whatever happened, they would go on building their marriage.

Whatever happened.

'All those nights in that freezing shelter. It was the war that killed her you know, and us and Robert being lost. You remember the night you first came to the house and we were having an anniversary party. How contented we all seemed and yet we weren't really. I wonder what it would have been like if none of this had ever happened.'

She paused a moment.

'I'd tell all the lies in the world to prevent anything like this happening again.'

'The truth doesn't hurt, you know,' he said.

She looked up at him, at the face she knew so well and all its funny eccentricities. She was beginning to love it again, that face.

'Doesn't it?' she said, wondering what would happen when he finally knew the truth as he would have to one day.

Yes, she knew he would have to. Her mother had died because of the lies and the half truths. She wasn't going to let her marriage die because she hadn't the courage to face up to the truth.

There were to be no more lies.

John looked up and saw his mother walking away from the grave with a strange woman. It was one of the old family nurses who had seen the children through the very first months of their lives.

He heard their words as they came near him.

'That's my brother over there,' said Mrs Porter.

'You mean the one with the grey hair?'

'No, the one with the white angel for a headstone.'

John smiled, knowing that she would never change. He could afford to smile now, because he had broken with his past and with the hold she had had over him.

Yes, he could smile now. It was from a distance, far enough for her not to be able to touch him.

David stood in front of his wife. There was little they had to say to each other, so, yet again they talked of the children. Empty, meaningless words that covered in the silence between them. He wondered what it was that he wanted. He didn't know and suddenly the prospect of his next tour of ops seemed an attractive one.

When you were up there in the air, there were only the definite, set down words to be said. It was not necessary to search through your brain for the right emotion and then to find that there was no emotion left.

Just a cold empty space.

Sheila looked at him and wanted to reach out. Colin had come to her a few days before and told her about a new girl-friend that he had found.

It made her sad to think that there was no more hope there. It could have become something in her life, and she had let it slip away.

She knew why she had let it slip away like that, it was because the strands of the past that existed between her and David were too strong.

She wondered when they would cease to exist. Looking at him standing among the rows of crosses she still felt them, and wondered if he did too.

Edwin and Sefton left the graveyard together. Memories of their previous history surrounded them, but the tensions and arguments, the envy and the hatred dropped away. She had been his wife and she had been his sister.

They were joined by a common bond.

It was a bond that had always existed, bringing them together through Jean, tying them inextricably into each other through her presence, and now she was gone.

They could go two ways. They could become more firmly joined, and they could split apart.

Edwin wondered which way it would be.

The grass ended and they came to the path. Turning towards the entrance to the graveyard, Edwin looked back a moment.

He saw the few people dotted around the graves and the mist making them into shadows, taking away their individuality and forming them into small wisps of flesh with little substance.

They were his family. He wondered whether it would be a family any more.

He wondered what the future held.

They had come so far, all of them, so far together and now, in more ways than one, the tide had turned.

'Funny,' said Sefton as they walked up the path, 'funny thing she said at the end.'

He repeated Jean's words.

Neither of them could really understand what she had meant but then, perhaps neither of them had ever really understood her.

'People say funny things at the end, Sefton.'

The end, and the few incomprehensible words that must have meant so much to her.

'Can I have a peach, Father?'

A past where peaches were nice, and where the world was fresh and bright, always growing.

Edwin knew that she had died because she was weary, was too tired to go on. She had come to a point where the eddy of the past was stronger than the current of the future. It had dragged her back into the bosom of memory. The stream had let her go.

There was a future too and he would face it as he had always done, only this time it would be just that bit more difficult, and the load just that bit heavier.

The fight just that bit harder.

The mist settled and the night closed in.

Edwin sat listening to the mild wind that curled around his house.

There were no messages there any more, and the violence had gone from its force.

Then there was a curious calm that settled about him and he became encircled by the silence of his own thoughts.

A curious calm and Edwin held still by the centre of the wind as its eddies touched his mind and brought back things that had mattered to him.

He tried to shrug them off, those thoughts, those memories that pricked him.

He looked into the fire and saw the flames there. They turned to embers, and as the rest of his family slept, he sat and watched them slowly die.

Finally, only a red glow of one coal, hanging on to its life. Edwin stood up and breathed on it.

It flared momentarily and he saw that there was still life in it yet.

With that in his mind, he went to bed.